*Do nothing out of
selfish ambition or vain
conceit. Rather, in
humility value others
above yourselves....*

–Philippians 2:3 (NIV)

MYSTERIES *of* LANCASTER COUNTY

A SLOWLY
DEVELOPING
STORY

MYSTERIES *of* LANCASTER COUNTY

Shaen Layle & Nancy Mehl

Guideposts
Danbury, Connecticut

Mysteries of Lancaster County is a trademark of Guideposts.

Published by Guideposts Books & Inspirational Media
100 Reserve Road, Suite E200
Danbury, CT 06810
Guideposts.org

This is a work of fiction. The village of Bird-in-Hand, and Lancaster County, Pennsylvania, actually exist, and some places and characters are based on actual places and people whose identities have been used with permission or fictionalized to protect their privacy. All other names, characters, businesses, and events are the creation of the authors' imaginations, and any resemblance to actual persons or events is coincidental.

Cover and interior design by Müllerhaus
Cover illustration by Bob Kayganich, represented by Deborah Wolfe, LTD.
Typeset by Aptara, Inc.

Printed and bound in the United States of America
10 9 8 7 6 5 4 3 2 1

CHAPTER ONE

Elizabeth Classen slipped on her coat and stepped out on the front porch of the old Victorian house that had been in her family for three generations. It was a particularly cold January in Bird-in-Hand, Pennsylvania. She pulled her coat tighter and walked down the porch stairs, heading for the shop that was also a family legacy. Secondhand Blessings had closed when her mother fell ill and subsequently died. Elizabeth's sisters moved back to Pennsylvania so, together, they could reopen the store situated in an old barn. Paint, repairs, and some elbow grease had restored the shop to life.

She tramped carefully through the snow. Only a couple of inches had fallen so far, but the forecast called for two or three more before it was over. The door of the store slid open, and her youngest sister, Mary, stepped out into the cold. She smiled at Elizabeth.

"I'm gonna bake those pies over lunch," she said. "I'll stick them in the oven and run a quick errand while they're cooking."

"Where are you going?"

"Remember that old camera Lauren Collier brought in?"

Elizabeth nodded. Lauren Collier's grandfather had recently died. Lauren, who was his only living relative, was in charge of his estate. She'd brought in several interesting possessions, including an ancient camera that still had film in it. Mary asked her if they could develop the film, and Lauren had said yes. It wasn't the kind of film you could just take to the local photo shop, though. Hardly anyone worked with film this old. It had to be developed very carefully, so Mary had contacted Todd Friesen, a man who attended their church who had his own darkroom. He'd offered to see if anything could be salvaged from the old roll.

"Todd called, and the photos are ready. He says he's found some pretty interesting stuff."

"Okay," Elizabeth said, "but don't take too long. I don't have time to keep an eye on your pies."

As Mary shook her head, her blond curls bounced. "I don't know why you're always telling me not to dawdle," she said with a dramatic sigh.

Elizabeth smiled at her. "You love to talk, and sometimes you forget the time."

Mary stared at her older sister for a moment before laughing. "Okay, you're right. I'll warn Todd up front that I need to get right back."

Elizabeth leaned over and hugged her. Mary might be a little scatterbrained and impulsive, but she had a good heart. Unfortunately, many times she allowed her feelings to lead her instead of her common sense. That trait had caused some problems in the past, but it also made Mary the special person she was.

Elizabeth said goodbye to her sister and went inside Secondhand Blessings. She was immediately greeted by Pal, their beloved border collie. Pal enjoyed staying in the shop during the day so he could greet their customers. Everyone loved him. Elizabeth scratched him behind the ears before looking for Martha. She spotted her talking to a customer Elizabeth didn't recognize. She nodded at Martha before hanging up her coat and taking her place at the front, near the cash register. Because of the snow, business was a little slow today, but there were several people in the store, looking through their inventory.

Elizabeth gazed around the large room. Although her intention was to find areas that needed to be cleaned or straightened, she couldn't help feeling a deep sense of satisfaction. She enjoyed the shop's warm, cozy feeling. Along with all the usual items brought in to a secondhand shop, she particularly loved the Amish items displayed on one side of the barn, including the gorgeous quilts and handmade items. In another area, Martha's baked goods, jams, honey, and maple syrup were showcased in a beautiful glass display case. It was hard to keep them stocked since Martha's homemade goods were such a big hit with customers.

Elizabeth couldn't help smiling at the antique cast-iron stove that sat in the corner. She could smell the wood burning inside. It was especially welcome today and helped to keep the old barn warm and toasty.

She noticed that the small tables and chairs set out for children needed a little attention. Crayons and coloring books were scattered across the tabletops, and some crayons had rolled to the floor. Before she had a chance to take care of it, Martha, who had finished talking to the older woman, noticed the mess. She hurried over and put everything in order within a few minutes.

"I noticed Mary leaving a little while ago," she said to Elizabeth as she walked over to where she sat. "Where's she going?"

Elizabeth told her about picking up the film. "She put some pies in the oven and promised she'd be back in time to take them out."

Martha rolled her eyes. Elizabeth didn't say anything, but truthfully, she was also a little skeptical about their sister's sudden interest in baking. She'd never been good at it. Martha did most of the cooking for the sisters. She was a natural. Mary's interest in a local group that worked with foster children had sparked her latest foray into culinary endeavors. Lancaster County Helping Hands was hosting a fund-raiser and had asked its supporters to assist with baked goods they could sell. Martha had offered to donate some pies and cakes, but Mary was determined to do the work herself.

"She really wants to do this," Elizabeth said. "I know you want to help her, but I think we should support her desire to tackle this on her own. She seems serious about her commitment to this group."

Martha sighed loudly. "She'll go to meetings for a month or two. Then she'll quit. Just like she has with every other so-called passion she's thrown herself into."

"Maybe it will be different this time. We need to give her a chance."

"You might be right. I don't mean to be critical, but I'm just going by past experience."

"You went over the pie recipes with her. She seemed to be listening carefully."

"*Reading* a recipe is a lot different than actually following one. I offered to at least help her with her first attempt, but she refused." Martha shook her head. "I'll back off, but let this be on your head."

Elizabeth couldn't hold back a laugh. "That's a little dramatic, isn't it?"

Martha shrugged. "Maybe, but I think she's being a little stubborn. That attitude doesn't usually end in success."

The woman Martha had been talking to came up to the register with several items. Elizabeth checked her out while Martha walked through the store making sure the shelves were neat and orderly.

As the afternoon proceeded, there was a break in the snow, and several people came in. A couple of times Elizabeth wondered where Mary was, but she didn't have much time to think about it. She assumed she was at the house, taking care of her pies.

A local Amish woman, Emily Miller, had her three children in tow, along with a foster child they'd recently added to their brood. Timmy was a darling four-year-old, but he had a bad habit of taking things. Emily had brought him back to the shop more than once to return something he'd stuck in his pocket. Elizabeth had heard from other store owners in the area that they'd had similar problems with him. Emily was doing her best to curb his behavior, but it appeared to be a struggle she wasn't winning.

It was a little after one o'clock when Mary came into the shop. Elizabeth breathed a sigh of relief. She'd thought about going into the house more than once and checking the pies. But true to her word, Mary had returned to take care of them.

Ignoring the customers, Mary called out, "Wait till you see what's on this old film of Lauren Collier's!" She jogged over to the large wooden counter and spread the pictures out on the top.

"There are old military pictures," Mary said. "And look at this. Some Amish man. Weird, since the Amish don't like to have their pictures taken. I wonder who he is."

A couple of customers drifted over to gaze at the photos. A youngish man with rather long hair and large black glasses reached over and began to riffle through them.

"These are great," he said. He looked up at Elizabeth, who was getting ready to ask him to stop touching the pictures. She wasn't sure they should be shown without Lauren's permission. "I think some of these may have historical significance. Could I use them for my photography class? I'm a student at the Pennsylvania College of Art and Design." He stuck his hand out and Elizabeth took it. "I'm Grant Slavick." He let go of Elizabeth's hand. "I promise to be very careful and return them in good condition."

"I'm sorry," Elizabeth said, "but they don't belong to us. All I can do is pass your request on to the owner."

Grant frowned but didn't argue. Instead, he pulled off his backpack and zipped open a pouch on the front. He took out a notebook and found a pen. "I'll give you my number. Maybe you could pass it along?"

Elizabeth nodded. "I'd be happy to do that."

Rather than walk away, Grant stayed where he was and continued staring at the pictures. Another man Elizabeth didn't know joined him. He also seemed engrossed by the subject matter exhibited in the photos.

Elizabeth was trying to figure out a way to put the photos away without seeming rude when Rosie Gittrich, an elderly woman who'd lived in Bird-in-Hand her entire life, walked up to the counter with two jars of Amish-made jam. She set them down on the counter and glanced over at the photos. Elizabeth heard Rosie take a sharp breath. She started to ask if something was wrong when she noticed an odd smell that seemed to be wafting through the shop. Was it the cast-iron stove? She watched as Martha, who obviously was wondering the same thing, went over to check it. After looking the stove over carefully, she turned to look at Elizabeth and shook her head. Then she went over to the front door and stuck her head out when it slid open.

"Fire!" she shouted. "The house is on fire!"

Mary ran to join her. "My pies!" she cried out. "I forgot to take them out of the oven."

Elizabeth ran out of the shop to join her sisters. Behind her, Pal barked his concern. The three of them entered the kitchen and found black smoke pouring out of the oven. After removing the blackened pies and turning the oven off, they realized the house was fine. The filling from Mary's pies had dripped down to the bottom of the oven, causing the thick smoke.

"Cheese and crackers, Mary," Martha fumed. "How could you forget to take these out of the oven?"

"I...I'm sorry," Mary said, looking embarrassed. "I got distracted. I put the pies in before I left. I intended to take them out when I got home. But when Todd showed me the pictures, I got excited. I wanted to show them to you. I guess I forgot about everything else." She swiped at the tears that sprang to her eyes. "I'm really, really sorry," she said again. "Sometimes I'm such a dope."

"You're not a dope," Elizabeth said with a sigh. "You just made a mistake. But you really need to concentrate when you're using the stove. This could have been a lot more serious." She was trying to be understanding, but thinking their cherished family home was ablaze had frightened her. She was still shaking. She noticed that their dachshund, Tink, and orange tabby, Butterscotch, were nowhere to be seen. They must have fled the kitchen, one of their favorite spots, for somewhere safer and less hazy.

"Mary and I will clean this up," Martha said, coughing through the smoke. She started opening windows. "You get back to the shop, Elizabeth."

Grateful for the chance to breathe some fresh air, Elizabeth headed for the front door. In the excitement, she'd left her coat in the shop, so the icy temperatures were a shock to her system. As she walked down the porch steps, she noticed it was starting to snow again. Through the white haze she watched two cars pull away. When she entered the barn, she found that except for Emily Miller and her children, the store was empty. Everyone else had left.

Emily was herding the children toward the door. "I felt I should stay until you returned," she said with a smile. "I hope everything is all right?"

Elizabeth nodded. "Just a couple of pies."

Emily laughed lightly. "I have done the same thing myself. I am grateful it was not anything more serious."

As they walked past her, Elizabeth said goodbye.

She sat down in a chair next to the cash register and took a deep breath, trying to calm her jangled nerves. She was just beginning to feel a little better when she stood to her feet and began to frantically search the countertop. "Where are the pictures?" she asked out loud of no one in particular. Her heart raced in her chest as she moved everything on the counter, hoping they were underneath something. But her efforts were in vain.

Every single one of the photos had disappeared.

CHAPTER TWO

Elizabeth couldn't believe her eyes. She must have made a mistake. Had she really left the pictures spread out on the counter, or had she absentmindedly stuck them somewhere safe before rushing out the door? Muscle memory was tricky. She'd lost plenty of items at home in the past, only to find her misplaced glasses or coffee cup perched on a random bookshelf. Maybe she'd done the same thing with the pictures.

Elizabeth searched all the nooks and crannies by the front counter. She checked every shelf, and behind them too, in case the photos had slithered to the floor. She gave the office a once-over but didn't find anything. Even the paper envelope that held the negatives was missing.

The pictures were really gone. Her heart sank. What was she going to tell Lauren? She had trusted them to take care of the photos.

There had been several people in the store a few minutes ago. Who had been there? Elizabeth ran through the list in her mind. The long-haired college student, Grant. He'd certainly seemed interested in the pictures. Another man she didn't know had been hovering close by the counter too. Maybe he was a friend of Grant's?

Elizabeth noticed two jars of elderberry jam sitting on the counter. Rosie had forgotten to take them with her. Elizabeth made a mental note to set the jam aside for Rosie. The only other people who had been in the store were Emily Miller and her children.

A thought struck Elizabeth. Emily! Emily had been the last one in the store. Surely she would have seen what happened. Maybe Elizabeth could still catch her. She rushed outside and saw that Emily was already nearing the end of the driveway. She watched as Emily maneuvered the horse down the snow-dusted road. Elizabeth wanted to run after the buggy, but the snow in the yard was accumulating, and the ground was too slick. Elizabeth pulled her coat close, then headed back to the house.

Mary stood at the sink, attempting to pry burned crust from a flowered pie pan with a spatula. She jerked her fingers back as they touched the dish. "Ouch! That's hot."

She sighed as she looked around the kitchen. The air in the room was still hazy, even though she and Martha had flung open all the windows to clear out the smoke from the botched pies. A thick, tarry substance coated the bottom of the oven where the pie filling had bubbled over. The counter was littered with burnt pies that she doubted even their goats would eat.

Martha sounded impatient. "Just leave the pies and the stove for now, Mary. Everything will have to cool down before we can even start to clean."

"I know. I just wanted to try before the filling dries and gets stuck." Mary felt awful. She'd offered to make pies for Lancaster County Helping Hands in part because she longed to be more like Martha. She admired her older sister's ability to take charge and get things done.

Responsible. Dependable. Someone who helped out and made a positive difference. Now Mary feared she'd gone and messed up again. The bumbling little sister in need of help. "What a disaster, Martha. I'm so sorry."

Martha sighed. "It's okay. We're only human." She grabbed a wet rag and started wiping down the counters. "I'm just glad no one got hurt."

Mary was surprised Martha wasn't more upset with her. She flopped into a chair. "Well, I'll get better. Practice makes perfect, after all."

Martha wrinkled her brow. "Practice?"

"Every cook has to start somewhere. I'm sure I'll improve."

"Yes, except you don't really need to." Martha rinsed out her rag and draped it over the sink divide to dry. She turned to face Mary fully. "Why don't you just let me make the pies? I enjoy baking, and it will get done quickly. You can move on to something else."

Mary brushed off her sister's offer of help. "There's no need. This was just a fluke."

Martha took a deep breath. "It was more than a small accident, Mary. The house could have caught on fire. Surely you see how serious that is."

"That's a little dramatic. The pies got overcooked, and the filling bubbled over. Nothing caught on fire."

"Nothing except the oven."

Mary glanced up, startled, when Elizabeth cleared her throat from the doorway. "Elizabeth, you're back. I didn't hear you come in. Did you close up shop for the evening?" Mary noticed Elizabeth's worried expression. Something was wrong.

"No, not yet. When I went back, Lauren's pictures were missing. I can't find them anywhere. Did one of you grab them and bring them into the house without me noticing?"

Mary shook her head, and so did Martha.

Elizabeth sighed. "That's what I was afraid of. Would you two help me search the store again? Maybe your fresh eyes will spot something I missed."

The sisters secured the windows on the house and made their way across the snow to Secondhand Blessings. They checked the store from top to bottom but found no sign of Lauren's missing photos.

"So, do we think someone took the pictures?" Martha stopped neatening shelves and straightened up.

"It's looking that way." Elizabeth's smile was tight, and Mary draped an arm across her sister's shoulders.

"It'll be okay, Lizzie. Was anybody in the shop when you came back?"

"Just Emily Miller and her children. I wanted to ask if she saw anything, but she left before I could."

"I trust Emily," Martha said. "She'll be honest with you. Though she did have her hands full with those kids. I wouldn't wonder if she was distracted."

Mary remembered Emily's foster child, Timmy. The little boy was sweet, but just today, she'd seen him pocket some crayons from the small children's table in the corner of the store.

She'd quietly mentioned it to Emily, so as not to embarrass the boy, and Emily had apologized.

"What about Timmy?"

"Emily's little boy? What about him?" Martha asked.

"I don't think he'd do anything wrong on purpose, but he has tried to take items from the store before. Today he put crayons in his pocket. When I mentioned something to Emily, she said stockpiling is a habit a lot of foster children pick up as a survival mechanism. You don't think Timmy could have taken the pictures?"

"I guess it's possible," said Elizabeth. "But how would he have smuggled out that many photos without Emily noticing?"

"There weren't that many. He could have figured something out. Or hidden them in here."

"I agree with Elizabeth," Martha said. "I think someone would have noticed a child grabbing a stack of photos."

"But shouldn't we at least check with Emily?" Mary asked. "Just in case?"

Elizabeth sighed. "I suppose I could pay Emily a visit tomorrow. Though I hate to cause her trouble or embarrass Timmy. He's had a tough enough time already."

"Maybe I could go with you," offered Mary. "We could treat it like a social visit. I could bring a pie."

Martha snorted, but Mary acted as though she didn't notice.

Elizabeth sighed. "That sounds good. I almost hope Timmy did take the photos. I don't like the idea of Lauren's family keepsakes floating around with a stranger. They're private, or they should be."

"We don't know that they're with a stranger." Martha raised an eyebrow. "What about Rosie Gittrich?"

Elizabeth gasped. "Oh, Martha! You don't really think Rosie would have taken them?"

"She did act a little peculiar when she saw them. Let's check with Emily first and make sure Timmy didn't have a hand in this."

"You're right," Martha said. "Why don't we go ahead and close up shop for the evening? I'll just put this jam in the back for Rosie in case she returns tomorrow." Martha grabbed the elderberry jam Rosie had left sitting on the counter. As she did so, a scrap of paper that had been weighted down by the jars fluttered to the floor.

"What's this?" Elizabeth bent down to pick up the paper.

"What does it say?" Mary asked. She tried to peek over her sister's shoulder, but she couldn't make out the words. "Is it a note from Rosie?"

"It doesn't look like her handwriting," said Elizabeth slowly. "I've seen her signature on quite a few receipts."

"The important thing is, what does it say?" Martha asked. She crossed the room to join them.

Elizabeth took a deep breath. "The note—no matter who wrote it—seems like a threat."

Goose bumps prickled along Mary's skin. "What do you mean? Who would threaten us?"

"How ridiculous," said Martha. "It must be a joke."

"If it's a joke, it's an odd one." Elizabeth turned the note toward her sisters. "It says, 'Forget the pictures.' That's it. There's nothing more. No name. Just 'Forget the pictures.'"

CHAPTER THREE

When the sisters sat down for supper, Elizabeth was anxious to talk about the missing photos. Why would anyone take them? It just didn't make sense. And the note? Was it a threat?

Martha had made pasta and salad. The sisters prayed over their food and then dug in. Martha's hearty pasta was comforting after a confusing day.

"I've got to call Lauren tonight and tell her the pictures are gone," Elizabeth said. "But I need to let her know that we're looking for them. That we're determined to find them and return them to her."

"I don't think you should promise something like that," Mary said with a frown. "They just might be gone for good."

"But why would someone take them?" Elizabeth asked. "If the pictures had nothing to do with you or your family, why would you want them?"

"There has to be a reason," Martha said. "We just have to find it." She focused her attention on Elizabeth.

"And what about that note?" Mary asked. "*Forget the pictures.* It sounds pretty sinister to me."

"But none of the people in our shop seemed *sinister*," Elizabeth said.

"Who was in the shop when you left?" Martha asked.

"You mean to save our house from destruction?" Mary asked with a sigh.

Martha didn't say anything, just shook her head. It was obvious she was still upset about the pie incident.

"Let me see," Elizabeth said, trying to recall everyone who was in the shop when she left. "Emily Miller was there with her kids. Rosie Gittrich came in to buy some jam, but she left it sitting on the counter."

"There was that strange man," Mary said. "You know, the one who kept trying to see the photos. He seemed really interested in them."

Elizabeth nodded after taking another bite of pasta. "I have no idea who he was. I'd never seen him before."

"Is that it?" Martha asked.

Elizabeth shook her head. "A young man with a backpack was also very interested in the photos. In fact, he asked if he could borrow them."

Martha's eyebrows shot up. "That sounds suspicious."

"It does, but I liked him," Elizabeth said. "He's a student at the Pennsylvania College of Art and Design. His name is…" Elizabeth put her hand into her pocket and pulled out a small piece of paper. "Grant Slavick." She shook her head. "I doubt that most thieves would give you their name and phone number."

"I agree," said Mary, pointing her fork at Elizabeth. "But how do we know if that's his real name or number?"

Elizabeth shrugged. "I guess we don't, but we can call and find out."

"What do we say?" Martha asked. "By the way, did you happen to steal those pictures you were looking at? And did you by any chance leave us a threatening note?"

There was silence as the women thought it over. "We could tell him they're missing and ask him if he noticed anyone fooling with the photos after we left," Mary said slowly.

Martha sighed. "I think that's a good idea." She ran her hand through her brown hair.

"Rosie seemed surprised by the pictures," Elizabeth said. "She gasped when she saw them. Of course, maybe she was reacting to something else. I can't be sure."

"There were a lot of people in the photos," Martha said. "Any idea which one upset her?"

Elizabeth shook her head. "I honestly don't have a clue."

"Maybe she knew someone in the war photos," Mary said. Her blond hair shone under the light that hung above the large kitchen table where they were gathered. She drummed her red fingernails on the table. Martha thought spending money on fake fingernails was silly. "Mama always said the most beautiful hands are the ones that create things," she'd say. Elizabeth really didn't care. Having her nails done made Mary happy. She couldn't see the harm.

The table on which Mary's nails tapped was old, built by their father many years ago. The women loved the table and the homey kitchen where they were gathered. Although they'd updated it a bit, for the most part it was just the way their mother had left it. It almost felt as if she were still here with them.

"Would Rosie have written that note?" Elizabeth asked.

"No," Martha said. "Nor would Emily Miller. That leaves this...Grant person. Or the man you didn't know."

"It would be almost impossible to find him," Elizabeth said. "Frankly, he sounds like our number-one suspect."

"I wouldn't let Grant off the hook so fast," Martha said, waving her fork around.

"Maybe," Elizabeth said slowly.

"Don't forget Timmy," Mary said.

"I haven't," Elizabeth said. "Trying to keep that many children corralled could cause Emily to lose sight of him for a minute or two. But then there's the note. Timmy certainly didn't write it." She frowned at Mary. "Did Todd give us the negatives for the photos?"

Mary nodded. "Sorry. They were in the package with the rest of the photos."

Elizabeth took a deep breath and blew it out. "I'd love to get a look at those pictures."

"Maybe if we could see them we could figure out why they were so valuable to someone," Martha said. "You know, whoever it was took a big chance grabbing them from our counter with people in the store. They could have easily been seen."

"You're right," Mary said slowly. "Makes the whole thing even weirder."

Elizabeth stared at the strange note lying on the table as the sisters finished supper. She couldn't help but worry. Was there something in the pictures that someone didn't want them to see? The note especially worried her. They had no choice but to look for Lauren's pictures since she'd entrusted them to the sisters. Did ignoring the note mean they were putting themselves in danger? Were they in danger?

CHAPTER FOUR

Elizabeth's stomach churned as she picked up the phone. She had dawdled over supper cleanup, helping her sisters put away the leftover food and wash the dishes. Then Mary and Martha got busy scrubbing out the cooled-off oven. As messy as the task was, Elizabeth would've preferred to help them than do what she needed to right now: call Lauren with the bad news about the photos. There was no way around it, though. The pictures were Lauren's property and unique memories of her family. She'd trusted the sisters with care of them. Elizabeth owed it to Lauren to be direct and honest with her.

She hesitated, her finger hovering over the numbers. Maybe she was worrying for nothing. It was possible Lauren wouldn't even be upset. After all, she hadn't noticed the vintage camera she'd sold to Secondhand Blessings had film in it. She'd seemed relaxed about the sisters developing the film for her. Maybe she was just curious about the photos but not horribly attached to the idea of having them as family keepsakes.

Lauren's excited tone when she recognized Elizabeth's voice on the phone instantly dashed Elizabeth's hopes.

"Elizabeth! How nice to hear from you. I'm so anxious to know if you got those photos back yet. I'm just chomping at the bit."

"We did get the photos back..."

Lauren gave a little squeal of excitement. "Oh, I've been thinking more about them, and I just can't tell you how thrilled I am that I might have some family photos from my grandfather's side. I know practically nothing about them. Not his mother or his dad. Only that they were Amish and that he'd had a falling out with them a long time ago. Granddad was very mysterious about his past. I can't wait to see these pictures. It could really fill in a lot of puzzle pieces."

Elizabeth swallowed. "I'm afraid I didn't finish my sentence. We did get the photos back...but now we don't have them."

"Don't have them? I don't understand."

"My sister, Mary, picked the photos up after they were developed. Then she brought them to the store so Martha and I could see them before we contacted you."

"And? I'm guessing this is the part where the other shoe drops."

"I'm afraid so. Mary forgot about some pies she had baking in the oven at the house, and when they started smoking, we thought the house was on fire. Everything turned out to be fine, but when we rushed out of the store to check on the house, the photos went...missing."

"Missing? Like misplaced?" Lauren paused. "Or like stolen?"

"I'm not sure. We've scoured the store but haven't turned anything up. It's looking like they may have been taken. We're hoping it's just a misunderstanding."

"How could someone accidentally take something that wasn't theirs?" Lauren sounded close to tears. "Those photos were so important to me. The basement in Granddad's house flooded about ten years ago, and we lost a bunch of shoeboxes full of photos. We managed to salvage a few but not many."

"I'm so sorry, Lauren. I know you trusted us, and we let you down. I promise you, we're doing everything we can to locate the pictures."

Lauren's voice was thick with emotion. "Do you have any idea who might have taken them?"

"We have a list of customers who were in the store at the time, yes. We're planning to talk with some of them tomorrow and see if we can figure out where the photos might have gone."

There was a long sniffle on the other end of the line. "I'd like to come with you if I could."

"Can I let you know? It might be better if I approach people on my own. The last thing I want is for anyone to get defensive or think I'm accusing them unfairly. It's a delicate situation."

"Whatever you think is best. As long as we get the pictures back." Lauren sighed, and Elizabeth heard a rustle like tissue on the other end of the line. "Did you at least see the pictures before they were stolen?"

"I did, but I don't remember much. I only had a moment before we ran out to check on the house."

"I'd appreciate anything you could remember." Lauren's voice was pleading, and Elizabeth searched her memory. Lauren was being so kind about the whole situation, but Elizabeth felt awful.

"Um... Let's see... There was a photo of a young man standing in front of a barn. He was dressed in Amish clothing.

Dark pants and shirt. Straw hat, so it must have been summer when the photo was taken."

"I wonder if that was my grandfather," said Lauren eagerly. "Before he left the community, I mean." Elizabeth felt a pang at Lauren's words. She had obviously been close to her grandfather and was probably still mourning the loss. Elizabeth knew how much it eased the grief of losing a loved one to have a physical memento of them. She kept a scarf of Mama's that held happy memories.

"There were a few other photos of a field and some outbuildings. Maybe a couple taken inside a home?" Elizabeth was apologetic. She wished she could help Lauren more. "I'm afraid that's all I remember right now. But we'll do everything we can to recover the pictures."

"All right." Lauren sighed again. "Will you please call me right away if you hear anything?"

"Of course."

The two women said goodbye and hung up. Elizabeth felt the weight of responsibility heavy on her shoulders. What was she going to do if she couldn't get the pictures back? She'd not only be letting down Lauren but also Lauren's entire family.

Tuesday morning dawned clear and cold. True to her word, Mary tried her hand at baking a pie to take to Emily. It was a good thing Martha was running the store again this morning; otherwise, Elizabeth suspected her younger sister would have been hovering over Mary like a hawk. Left on her own, though,

Mary seemed to do well. She watched her timer carefully, and the pie came out nicely browned but not overly so.

Mary looked satisfied. "There. That's not too shabby, is it?"

"Not at all."

Mary cheerfully plunked the pie on a pot holder and lowered it into a cardboard box. "Oh no!" she said. "There goes another one."

"What? Is the pie okay?"

Mary pulled the pie out of the box again and looked sheepish. "No, the pie's fine. It's my nails that are worse for wear." She held up a hand which now only sported three red nail tips. "I lost one earlier today, and just now, I caught one on the box edge."

Elizabeth reached into the box and pulled out a detached acrylic nail. "Be glad it didn't fall in the pie. Close call," she said with a wry smile. She handed the nail to Mary, who made a face and tossed it in the trash. Mary frowned but finally saw the humor and smiled back.

"That's what I get for getting a manicure at a cheap place."

The two women went out to the idling car, which Elizabeth had let run to warm up. Mary sat in the passenger seat, cradling the pie protectively in her lap, while Elizabeth drove. Emily's house was only a few miles away, and they soon arrived. Like many of the Amish homes in the area, the Millers' farm was large, to accommodate a life focused on family and agriculture. The house was white with a brown roof and a generous expanse of front porch, and it looked pleasantly well kept.

Elizabeth navigated up the steps with Mary lagging behind, going slowly so as not to drop her pie.

Emily answered the door, a smudge of flour on her cheek and several of her little ones crowded at her hip. "Elizabeth, Mary, what a pleasant surprise to see you both. I was not expecting company today."

"We thought it would be a nice day for a visit," Elizabeth said, though she felt the strain of the half-truth in her tight smile.

"We brought a pie. Blueberry," Mary said proudly, holding the dish out. "Though I'm sure it's not as good as yours."

Emily graciously accepted the gift and motioned for Elizabeth and Mary to enter. "Come in, come in." When Elizabeth entered, she saw evidence that Emily had been hard at work already that morning. Her kitchen counters were liberally dusted with flour, and it looked as though she was preparing a variety of baked goods: bread, cookies, and also a few pies of her own. Their delicately cut lattice crusts looked like works of art.

"I'm sorry," Elizabeth said. "We've interrupted you."

"Oh, the baking will wait a few minutes for a visit." Emily shrugged off Elizabeth's concern. She brought cups of steaming coffee to the table for her guests and fished around in a drawer before removing a pie server.

"Let me offer you some of this lovely dessert Mary brought to go with the coffee. You were so kind to bring it." Mary blushed, but Elizabeth could tell she was pleased.

Emily cut into the pie but stopped before sliding a wedge onto a plate. A puzzled look crossed her face.

"Is something wrong?" Mary asked, rising to Emily's side.

"I think there's been a mistake," Emily said.

Mary knit her eyebrows and leaned over the pan. "Did it not cook all the way through? The top was so perfectly brown."

"No, but there is something unusual about it," said Emily, her eyes wide. She reached into a nearby drawer and grabbed a teaspoon. She fished around in the pie to pull out a bright red fake fingernail. "I am fairly sure this was not supposed to be one of the ingredients in your pie."

Elizabeth thought Mary would die of embarrassment then and there.

Her sister turned beet red and stared at the pie with a horrified look. "I am so sorry, Emily. It must have slipped into the bowl when I was mixing."

To Elizabeth's surprise, Emily burst into laughter, but seeing Mary's reaction, she pressed a hand to her mouth to quell her amusement. "Please do not think me impolite. I only laugh because I made many mistakes when I first started baking."

"Nothing as bad as this, I'm sure," said Mary, looking pained.

Emily quickly cleared her throat. "I have another pie that just finished cooling on the drainboard. Let me fetch it for us."

As Emily busied herself cutting fresh slices of pie, Mary whispered to Elizabeth, "See? I told you her pies would be better than mine. I'm a hopeless case."

Elizabeth slipped an arm around her sister's shoulders. "Don't be so hard on yourself. Everybody makes mistakes when they're learning. You'll do fine after some more practice."

Emily handed the sisters plates of warm lingonberry pie before settling in at the table herself. "And how is everything at the store?"

Elizabeth paused with a bite halfway to her mouth. Suddenly, she felt as though she'd been exposed to an X-ray machine. She wondered if Emily, as polite as she was, had guessed the real reason for their visit before they'd even stepped inside. She shook her head. "I seem to have misplaced some photographs I had in the store. I was wondering if maybe you moved them somewhere for safekeeping while I was gone?"

Emily frowned. "I am sorry to say I did not. I kept an eye on the register for you, but other than that, I was busy minding the children."

"So you didn't see anyone else pick up the photos?"

"No, I did not. You do not think someone took them? Surely it would be a misunderstanding if they did?"

Elizabeth smiled. Emily always assumed the best of people. Elizabeth tried to do the same, but she wasn't quite as practiced at the art as Emily.

"You know, Timmy sometimes takes things," Emily said, "but he would not take your pictures. Besides, if he had, I would have found them last night when the children got ready for bed."

"Thank you, Emily," Elizabeth said, grateful that Emily had mentioned Timmy before they had. She still felt Timmy wasn't at fault. He wouldn't have written the note they found. She glanced at Mary, who looked satisfied with Emily's comments.

Emily's frown deepened. "I do not want you to worry." She called Timmy into the room. She got out of her chair and knelt down to his height, looking him in the eyes.

"Timmy, there are some items missing from the Classens' shop. Some photographs. Did you take anything yesterday that did not belong to you?" At first, the little boy fought meeting Emily's gaze and tried to twist from her grasp.

"Lemme go. Lemme go," he muttered as he struggled against her.

Emily kept her voice smooth and level. "You are not in trouble, Timmy. I only want you to tell the truth to me, *ja*?" She held him firmly but gently and waited patiently as he struggled to interact with her.

Elizabeth's heart nearly broke watching the tender interaction between caregiver and child. A four-year-old child unable to be cared for by his birth parents. A child who had likely been neglected his whole life, and maybe accused like this many times. Her heart ached, and she swallowed hard.

Timmy finally calmed down and held eye contact with Emily for a moment before looking away.

"Timmy? Did you take anything from the Classens' store yesterday?" Emily asked again.

"No," the boy finally said. "I didn't take anything." He swiped at his nose with his shirt sleeve. He finally pulled himself out of Emily's grasp and ran out of the room.

Emily stood to her feet. "I am sorry we can't help," she said, "but I believe him. Your thief is not Timmy."

Elizabeth thanked her. Now they knew more about who hadn't taken the photos, but when would they learn something that would lead them toward the real thief? Were the photos gone for good?

CHAPTER FIVE

It's all right," Elizabeth said in response to Emily's statement. She smiled through her disappointment. She'd hoped to find the pictures today.

"If it would set your mind at ease, I will look through his things just in case he took your photos," Emily said, "but I have not seen any sign of them. I believe I would have found them by now if they were here. I truly do believe him, though."

"Thank you for looking anyway," Elizabeth said. Since she didn't want to mention the threatening note to Emily, she couldn't tell her the reason they hadn't really suspected Timmy.

Emily smiled at Mary. "I hear you are also baking for the Helping Hands fund-raiser."

Mary laughed. "Yes, if I can keep my fingernails out of the pies."

"You will be fine." Emily laughed with her. "I must tell you that my first few pies were a disaster. My worst experience happened when I substituted salt for sugar. My *maam* had changed the containers, and I did not know." She wrinkled her nose and giggled. "My *daed* took the first bite of my pie. Not wanting to hurt my feelings, he tried to say something nice, but in the end, he had to spit it out." She nodded at Mary. "You will outdo me, I believe."

Mary laughed with her. "Thank you for that story, Emily. It really does make me feel a little better."

Elizabeth and Mary said goodbye and went out to the car. There was still snow on the ground, so they had to walk carefully to keep from slipping.

"I'm afraid this didn't help us much," Mary said once they were in the car.

"I'm really worried about those photos. If they weren't so important to Lauren, I wouldn't be so upset about losing them. But she has so little of her family history."

Mary reached over and patted her sister's arm. "I know. I'm sure they'll turn up. But I still don't see why anyone would want old photos that had nothing to do with them."

"I don't either," Elizabeth said. "This might be the oddest theft we've ever experienced."

The two women stopped at a favorite local sandwich shop and picked up lunch. Martha had been handling the store for a while. It was only fair she get a break. Mary and Elizabeth planned to eat their sandwiches inside the store when there weren't any customers.

When they arrived there was only one car parked near the barn. The sisters got out and went inside. Elizabeth's stomach tensed when she saw Lauren Collier talking to Martha. She hated to give her bad news.

Lauren looked at her and smiled. "I heard you might know where my pictures are."

"I told her it was only a possibility," Martha said quickly. Elizabeth was sure her sister could tell by looking at her that she hadn't recovered the photographs.

"I'm sorry, Lauren," she said, "but it didn't pan out. We have some other ideas, though. We're not done."

Lauren was in her twenties, but she looked tired beyond her years. Elizabeth couldn't imagine the stress she was under, having to clean out her grandfather's house by herself. She was shocked to see tears spring into Lauren's eyes. She hurried over to her. "We're doing our best to find them—"

Lauren waved her comment away. "It isn't that," she said, wiping her face. "My grandfather left some debts. I had no idea about them until after he died." She took a deep breath. "He'd gotten a second mortgage on the house. I don't have the money to make the payments." She sniffed several times. "He left the house to me. I love that house. I don't want to lose it. I've sold enough things to keep the bank happy...for now. But unless I find something pretty valuable, I'll lose it." She looked at them with a tear-stained face. "I know that has nothing to do with the photos. I'm sorry I brought it up."

Elizabeth put her arm around the young woman's shoulders. "I'm glad you told us. We'll keep going through his possessions. Surely there's something that will help."

"We'll do everything we can," Mary said. "Don't give up."

Lauren's gloomy expression lightened, and she smiled. "Thank you. I really appreciate that."

"Lauren, I know you don't have any other family here, but don't you have friends who can help you?"

"I moved here a couple of years ago to take care of my grandfather. He was ill, so I never really got out much. I don't know a lot of people." A sudden smile played on her lips. "I did meet a nice guy at church. Peter. He's been coming over to the house in the afternoon and unpacking boxes so I can find out just what I have. He's been such a big help."

Mary smiled. "Sounds like you like him."

Lauren blushed. "I...I don't know him that well yet, but yes, I guess I do. He certainly has helped take some of the weight off my shoulders." She shook her head. "You wouldn't believe all the junk my grandfather had. The attic is full. The basement is full. And the furniture in the house was covered with piles of stuff. I'm convinced he never let go of anything."

"Was he a hoarder?" Martha asked.

"Just a few degrees shy of it, maybe. I tried to talk him into getting rid of some things, but he wouldn't allow it. I knew the basement was a mess, but I'd never gone into the attic. It's even worse. Grandfather wouldn't let me go up there. Now I know why." She sighed deeply. "At least he allowed me to throw his trash away." She frowned. "I found a bunch of old letters and quite a few magazines in the basement. I'm pulling out any that mark important historical events. Just in case."

"You should also keep copies of the first magazine from a publisher," Elizabeth said. "Some of them can be valuable. Of course, condition is everything."

"Unfortunately, most of them were just shoved in boxes. Mice got into a bunch of it. We've had to throw a lot of boxes out without going through them."

"I can understand that," Mary said. "Yuck."

Lauren nodded. "Yuck indeed."

The door to the shop opened, and Mrs. Andrews, a woman who lived in Bird-in-Hand, came in with a large bag. She was downsizing and had mentioned she had some kitchen items she couldn't use anymore. Quality glass baking dishes went like hotcakes in the shop. Mrs. Andrews insisted she had a great collection.

"You need to work," Lauren said. "I should go."

Elizabeth thought of asking Lauren if she wanted to stay for lunch. She planned to give the young woman her sandwich. There was plenty of food in the house. She didn't need the wonderfully fragrant meatball sub sitting in the bag next to her. Before she could make the supreme sacrifice, Lauren's phone rang.

She looked at the phone's display. "It's Peter," she said. "I left him the key. I hope he didn't have trouble getting in." She said hello, and within seconds, her face fell. She only said a few words and then hung up.

"Is something wrong?" Elizabeth asked.

"When Peter got to the house, he found the back door kicked in. Someone was in the house. Peter thinks they may have stolen something."

CHAPTER SIX

Let's step back in the office for a minute." Elizabeth ushered Lauren toward the back of the shop so they could talk in private. Mary and Martha stayed out front to help Mrs. Andrews.

"Why don't you have a seat?" Elizabeth pulled a chair out of the corner, and Lauren sank into it. "You look pale. Has Peter contacted the police yet?"

Lauren ran a trembling hand through her hair. "Yes. He said he called them before he phoned me to break the news. He's sitting out in his car right now in case someone's still in the house." She shuddered. "Can you imagine running into someone as they're trying to rob you? How scary. I'm so glad Peter's okay. Now I just hope the thief didn't take anything too sentimental."

Elizabeth felt a fresh pang of guilt. That was the last thing Lauren needed, since the photos had gone missing. She rested a reassuring hand on Lauren's shoulder. How relieved she'd been when the farmhouse had turned out to be safe, if a bit smoky, after yesterday's pie fiasco. All the memories held within those walls. All the times she remembered, of holidays and special occasions spent with her sisters and her parents. She identified with what Lauren was feeling, and she ached for her.

Lauren eyes misted, and she removed a tissue from her bag to dab at her face. "I'm sorry. I'm not usually emotional like this."

"No need to apologize. You've dealt with a lot the last few months. Lauren, didn't your grandfather have anything saved? Any money put aside for emergencies?"

"Not really. What little bit he did have went toward funeral expenses. And then I maxed out my credit cards to cover the rest."

"He didn't have life insurance?"

Lauren shook her head. "He grew up Amish, you know. Even after he left the community, he still didn't like the idea of buying a life insurance policy." She dabbed at her eyes again.

"You mentioned you're still going through his belongings. I know you'll want to keep some items, but is there anything you could sell to gain some money to put toward the house?"

"Maybe. He had a lot of possessions. I'm trying to sort through them, room by room, but it's…overwhelming."

"It sounds like he was a collector. Why don't you let me work with you to go through everything? Assess the value. Of course, I'd need to refer you to an antique shop if we find anything really valuable, but otherwise, my sisters and I would be glad to help."

Lauren looked as though she were about to mist up again. "That would be really helpful, thank you." She pressed a hand to her forehead. "What I don't understand is why someone would break into my grandfather's house in the first place. It's old. Run-down. Granddad lived simply. It doesn't seem like the best target for a burglar."

"Maybe someone thought it was empty, since your grandfather died. Someone who wanted to get out of the cold."

"Like a drifter?" Lauren sounded doubtful. Her cell phone rang again from the recesses of her bag, and she answered it quickly. "Hello?" After exchanging a few brief sentences, she hung up.

"That was Peter again. I need to head back to the house right away. The police are there, and they want to talk with me." Lauren slung her purse over her shoulder. "Listen, why don't you come with me?"

Elizabeth shook her head. "Oh, you don't need me there. I'd only be in the way."

"You wouldn't be. I have to check the house for missing items. We could look through things together at the same time. You could let me know if you see anything of value that I could sell. Plus, it would make me feel better to have you there."

Elizabeth smiled. "Let me get my coat."

When they pulled up at the house, two police cars sat out front, their lights flashing red and blue streaks across the snow. A group of officers stood in the front yard. Elizabeth scanned the faces to see if Officer John Marks was in the group, but she didn't see him. She and John had been seeing each other, although they were just friends. They got along well, and she certainly enjoyed his company. She was disappointed he wasn't in the crowd. She blushed, feeling like a silly schoolgirl. She pushed thoughts of him out of her mind as Lauren jumped out of her car and ran over to Peter.

"Did they catch anyone?" she asked breathlessly.

"No, I think he—or she—must've left when I came in the front door. The police have combed the place, but they didn't find anybody."

"Is anything missing? Could you tell?"

"I'm not sure. Nothing struck me off the bat. You'd probably have a better idea of that than I would, though."

An officer pulled Lauren aside to ask her a few questions. Elizabeth introduced herself to Peter.

He smiled. "You're the one who has the thrift shop, right? Lauren talks about you. She really appreciates what you've done so far to help her with her grandfather's estate. His death has been tough on her. She doesn't have a lot of other family."

Peter was tall, with wavy black hair and a kind smile. Elizabeth liked him immediately. He seemed very devoted to Lauren and committed to helping her get through the loss of her grandfather. Elizabeth was glad Lauren could count him as a friend.

"I know what it's like to lose a dear family member. My mother died not too long ago. Lauren is a strong woman. I know she'll get through this just fine. It takes time."

"I'm sure she will. It's just a shame she has to deal with a break-in on top of everything else. When it rains, it pours, I guess."

Elizabeth smiled. "Things will look up soon."

"I hope so."

The police officer walked back across the yard with Lauren. "Let's check out the inside, see if you notice anything missing."

Lauren shot Elizabeth and Peter a tight smile and entered the house. After a few minutes, she came back outside.

"Anything gone?" Peter asked. He slipped a protective arm around her shoulders, and she leaned into him gratefully.

Lauren shook her head. "Not that I can tell." Peter looked relieved, and Elizabeth knew how he felt.

"Sorry we can't do more right now," the officer said, looking apologetic. "We'll make sure to keep a close eye on the place, and we'll let you know if we get any leads. You be sure to call us if anything else out of the ordinary happens."

"Thank you," said Lauren. "I will."

The officers loaded up and drove off, and Peter jabbed a thumb over his shoulder at the house. "Why don't I go see if I can get that busted door secured, at least temporarily."

Lauren shot him a smile as he disappeared toward the back of the house.

"He seems like a good guy," Elizabeth said.

"He is. I'm so thankful for him. When you're going through a tough time, it helps to have people who support you." She gave Elizabeth's hand a quick squeeze.

"That's certainly true."

Lauren wrapped her coat tighter around herself. "Why don't we go inside? It's freezing out here."

Elizabeth glanced at her as they walked across the yard to the large two-story home. "Are you sure you're okay?"

"I'm fine. A little shaken up, but that's to be expected, I guess. It feels like such a violation to have your door kicked in and to know somebody was looking at your personal belongings.

It creeps me out to know the thief is still out there. What if he or she comes back?"

"I have a friend on the force here. The police department is very thorough. I know they'll do their best to find whoever broke in."

Lauren gave a little shiver. "I hope you're right."

The inside of the house was a mess, though Elizabeth had no way of knowing if the chaos was due to the attempted burglary or if it had been left in that condition after Lauren's grandfather died. She could see that the house, with its braided rugs and hardwood floors, would be considered cozy and cute if it was cleaned up. Right now, though, it bombarded the eye with visual clutter. The space felt cramped due to the random piles of cardboard boxes, stacks of books and papers, and various knickknacks cluttering every flat surface. Elizabeth wouldn't be surprised if the robber ran out because he had no idea what to grab first.

Wandering into the den, she picked up a scrapbook that lay open on the floor. She turned the crackling cellophane pages carefully. The album was filled with newspaper clippings from World War II.

"Was your grandfather a history buff?"

Lauren stopped her perusing to peer over Elizabeth's shoulder. "I don't know about him being a history buff in general. He was very interested in World War II, though. He served in the army."

"Really? How very interesting. That's quite unusual, given his Amish background."

Lauren lowered her voice, though there was no one around to eavesdrop. "I think that's why he wound up leaving the Amish community. He was raised to be pacifist, but he also felt a responsibility to help out in some way with the war effort."

Elizabeth mulled the information over in her mind as she walked slowly through the rest of the house, checking for items that might be valuable antiques. She made mental notes about a few pieces of furniture in good condition, and some unusual items, like a particularly intricate cuckoo clock and an item that looked similar to an old typewriter that warranted a second look.

In the back of the house, Elizabeth found a room that must have served as an office. A rolltop desk was shoved against one wall, and stacks of newspapers lined the other walls. Cardboard boxes held a jumble of random items.

"It's like Granddad never threw anything away," Lauren said. She put her hands on her hips and looked around the room in disbelief. "I don't even know where to start."

"We'll start in one corner and work our way to the next. My mother always used to say that you can't do everything at once, but you can do something at once."

Lauren let her arms drop and grinned, the first real one Elizabeth had seen on her face that day. "Smart lady."

"She sure was." Something on a cluttered end table caught Elizabeth's eye. "What about this?" She held up an amber-colored stained-glass lamp. When the light from the window shone through it, it gleamed. "Look how beautiful this is. The style looks similar to a Tiffany lamp. I'm certain this would sell well at an antique store. I'd estimate you could get a few hundred dollars out of it, at a minimum."

Lauren drew in a deep breath. "That is lovely. What a find, Elizabeth." She carefully packed the lamp in newspaper and nestled it in its own box.

"There are a few other items I've noticed that you might have checked out." Elizabeth pulled her cell phone out of her bag and read off the name and number of a friend who owned a local antique shop. Lauren dutifully typed the information into her contacts.

The women worked for several hours. Finally, Elizabeth suggested that Lauren and Peter pack up items they thought could be valuable and bring them to the shop where she and her sisters could sort through them. Lauren loved the idea and promised to do just that.

Elizabeth couldn't help but shiver as she headed back into the cold. She waved goodbye to Lauren and Peter as she climbed into her SUV, but her head was full of questions. What was in Lauren's photos that was so important? Who would want to break into an old man's house? And most worrying of all—what if the events were connected in some way, and Lauren and the sisters were being targeted by someone?

CHAPTER SEVEN

By the time Elizabeth got back, it was late afternoon, and the sun was low in the sky. She noticed the lights on in the shop and went inside. Martha and Mary were stocking some new items from a local woman who created handmade kitchen items. When she entered the store her sisters had nothing but questions.

"So, what happened?" asked Martha. "Did they catch the person who broke in?"

Elizabeth sighed. "No. Lauren thinks Peter scared off whoever it was before they were able to take anything. The police are going to keep a close watch on the place in case the thief comes back."

"I'm so glad nothing was missing," Mary said, her eyes wide.

"I am too," Elizabeth replied. "I had a look around, but there is so much stuff. Lauren and Peter are going to box some of it up and bring it over here so we can go through items. Lauren does have some nice pieces from her grandfather. He owned a few antiques, some World War II memorabilia. There was also a beautiful stained-glass lamp that looked like a Tiffany. I gave Lauren the information for Loretta at Sweetbriar so she could help her price it properly if she chooses to sell. In fact, I wouldn't wonder if that was what someone tried to make off with."

Mary nodded, but Martha looked thoughtful for a moment. Her brow furrowed. "How would someone have known the lamp was there? Or that there was anything of value inside the house, for that matter?"

"Hmm," said Elizabeth. "I'm not sure. Maybe it was a wild guess. Or perhaps the thief had visited the house before?"

Mary jumped in. "Do you mean like a friend of the grandfather's? Yikes, what an awful friend."

"It would make sense." Elizabeth warmed to the idea. "He—or she—would've known there were valuable items. It's possible the thief assumed the house was empty after Lauren's grandfather died and thought he'd take his chance?"

The women's conversation was interrupted when Rosie Gittrich burst in the door, bringing a gust of cold air with her. "Oh, good. You're still open. You didn't sell my jam, did you?" Her presence was abrupt, and it took the sisters a few seconds to respond.

"Actually, we're closed," Martha snipped.

"No, of course not," Elizabeth said, frowning at Martha. She fetched the two jars from the storeroom and started to ring Rosie up.

"Were you all right yesterday?" Mary asked Rosie. "We were worried about you."

"Of course I was all right. Why would you think I wasn't?"

"You left so quickly. You didn't stay to buy your jam."

"Oh, that." Rosie shrugged off the comment. "I have low blood sugar. I needed to get home to get something to eat. I knew you'd be dears and hold my items back for me."

What she said made sense, but Rosie's skittish gaze and tight cross of her arms across her body made Elizabeth wonder if she was being entirely truthful. But what would Rosie have to hide?

Martha handed the elderly woman her change, while Mary carefully wrapped the jam in newspapers and lowered it into a paper sack.

Mary acted nonchalant as she folded down the bag's top. "We also found the note you left for us?"

Elizabeth nearly gasped. What was Mary doing? The note had obviously not been left by Rosie. It wasn't her handwriting, for one, and two, leaving threatening letters didn't really seem like Rosie's style. All Mary was going to achieve was offending a regular customer.

Rosie narrowed her eyes. "What makes you think I left you a note?"

Elizabeth noticed she didn't answer the question, but she wasn't sure what to make of it. She tried to smooth the situation over. "Never mind, Rosie. It's just a misunderstanding."

The sisters had known Rosie for years. She'd watched the three of them grow up, and she'd always been a loyal customer and friend. It just didn't sit right that she'd steal from them and then threaten them as well. Elizabeth just couldn't believe she was involved.

Rosie took a step toward the door. "Now, if you're looking for a suspicious character, why don't you talk to that Arthur fellow?"

Elizabeth's face felt as blank as her mind. "Arthur?"

"You know, that guy in here yesterday who was crazy about war artifacts. He was sniffing around those pictures like a puppy tracking a scrap of meat."

Arthur had been the older man who was in the store when the photos were taken, and he was the only person they didn't know how to track down. "You don't happen to know Arthur's last name, do you, Rosie?"

Rosie scrunched up her face in thought. "Maybe Grand? Or was it Granger? Oh, I'm just not sure. But I know who you can ask. That skinny college kid with the Coke-bottle glasses. They were hanging around each other, thick as thieves, like they were friends. I bet he'd know his name." Elizabeth imagined Rosie was referring to Grant Slavick, the college student who'd been interested in the pictures for his photography class.

As Rosie left the store, John Marks came in. He waited as Rosie shuffled across the threshold. Then he helped her to her car to keep her from slipping on the snow-covered ground. Elizabeth felt herself blush as Mary nudged her with her shoulder and gave her a tiny wink. Elizabeth prayed John didn't notice her red-stained cheeks when he came back inside.

He walked up to the counter and smiled at Elizabeth. "One of my buddies told me they saw you a few hours ago at the site of a break-in. I wanted to come by and check on you. Are you all right?"

His concern made her feel warm and safe. "I'm perfectly all right. I was just helping my friend Lauren. It was her grandfather's place that was broken into. He has some antiques, and I've no doubt someone thought they'd make a quick dollar if they thought the house was unoccupied."

"Did the place have an alarm system?"

Elizabeth shook her head. "No. I'm sure it would give Lauren piece of mind to know her grandfather's house is secure, but she doesn't have any spare money right now. In fact, she's concerned the bank might foreclose if she can't pay the mortgage in time. That's one of the reasons I was there, to help her look through her grandfather's antiques. We're hoping there's some things she can sell."

"I'm sure Lauren appreciates your friendship. You're a good person to know, Elizabeth."

His gaze was so honest and kind, it made her heart hammer away in her chest and her cheeks flame afresh. Out of the corner of her eye, she saw her sisters exchange knowing smiles.

Thankfully, John continued talking. "Didn't Lauren already sell you some items from her grandfather's estate?"

Elizabeth swallowed and forced herself to regain her composure. "She did. A vintage camera with some undeveloped film in it."

Martha raised an eyebrow at Elizabeth's comment. Elizabeth was certain it was because she hadn't mentioned that the pictures had been stolen. But thankfully, Martha didn't say anything. Elizabeth was grateful. She didn't really want to involve the police in something like the theft of a few pictures. Besides, they were working their way down the suspects list pretty quickly. Surely they'd find the photos soon. Of course, there was the note. But again, was it worth John's time? She just couldn't be sure. Maybe if they didn't find the photos soon, she'd mention it to him.

She thought of what Rosie had said a few minutes earlier about Grant Slavick knowing Arthur, the man who'd seemed so interested in the pictures. Maybe if she tracked down Grant, she could find out more about him. She knew John had some friends at the college, people he'd gone to high school with many years before and still kept in touch with.

"Actually, I have a favor to ask you, John."

"I'd be happy to help any way I can."

"I want to know more about someone who was in the store yesterday. A young man, Grant Slavick, who takes photography classes at college. He gave me his phone number, but I wondered if you know someone who works at the college. Someone who can tell me more about his background."

"I do know the professor who teaches photography." He paused, and now it was his turn to turn red. "Maybe we could talk about it over dinner? Tonight?"

Martha made a big show of clearing her throat and noisily moving toward the office to start shutting down the shop for the evening. But Mary hung on, seemingly oblivious to the fact that John and Elizabeth wanted a moment alone.

"Mary?" John finally asked. "Do you have any of those wonderful Million-Dollar Pickles that I bought last time I was in here?"

Elizabeth held her breath as Mary tipped her head to one side. "I think so. Let me check in the storage area."

John waited until Mary left to lean close to Elizabeth over the desk. "I know it's short notice, but I switched shifts unexpectedly and was hoping you were free tonight."

He was so near to her, she could smell his cologne. Her heart beat fast. "I am, and I'd love to. Where are we going?"

John smiled. "It's a surprise."

CHAPTER EIGHT

Mary and Martha had a quick supper while Elizabeth got ready for her date with John. When Elizabeth walked into the kitchen, Mary gasped. Elizabeth looked lovely. Due to their Mennonite background, Elizabeth had grown up dressing plainly. No makeup. A trait she carried with her into adulthood. But after Martha and Mary moved in, they began to urge her to expand her wardrobe. And to experiment with cosmetics. Although Elizabeth had always been attractive, recent changes had really enhanced her beauty. She wore dark slacks with black pumps. Her gray sweater had silver threads running through it.

"Oh, Lizzie. You look beautiful," Mary said, feeling a little emotional.

Elizabeth's brown hair was brushed back, and feathery bangs framed her face. Her dark eyes shone. Mascara and eyeliner made her eyes stand out. A touch of red lipstick highlighted her full lips.

"So pretty," Martha agreed, her voice choked.

Mary was moved by Martha's reaction. Martha was the sensible sister, but she felt the same way. Elizabeth had been engaged once, but it hadn't worked out. Then she'd spent several years taking care of their parents. Over the years, her looks had taken a back seat. To see her now, caring enough to make herself look nice, and going out with a good man who appreciated her, made Mary want to cry.

"You two need glasses," Elizabeth murmured. But the sides of her mouth twitched up. It was obvious she was touched by their response.

"So where are you going?" Mary asked.

Elizabeth laughed. "John said it was a surprise. I have no idea. Hopefully we're not getting hot dogs and going to the park. If so, I'm overdressed."

"If he's taking you to the park in January, it's a sign that you need a new boyfriend," Martha said dryly.

Elizabeth and Mary laughed. Just then a car pulled up to the house. Elizabeth hurried to the hall closet to get her coat while Martha went to the door. When John stepped inside, it took all of Mary's self-control not to whistle. Although she thought it would be funny, her sisters had talked to her more than once about being inappropriate. It seemed that sometimes her first response wasn't always the right one.

"Elizabeth is just getting her coat," Martha said.

John was a handsome man. Tall with dark hair and blue eyes, he had a commanding presence. Probably had something to do with his job as a police officer. His hair had streaks of gray, but they only made him look even more distinguished. His dark suit and blue shirt brought out his features, especially his eyes.

Elizabeth came around the corner, struggling with her coat, and John hurried over to help her. As he held it, she slipped her arms into the coat sleeves. "I wasn't sure how to dress since you wouldn't tell me where we were going," she said.

"You look wonderful," he said. "Every man in the place will be jealous of me."

Mary was tickled to see Elizabeth's cheeks turn red.

As they headed toward the door, Mary and Martha said goodbye. Mary watched them as they walked down the front steps and to John's car. He opened the door for her and then closed it once she was safely inside. Such a gentleman. As they drove away, Mary asked, "Didn't she look happy?" She had to blink away quick tears that sprang to her eyes.

Martha put her arm around her sister. "You have a good heart, Mary."

"Just not a good head?"

Martha let her go and stepped back. "Don't be silly. You're one of the smartest people I know. Perhaps you're just a bit... impulsive."

"You mean I don't look before I leap."

"Possibly. But you make life interesting." Martha grinned. "And I wouldn't trade you for anyone else in the whole world."

"Well, I hope you feel the same way after I tell you where I'm going."

Martha put her hands on her hips. "I have a feeling I'm not going to like it."

Mary took a deep breath. "I'm going over to Rosie Gittrich's house."

"Whatever for?" Martha's frown deepened as she stared at Mary. Not a good sign.

"I'm going to ask her to bake one of her famous Italian cream cakes for the Helping Hands benefit."

Martha's concerned expression turned to puzzlement. "Why wouldn't I like that?"

"Because I'm also going to nose around a bit. See if I can find out why she left the store so quickly the day the photos were stolen. Low blood sugar, my foot. Something else was going on."

Martha smiled at her. "Believe it or not, I think that's a great idea. Do you want me to come with you?"

Mary shook her head. "I don't want her to feel outnumbered. I think taking on one of the Classen girls at a time is more than enough."

Martha laughed. "I believe you're right." She sobered. "Don't be too direct, Mary. We don't want to make her suspicious and refuse to talk to us."

"I know. I intend to be careful. If she starts to get offended, I'll change the subject. Talk about the benefit or something. Or maybe I could ask for her recipe. That cake is out of this world."

"She won't give it to you. I tried once. She acts like she's protecting nuclear launch codes."

Mary giggled. Martha was her funniest when she wasn't trying to be humorous.

She helped Martha clean up the kitchen. Then she left to go to Rosie's. Mary had only been to Rosie's once before. Rosie had sprained her ankle and couldn't drive, so Mary delivered her order of jam. Although Mary hadn't seen much of the house, she was impressed by Rosie's decorating skills. The classic craftsman bungalow was attractive from the outside, but inside, the attention to detail was notable. Solid wood floors, overhead beams, built-in oak bookcases, and oak trim were appropriate for the style.

When Mary got out of the car, she pulled her coat closer. The sharp winter wind bit through the fabric. By the time she got up the steps to Rosie's front door, she was praying Rosie didn't take too long to answer. Thankfully, Mary's prayer was answered. Rosie opened the door a few seconds after Mary knocked. Rosie's frown certainly didn't give Mary confidence.

"I'm sorry to just stop by, Rosie," Mary said. "If you're busy or something, I could come back another time."

Rosie seemed to consider Mary's offer, but in the end, she pulled the door open. "You're already here. You might as well come in."

Not the most gracious invitation she'd ever received, but Mary smiled and stepped inside anyway. The warmth of the fire crackling in the living room fireplace made her shiver with pleasure.

"It's so cold this evening," she said, hoping to start a conversation.

Rosie nodded. "Colder January than last year. And my bones feel it." She gestured at Mary's coat. "Might as well take that off and sit down."

Two *might as wells* in one visit. Hopefully, Rosie's mood would improve. Mary shed her coat and put it and her purse on the chair next to her. As if she'd read Mary's mind, Rosie suddenly smiled. "How about a cup of tea?" she asked. "And a slice of my Italian cream cake?"

Mary returned her smile. "I would love that. In fact, the reason I came by has to do with your wonderful cake."

"Come into the kitchen," Rosie said. "I'll put on the tea, and you can carry our cake into the living room."

Mary dutifully obeyed her instructions. The cake was in a large glass cake holder. After setting the teapot on the stove, Rosie brought over a cake knife, removed the lid, and sliced two large pieces of cake, putting each one on a plate. After putting the cover back, she got forks and napkins.

"Put these on the coffee table, and I'll be there in a moment," she said. "I must admit, I was surprised when you knocked on the door." She gave Mary a rather disapproving look. "Most people call first, you know."

"I realize that, Rosie. I'm sorry. I was just anxious to see you."

Rosie shrugged. "Actually, I was feeling a little lonely. I'm glad for the company."

After being scolded and then being told she was grateful Mary had stopped by, Mary was more than a little confused. She decided to let it go and pretend as if the last thing Rosie said was the truth.

Mary picked up the plates and headed to the living room. After she set them on the table, she walked over to gaze at the pictures that lined the mantelpiece. Rosie when she was younger. Very pretty. She was still attractive, even though she had to be in her nineties. Gray curly hair, dark blue eyes, and a trim figure. She'd kept her looks, but she didn't fix herself up much. She dressed like Elizabeth used to. Sensibly. Sensible shoes. Sensible, plain dresses. Mary had never seen Rosie in pants.

There was an older couple in one photo that Mary assumed were Rosie's parents. The other photos were people Mary didn't know. She was starting to go back to the table when she noticed a small room off to the side. She walked over to the doorway and glanced inside. It was too little for a bedroom. Rosie had placed an overstuffed chair in the corner with a matching footstool. It was an attractive room, but the thing that stood out was an entire wall filled with pictures of a famous movie and theater actor. Mary had seen him in *Les Miserables* on Broadway twenty years ago. He had been amazing. She wondered if he was still alive. She wasn't sure. She could remember almost every moment of that trip. Brian had surprised her with the trip for their wedding anniversary. It had been magical, but now, thinking about it only brought sadness. She turned around and went back into the living room, blinking back inconvenient tears that filled her eyes.

Rosie walked into the room with a small tray. There were two teacups, some milk, and sugar. She set it on the coffee table, next to the plates of cake.

"I hope you like Earl Grey," she said. "I serve it with milk, the English way. But I'd be happy to get you some cream if you'd rather have it."

Mary smiled. "I love Earl Grey and drink it with milk too. Tastes so good that way."

Rosie suddenly got a strange look on her face. Instead of sitting down on the couch with Mary, she hurried over to the small room Mary had inspected. She closed the door and returned to the couch. Obviously, it was a place she didn't want anyone else looking into. Mary wondered why. Maybe she was embarrassed that she had a crush on someone at her age.

"You said you wanted to talk to me about my cake?" Rosie asked after she sat down. She picked up the teapot and poured tea into both cups. Then she put sugar and milk into her cup. "I hope you're not going to ask for my recipe. I don't give it out."

"Well, I'd love to have your recipe, of course, but that's not why I'm here." Mary told her about the Helping Hands benefit. When she finished, Rosie smiled.

"I'd be happy to bake an Italian cream cake for your event. It sounds like a worthy cause."

Mary was actually very grateful for Rosie's contribution. She was glad she'd used that excuse to come over.

They talked for a while about Helping Hands and what they did. Then Mary asked about the older couple in the picture on the mantel. Sure enough, they were Rosie's parents. She told Mary about them. It was obvious she'd loved them very much.

After drinking her tea and finishing the cake, which practically melted in her mouth, Mary decided it was now or never. "I hope you're feeling better, Rosie. Low blood sugar can be serious." She wanted to ask her how she could eat cake and put sugar in her tea if her sugar was out of whack, but she kept quiet.

Rosie put her cup down and cleared her throat. "Yes. Silly of me. I'll make sure not to skip meals from now on."

"At first I thought you were shocked by something in the pictures from the camera Lauren Collier brought in." She smiled at Rosie. "I guess I misunderstood the situation."

"Yes, I guess you did."

Rosie's tone had turned decidedly icy. She stood to her feet. "I'm sorry, Mary, but I have a rather severe headache. I need to take some aspirin and lie down."

"Oh, certainly. I'm sorry, Rosie. You should have told me sooner. I wouldn't have stayed for tea." She got up and gave Rosie a quick hug. It was like hugging a stone statue. Mary retrieved her coat and purse. By the time she had her coat on, Rosie was already holding the door open.

"Thank you so much for the tea and cake," Mary said as she walked out on the porch. "And thank you for offering to bake an Italian cream cake for—"

She didn't get a chance to finish her sentence. Rosie had shut the door in her face.

As Mary hurried down the sidewalk toward her car, she wondered about Rosie's odd reaction. Could she have taken the pictures? The handwriting on the note didn't look like hers, but maybe she'd purposely tried to disguise it. Something strange was certainly going on, and Mary was determined to find out just what it was.

CHAPTER NINE

"So, are you going to tell me where we're going? Or am I going to have to guess?" Elizabeth found herself teasing John, a playful lilt to her voice. They drove for a while, John still silent about their destination.

"Just hold your horses," John said. "You'll find out soon enough. Let a man keep some secrets."

Elizabeth grinned too and leaned back in the passenger seat. Before long, they pulled up across the street from a large building. John opened the car door for her, and she gingerly stepped out, trying to avoid the slushy snow piles at the curb's edge.

"Ta-da! Your evening of mystery awaits, milady." John swept his arm in a grand gesture that made her laugh as he escorted her across the street. She glanced up at the impressive Victorian structure in front of them. It was a theater, with a lean, beige main face and red brick buildings flanking it on either side. The blazing marquee sign in the middle read FULTON in thick, blocky capitals. She'd lived in the area her whole life, so she'd passed by the Fulton on occasion before, but she'd never attended a performance there. She suddenly felt like a tourist in her own town. Her eyes trailed upward, to a statue of a man standing in an alcove.

John followed her gaze. "Robert Fulton," he said, pointing to the statue. "He developed the first working commercial steam engine. The building's named after him." John looked back at her. "I wasn't sure if you'd been here before. It's a special place for me, so I thought I'd share it with you."

"No, I haven't had the chance to visit. Mystery indeed. You are surprising," Elizabeth said, fighting to keep a smile off her face. They'd been to a concert before, but she didn't realize he was a theater buff.

"My mother loved this theater," he said by way of explanation.

"You haven't talked about her much." Elizabeth knew John's mother had died sometime before her own mother had passed away, but John rarely mentioned her. She was pleased he considered her a good enough friend that he could share a memory of his mother.

"My mother was for me what I imagine your mother was for you and your sisters," he said. "She was a shelter in times of storm. A constant rock."

They paused together in silence for a moment, as a tiny gust of snow blew off the building. The snowflakes shone like glitter in the light of the marquee sign.

"Thank you for telling me about your mom," Elizabeth said softly. "That makes me feel closer to you, to know we have that in common."

John nodded slowly, then cleared his throat, as though he didn't want emotion to get the best of him. "I figured, since it's early, we could catch a show first and then have dinner? Unless that's too out of order for you." His tone was teasing. She could tell he was enjoying himself and her company.

"That would be lovely. I can wait to eat. What are we watching?" A gust of particularly frigid wind whipped the ends of Elizabeth's scarf, and she shivered.

"Why don't we get inside where it's warm, and then I'll fill you in," John said. She nodded gratefully, and they headed toward the entrance.

The building was lovely inside. Soaring ceilings, rich colors in rugs and carpets, and ornate architectural details made the place feel like a lavish palace. They navigated to the front desk, and John held up two fingers to the employee seated at the farthest side of the counter.

"Two, reserved for Marks." He glanced over at Elizabeth and smiled as the employee sorted out their reservation. She found herself glad that she'd paid a little more attention than normal to her appearance this evening. Not that John would feel differently toward her without the extra trappings of makeup and jewelry, of course, but it was like icing on a cake. Not necessary, by any means, but it sure made things seem more festive.

After being cleared by the ticket taker, they walked farther into the theater. "This building actually started out in colonial times as a jail, believe it or not," said John. He pointed to the brick wall directly across from them. "That wall is original to the jail, though it was located on the exterior of the courtyard then." They continued meandering, and every once in a while, John would point to something and spout a few interesting facts.

Elizabeth looked at him in amazement. "How do you know all of this? You could practically be a tour guide."

"I told you. My mother loved music. We came to the Fulton often until she became ill."

"You came here with her?"

John nodded. "It wasn't really my cup of tea at first, but my father, good as he was, couldn't stomach live theater. Mother loved it, though. I grew to enjoy the music and the plays over time. The performance we're seeing tonight used to be one of her favorites."

Elizabeth had appreciated John for the kind person he was before, but now she really found herself proud to be in his company.

"And what performance are we seeing exactly? Since you prefer to keep me in the dark."

She smiled, and he returned the grin.

"Enough being mysterious, I guess. We're going to be listening to Beethoven's Symphony No. 7. The Lancaster County Orchestra is performing. Should be excellent."

The performance was breathtaking. Elizabeth enjoyed every minute, snuggled in her seat among the crowd, listening to the energetic piece. She noticed that John had been sincere when he said he had grown to enjoy classical music. He watched the performance attentively and clapped loudly at the conclusion of the concert.

After the performance, they got back in the car and headed a short distance down the road to the Stockyard Inn, a restaurant Elizabeth had been to before and which was well-known for its seafood, steaks, and pork chops. She ordered the Chef's Special, and John chose the French Rib Pork Chop with a side of sautéed mushrooms.

"So," he said, after they'd been served, "we didn't get much chance to talk at the theater. You mentioned at the store that you wanted my help to check up on someone?" He speared a mushroom on his fork before taking a bite.

Elizabeth quickly chewed and swallowed her own food before answering. She decided to tell him about the theft of the photos. "I do. Remember the camera that belongs to Lauren that I mentioned?"

John nodded, looking attentive.

"What I didn't tell you is that there was some old film inside. We had it developed, and someone took the pictures from the store."

"They're missing?"

"No, we think they've been stolen. I didn't want to bother you about it. It seems so unimportant."

"Don't be silly. You're not bothering me at all. I'd like to help if I can. So you think that this Grant character might have taken them?"

Elizabeth set her fork down. "I don't know. Maybe. He seemed awfully interested in the photos. He wanted them for some intro to photography class he was taking at college. He left his name and number for us if we decided to let him make copies, but what if he decided he didn't want to wait? He would've had ample opportunity to grab them while I was in the house with Mary and Martha."

"I know the man who's probably Grant's professor. He's an old buddy of mine from high school. Believe it or not, we used to play football together." Looking at John's square shoulders and strong bearing, Elizabeth could believe it. It was easy to turn back the clock in her mind and imagine John as a fresh-faced student himself.

"I hate to think ill of anyone. It's possible Grant intended to borrow the photos, but I have to have them back. They mean so much to Lauren."

John reached across the table to place his hand over hers. "I promise I'll do anything I can to help you find them."

A warmth surged through her. He really was a good man, kind and thoughtful. She'd thought she'd never find companionship as her sisters had, but she found herself liking John more and more as they spent time together.

A man passing by Elizabeth jostled her arm as he headed for the exit. Startled, she looked up to see a familiar profile walking past her. The man turned his head as he bid goodbye to the hostess, and she nearly gasped. It was the man from the shop, the one who had been talking to Grant. The man whose name she didn't know. What were the chances of running into him here? She supposed Lancaster was a fairly small community, but still, it seemed providential.

She quickly stood and tossed her napkin on her empty chair. "John, I'm sorry to be so abrupt, but can you get the check while I go outside for a moment? I saw someone I need to talk to immediately."

"Of course. I'll be right behind you." John looked concerned as he flagged down the waitress, but Elizabeth had no time to explain. She trailed after the man, just in time to see him climb into an old green truck with rust on the hubcaps.

"Hello? Hello!" she called out after him, but he either didn't hear her or chose to ignore her. His truck engine sputtered to life just as John exited the restaurant with the rest of their food corralled in Styrofoam to-go containers.

"We need to go. We need to follow him," she cried as the truck pulled away and headed down the street. John obediently climbed into his vehicle and began chasing after the man. After a few turns, though, Elizabeth sensed the stranger realized he was being tailed. He quickly lost them in a series of complex twists and turns that left them a few miles away from downtown.

John pulled the car over and parked, then looked at Elizabeth and laughed. "I didn't expect our date to end with a high-speed chase." He was joking, though Elizabeth could see his brows were furrowed with concern. "What was that all about?"

"I suppose I really am a woman of mystery," she kidded back. But in her mind, all she could think of was how everyone who was in the store when the photos were stolen seemed suspicious. Emily Miller was the only person who didn't seem to be hiding anything. What were the secrets surrounding Lauren's grandfather's photos, and why were they so valuable?

"That man, the one we just followed? He was in the store when the pictures were stolen."

CHAPTER TEN

Martha woke up before her alarm clock rang. There was an odd aroma in the air. She turned off her clock and swung her legs over the side of the bed. Butterscotch opened one eye as if asking why Martha felt she had the right to disturb his sleep.

"Sorry, sweetie," Martha said. She hurried over to the chair near her bed and grabbed her robe. After slipping it on and tying the belt, she slid her feet into her slippers and padded down the stairs to the kitchen. What she saw made her mouth drop open. The kitchen was in a shambles. It looked as if every dish the sisters owned was out of the cupboards and sitting on the counters. Suddenly, a blond head popped up from behind the table. Mary.

"Cheese and crackers, Mary. What happened in here?" Martha asked. She expected her sister to tell her there was a mouse in the kitchen, and she was trying to find it.

Mary stood to her feet, her face smudged with something white. Flour. "I thought it would be a good idea to bake my pies before you and Elizabeth got up. I don't want to be in the way."

Martha stood frozen, unable to find a response. In her entire life she'd never seen their mother's kitchen this messy.

"I…I was on the floor trying to clean up some butter I dropped. Really hard to wipe up."

At just that moment Elizabeth came into the kitchen. Martha assumed the look on her older sister's face was pretty close to her own. Shock, disbelief, tinged with a touch of irritation.

While Martha stood there, trying not to lose her temper, Elizabeth said, "Mary, what in the world are you doing?"

Mary frowned at her sister like she was simple. "Like I told Martha, I got up early to make pies so I wouldn't bother you." She looked back and forth between her two older sisters. "Are you upset about something?"

Elizabeth had started toward Mary when her feet slipped out from under her. Martha, still in shock, called out Elizabeth's name.

Mary leaned down and helped Elizabeth to her feet. "Are you okay, Lizzie?"

"Yes, I'm fine." She pointed at the floor. "What is that?" she asked.

"Butter," Mary said. "It fell on the floor. Sorry. It's really slippery."

Finally, Martha got her feet to move. "Oh really? Butter is slippery? So glad you figured that out."

She took Mary's sleeve and pulled her away. "Just…just go get the eggs. Give me some time to clean this floor before one of us gets hurt." She turned her attention to Elizabeth. "Are you sure you're okay?"

"Absolutely. I'm sure Mary didn't mean to—"

Martha put her hand up. "Don't defend her. You could have been badly hurt." She glared at Mary. "Didn't I ask you to get the eggs?"

Mary, wide-eyed and looking ashamed, grabbed the egg basket and fled out the front door.

"She forgot her coat," Elizabeth said quietly. "I think you frightened her."

Martha shook her head as she got a dishrag and some soap from the sink. "I doubt seriously if she's really afraid of me. But I am upset, Elizabeth. Don't try to talk me out of it." Before kneeling down to clean the floor, she swept her hand around the room. "Look at this mess. You keep making excuses for her. Mary's not stupid. There's no reason for clutter like this."

Elizabeth sighed. "She's trying, Martha. Helping this foster child organization is important to her. She wants to be useful. And I know the kitchen's a mess, but I'll bet she would have cleaned it all up on her own if we'd given her time."

Martha put a hand on her hip. "Maybe you have confidence she could put this room back together, but I don't. You could have broken a hip or something, Elizabeth. The kitchen is one of the most dangerous places in the house."

"Broken a hip? Just how old do you think I am?" Elizabeth raised an eyebrow in obvious annoyance.

"I'm sorry. I'm just upset." She tossed the dishrag in the sink and grabbed some paper towels to dry the floor. "You know, I've been cleaning up after Mary our entire lives. When we were kids, you and I would get scolded for making messes. But it was always Mary." She pointed the roll of paper towels at Elizabeth before removing some. "You know that's true."

"Yes, I do. But why did we always take the blame?"

Martha leaned against the sink and stared at her sister. She knew the answer, but she wasn't in the mood to offer it.

"Because we both knew Mary had a good heart," Elizabeth said after a long silence.

Martha sighed loudly. "Yeah, you're right. But still, Elizabeth, she needs to grow up. This is ridiculous."

"I agree. So leave it. Don't take care of this for her." Elizabeth sniffed the air. "What is that?"

Martha's eyes widened. "Oh brother." She grabbed some mitts and opened the oven. She was surprised to see two absolutely beautiful pies. She carefully took them out and put them on the hot pads that sat on the counter. "Look at these," she said. She leaned down and sniffed them. They smelled great. "I'll be a monkey's uncle," she said in subdued tones. "They're perfect."

Elizabeth got up and came over to look. "Oh, Martha," she said, her voice breaking a little. "She kept at it until she got it right."

Martha felt her eyes mist over as well. She reached over and turned off the oven. "You're right," she said. "Anyone who can turn out pies like these can clean up a kitchen." She walked over to the coffeemaker. Thankfully, there was hot coffee. She got out two cups and poured coffee for herself and Elizabeth. "This place is too big a mess for me to cook breakfast," she said, "but I still have some muffins from the other day. How about a banana nut muffin and some fruit?"

"Sounds great," Elizabeth said.

A few minutes later they were eating delicious muffins which Martha warmed up in the microwave. She put butter on the table along with sliced cantaloupe.

"So tell me about your date last night," Martha said. "I was already in bed when you came in."

Elizabeth smiled. "Well, it was certainly exciting."

Martha frowned. "Exciting. Not the response I was expecting. What do you mean?"

Elizabeth told her about following the green truck. Martha found her story extremely humorous. Elizabeth on a car chase was so out of character.

They were both laughing when Mary came inside with a basketful of eggs. She was shivering from the cold. She looked at them in surprise. Probably not the reaction she expected, Martha mused.

Mary put the basket on the counter. "What's so funny?" she asked, as if almost afraid to hear the answer. Elizabeth recounted her story while Martha got up and prepared breakfast for her younger sister. Mary looked confused to be the recipient of Martha's kindness.

Mary sat down and listened to Elizabeth until she was giggling too. Martha felt badly for her reaction toward Mary. It wasn't the first time she'd gotten irritated with her. She had to admit that sometimes she felt a little jealous of Mary. She was younger and prettier than Martha. But the truth was, she wouldn't trade her life for Mary's. Mary's husband had betrayed her. Maybe Chuck, Martha's husband, was gone, but he had loved her with his whole heart. Martha couldn't imagine the hurt Mary had gone through. It probably made her feel insecure, a condition Martha rarely battled. She was a pragmatist, but she was also confident in her abilities. She suddenly felt really ashamed. Here Mary was, trying something new, and all Martha had done was complain and criticize. Philippians 2:3 popped into her mind. *"Do nothing out of selfish ambition or vain* conceit. *Rather, in humility value others above yourselves."* When Elizabeth finished her story, Martha picked up the two pies Mary had left in the oven and carefully carried them over to the table. "Look at these beautiful pies," she said to Mary. "You did a perfect job."

Mary looked up at her with tears in her eyes. "But I made such a mess in the kitchen."

Martha shrugged. "No big deal. When I started baking, the kitchen looked like a bomb had gone off. You'll learn how to clean up as you go along. It comes with practice."

Mary sniffed. "Thank you, Martha."

"You're welcome. Elizabeth and I are going to open the shop."

Martha reached over and gave Mary a hug. "I don't say it enough, but I love you, and I'm proud of you." She let Mary go and pointed at the pies. "It took me a lot longer than you to turn out pies like that," she said. "Seems you're a natural."

"I really appreciate that coming from you, Martha," Mary said, wiping away a tear. "I promise I'll make this kitchen shine."

Elizabeth and Martha had started upstairs to change their clothes when Mary called out, "I want to share these pies with you. I'll make more tonight for Helping Hands."

Elizabeth nudged Martha. "Your faith is being tested," she whispered with a grin.

Martha sighed. Sometimes life just wasn't fair. "God help me be humble…and patient," she prayed softly as she climbed the stairs.

CHAPTER ELEVEN

The morning started out a little slow, but after a few hours, things picked up. The shop stayed rather busy even though it was snowing again. Elizabeth looked out the window to see feathery flakes floating down, drifting on a light wind. Not too intimidating. Probably wouldn't scare people away, although the weather forecasters felt things could take a downward turn later in the day.

Martha's baked goods were certainly popular. The winter storm warning probably had something to do with it. Nothing better than getting cozy inside a warm house with a cup of coffee and some of Martha's chocolate fudge brownies.

Pal was having a blast greeting everyone who came in. Children gravitated toward him. If she didn't know better, Elizabeth would have bet he knew somehow that parents spent more if their children were occupied.

Elizabeth was checking out one of their frequent customers when John walked into the shop. She was surprised to see him again so soon. He waited until she was finished before approaching the counter. "Can you get away for lunch?" he asked.

She looked at her watch. Mary had joined them around eleven. "I think so. Let me check with Mary and Martha." She left the counter and found her sisters refolding some quilts and lap robes left in disarray after a couple of overly exuberant customers.

She didn't even get the chance to ask before Martha waved her comment away. "Go. We'll be fine. Just keep an eye on the weather. I heard from a customer that the storm could be coming in a little sooner than expected."

"Thanks. Be back soon."

Mary grinned at her. "Two dates in two days?" she asked in a low voice. "Sounds like it's getting serious."

"Don't be daft," Elizabeth huffed. "It's just lunch."

As she walked away, she heard Mary laugh. She felt her cheeks burn. John Marks wasn't in love with her. They were just friends. But if that's what she really believed, why did her heart beat faster whenever she looked at him?

When she told John she could leave, he took her coat from the coat rack near the door and helped her into it. Then he held out his arm, and she took it. As they walked out to his car, Elizabeth noticed the snow was getting a little bit heavier. Still, it didn't appear to be anything to be overly concerned about.

John helped her into the car and then went to the driver's side. He got inside, but before he started the engine he leaned toward her and said, "I did some checking on our friend in the green truck this morning."

"Checking?" Elizabeth asked. "What do you mean?"

John smiled. "I'm a police officer, Elizabeth. I looked up his license plate. I know who he is."

Elizabeth gasped. "You do? I never thought... I mean, I should have realized." She stopped and frowned at him. "Can you get in trouble for that?"

John burst out laughing. "No, I won't get in trouble. I'm allowed to check up on anyone I want to."

Elizabeth blushed with embarrassment but had to laugh along with him. As the big sister, she kept an eye on Mary and Martha, making sure they weren't doing anything that might get them in trouble. Now she was doing the same thing with John.

"Sorry," she said. "Old habits."

"Don't apologize," John said good-naturedly. "I kind of like knowing someone is concerned that I'm walking the straight and narrow."

Elizabeth smiled at him, relieved. "So what did you find out?" she asked excitedly.

John started the car and turned up the heat. "His name is Arthur Graves. That's all I know. Except for his address. How about we pick up lunch and set up a stakeout?"

Elizabeth grinned. "I've never been on a stakeout. Let's do it."

John drove out of the sisters' long driveway and headed toward town. They stopped by the Two Bird Café first. John went inside and came out with two boxes. Two Bird was famous for their box lunches. Elizabeth had tuna salad on a croissant along with chips and an apple. John had a roast beef sandwich on sourdough, chips, and orange slices. He put two cups of steaming hot coffee into the cupholders in front of them.

About ten minutes later he pulled up in front of a small green house with white shutters. "This is where Mr. Graves lives," he said.

Elizabeth pointed at the attached garage. The door was open. A green truck sat inside. "You're right."

John backed down the street until they were parked behind a huge tree. He turned off his lights but kept the engine running.

"I get the feeling you've done this before," Elizabeth said.

"A few times." He nodded at the boxes Elizabeth had on her lap. "Should we start eating?"

"Sounds good." Elizabeth handed John his box.

Within minutes they were enjoying Two Bird's excellent food. Elizabeth stared out her window and watched the snow dancing around them. She felt so cozy and safe inside John's car. She swung her gaze back toward the green house. No activity yet.

"With bad weather coming in, maybe he plans to stay inside today," she said.

"It's certainly possible. How about we finish lunch and then head back to your place? The snow is getting thicker. No point in taking chances."

Sure enough, in the last couple of minutes, things had changed quickly. Elizabeth began to worry a bit. Before she had a chance to voice her concern, however, the door to the green house opened, and Arthur Graves came out. He headed to his garage, started his truck, and took off down the street.

"We can either follow him or go home," John said. "What do you want to do?"

Elizabeth, always the cautious sister, decided to take a chance for once. Being on a stakeout, following a possible thief…it was exciting. "Follow him!" she exclaimed.

John closed his lunch box and handed it to Elizabeth, who folded hers shut as well. John pulled out carefully, staying far enough back from Graves so he wouldn't realize they were behind him.

Graves turned a corner and headed toward the highway. They followed him, but as their speed increased, the snow got heavier, and the wind suddenly picked up, blowing the frozen flakes across their path, almost blinding them to what was ahead.

"I'm sorry, Elizabeth," John said, "but this is too dangerous. We need to let him go. We'll try again some other time."

"I understand," she said, relieved. She wanted to be adventurous, but this had become too treacherous.

John turned on his blinker and was getting ready to exit the highway when up ahead the green truck suddenly skidded, hit a guardrail, and began to slide across the road. Elizabeth gasped as it turned over, slipped off the shoulder, and hit a tree.

John drove up close to where the truck had stopped upside down. "Call 911," he told her. "Tell them we're on Highway 30." He mentioned the mile marker, but he'd already opened the door and stepped out. She wasn't quite sure she heard it over the roar of the wind. She looked out the window but couldn't see any marker.

She put the boxes in the driver's seat and grabbed her purse, fumbling for her phone. Her hand shook as she dug for it. When her fingers closed around it, she pulled it out and quickly dialed 911. She tried to tell the dispatcher where they were. "We're on Highway 30. I'm not sure about the mile marker," she said, "but we were getting ready to exit onto Highway 283."

"Yes, ma'am. We already have that phoned in. Emergency vehicles are on the way."

Elizabeth thanked the woman and hung up. Then she offered up a prayer for Arthur Graves. She peered through the windshield, trying to spot John, but she couldn't see anything. She was just thinking that being more daring wasn't all it was cracked up to be when through the sound of the wind and the steady whooshing of the car heater she heard an explosion. Her heart thudded in her chest as she watched a large fireball erupt from the spot where the green truck had landed only minutes before.

CHAPTER TWELVE

Elizabeth watched in horror as the fireball lit up the sky. The scene was like something out of an action movie. She couldn't believe her eyes. Adrenaline flooded her body, and her heart dropped as she realized she couldn't see John or Graves. What if Graves was still trapped inside the truck? What if John got hurt trying to get him out?

She pulled her coat tighter around her body and slipped out of the vehicle. Snow seeped into her shoes, but she pressed forward, making sure to stay in the ditch as far away from the road as possible. If Graves had had trouble keeping his truck on the road, she wouldn't be surprised if other people did too. It wouldn't help the situation to get injured herself.

She squinted against the snow blowing into her face. "John? Mr. Graves? Are you all right?" She didn't hear an answer, so she tried again, yelling this time. To her frustration, the wind carried her words away as though she'd whispered them.

She made sure to keep a respectable distance from the truck and nudged up against the fence line of an empty field. She carefully skirted around the front of the vehicle. To her relief, she saw John off to the side, his arms looped under Graves as he pulled him away from the truck and the fire.

"Help me," yelled John. She hurried over to him and helped him support the man, who was conscious but seemed shaken up. He sported a nasty-looking bump on his forehead. John slipped out of his jacket and wrapped it around Graves's thin shoulders. He started to protest, but John cut him off.

"You need it more than I do. It's cold enough out here as it is, and if you go into shock, your temperature could fall even more."

Graves shook his head and pushed to his feet while Elizabeth tried her best to calm him. "Don't move. An ambulance is on the way."

"You don't understand." He fought against her, finally breaking free to lunge toward the burning wreck. John grabbed him just as he was about to take hold of the door handle.

"It's not safe," John said. "Not to mention that metal's boiling hot. You'll get burned."

"I'm not an idiot." Graves spat the words. Elizabeth was surprised by the ferocity in his tone. He held up one hand, the fabric from John's coat pulled down to protect his palm. "There's something very valuable in that truck. I can't let it get destroyed." He tried to stagger around to the other side of the vehicle, its door busted and hanging open, but John held him off again.

"Stay away," he yelled with the authority of an officer, and this time, Graves shrank back. He must have been carrying tools in his open truck bed because Elizabeth noticed an assortment of items scattered across the snow. They'd probably spilled out when the vehicle flipped. John saw them at the same time Elizabeth did and pawed through them until he found a shovel. He started hefting large scoopfuls of snow onto the fire. At first, it looked like the flames wouldn't be put out, but slowly, the fire fizzled to smoke.

Off to the side, Graves groaned. "My truck...," he said mournfully, looking at the mangled heap of green metal in front of them.

"I'm just glad you're not in as bad a shape as your truck is," said John. Elizabeth had to agree. She silently sent up a prayer of thanks that the man was safe, if a bit bruised.

Emergency workers arrived quickly and loaded Graves onto a stretcher. John and Elizabeth followed close behind the ambulance en route to Lancaster General Hospital.

After a brief checkup, Graves was pronounced well, with no injury other than the goose egg on his forehead and a few minor scratches from climbing out of the flipped vehicle. "It's a miracle he wasn't badly hurt," Elizabeth whispered to John as they headed into Graves's hospital room.

Elizabeth walked to Graves's bedside. "How are you feeling? I was pleased to hear you got a clean bill of health."

To her surprise, Graves frowned at her and John. "No thanks to you two."

Startled, Elizabeth blinked. "What do you mean? John saved you. He pulled you from the wreck just before the engine caught fire."

Graves snorted. "I was doing just fine on my own. I wouldn't have gotten in a wreck in the first place if you hadn't been following me." John and Elizabeth exchanged a glance, which Graves intercepted. "I told you earlier, I'm not an idiot. I saw you parked down the street, all cozy, eating your lunch. What I want to know is, why you were watching me?"

It didn't feel like the time or place to be bringing up the missing photos, but Graves was asking. "We hadn't intended on following you. And we stopped as soon as we felt the weather was getting bad," she added hastily.

"Too little, too late," Graves muttered.

"I'm sorry," said Elizabeth. "I'm just trying to be honest with you."

Graves narrowed his eyes. "Honest? I know what you are, lady, and it's not honest. You were trying to steal my antiques so you could sell them yourself." He jabbed a thumb at John. "And somehow you talked your crooked boyfriend here into helping you out!"

John, who up until this point had been silent, jumped into the conversation. "Now wait just a minute, sir. I happen to be a police officer."

"Well, goodie for you," Graves said sarcastically. "I don't really give two rats if you're the king of England. I just want to know why you're here right now. No, wait, let me guess. You're here to tell me that you couldn't salvage any of the items from my truck. Bet you filched them for your own benefit."

"Mr. Graves." Elizabeth cut him off. His hostile attitude had intimidated her at first, but now she regained her footing. "I've never stolen a thing in my life. In fact, one of the reasons John and I stopped by was to tell you that the police saved some of the items from your vehicle. A box of WWII medals and an old rifle? They were undamaged."

Graves's shoulders relaxed. "Really? That's good news."

Elizabeth took advantage of his softened demeanor to try to make conversation. They'd started off on the wrong foot, and she longed to fix things. "So you collect antiques?"

"Not that it's any of your—or anyone's—business, but yes. I study war history, and I enjoy collecting antiques to resell to museums. I do pretty well too. That is, when people are willing to part with items. The worst thing is to have a rare antique gathering dust in someone's basement."

"Is that what you were doing in Secondhand Blessings? Looking for antiques to resell?"

"No crime in that." Graves raised his chin a notch. "Shops like yours often have diamonds hidden among the rocks. It's a crying shame when you don't have a professional assessor on staff, though. You'd probably sell *Guernica* for the same price as a Velvet Elvis."

Elizabeth bit back a sharp retort. *Guernica*, the Pablo Picasso painting he referred to, was perhaps the most famous piece of art depicting war in the world. She knew as much, and she bet her sisters did too. The fact that Graves condescended to think them foolish and uneducated angered her, but she didn't let him know that. "We're not in the business of hawking Velvet Elvis pictures, Mr. Graves. Or poker-playing dogs, for that matter. Nor do we scalp antiques from other dealers."

Suspicion clouded the man's hawk-like features again. "So, if you weren't trying to get my antiques, what did you want?"

This time, John answered. "We just wanted to talk. Elizabeth had some pictures go missing from her store, and she wanted to know if you saw what happened."

"Ah, I see. I'm suspicious of her, she's suspicious of me. I can read between the lines. You mean she wants to know if I took the photos." Graves sat up a little in his bed. "The answer is no. I didn't take a dime or a drop from her store."

"I'm not accusing you of taking them," said Elizabeth. "Did you see anybody else who might have, though?"

"I didn't see anything." Graves snapped his mouth shut like a turtle. "Is there anything else I can help you with? If not, I'd like to get back to recuperating from the nearly fatal wreck I was just in."

Elizabeth sensed that the man knew more than he was saying, but she could tell they weren't going to coax anything from him but pithy put-downs today. She looked up at John. "Why don't we let Mr. Graves get some rest?"

Graves exhaled a dramatic breath. "Finally! The lady takes a hint."

Elizabeth saw John clench his jaw, but she shook her head at him. They headed out into the hallway. When they were out of earshot, she turned to John. "So, what do you think about our friend Mr. Graves?"

"Truthfully?" John raised an eyebrow. "I think he protests a bit too much for someone who's completely innocent. I've interacted with an awful lot of criminals over the years, and pretty much anytime someone crossed over the line from grumpy to hostile it was because they were hiding something. Strong fear provokes strong emotions."

Elizabeth couldn't help but agree. What could Graves be hiding? He'd been so quick to assume they were following him to steal his antiques. Did that mean he had stolen items from others before, or that he'd had items of his own stolen? Was he a victim? Or a vulture, scavenging opportunity when he saw it? The way he'd looked at her, as if she was nothing more than a bug he'd like to squash under his shoe, set her nerves on edge. If looks could kill, she'd be six feet under.

CHAPTER THIRTEEN

By the time Elizabeth and John got back to the shop, it was obvious Martha and Mary had closed for the day. The snow was coming down even heavier.

"I'm going to let you off and head home before it gets any worse," John told Elizabeth.

She gestured toward the windshield. "I think it's too late. The roads are pretty bad. Maybe you should come inside. Have some pie and coffee. We can check the weather report and see when there'll be a break in the snow. Wouldn't that be safer?"

John glanced out his window and nodded. "I think you're right. Let me pull closer to the house. It's liable to be slippery."

"Thank you," Elizabeth said. "We have ice melt, but we usually don't put it out until it stops snowing."

John pulled his car as close to the front porch as he could. He insisted that Elizabeth wait for him, but as he came around the side of the car to open her door, he suddenly disappeared.

"Oh dear," Elizabeth said. She started to open her door to check on him but decided at the last second she might accidentally hit him. After waiting a few moments without any sign of John, she felt she had no choice but to see if he was all right. She put her hand on the door handle, but before she could push it open, John's face suddenly appeared at her window. He slowly opened the car door.

"Sorry," he said. "It's really slick out here. You need to hold on to me."

Elizabeth put her purse over her shoulder and reached for his extended arm. It was then she noticed his pant leg was torn. Was that blood?

"Oh, John. You've hurt yourself!"

"It's okay," he said, dismissively. "I'm fine. Just a little scratch."

It certainly didn't look like a scratch to her, but she decided to wait until they were inside before looking a little closer. They took it slowly, holding on to each other until they reached the railings on the porch. Then they pulled themselves up toward the front door. Elizabeth opened it and stepped inside, John right behind her. Mary and Martha were waiting in the kitchen.

"Are you sure you're okay?" Martha asked, jumping to her feet. Elizabeth had called her from the hospital to let her know what had happened.

"Perfectly fine," Elizabeth said. "Except for John. He fell on the slick sidewalk outside."

Martha hurried over and took his coat. Then she looked down at his torn pant leg. "Oh my," she said. "You've got a really deep cut." She drew herself up to her full height, which was about a foot shorter than John. Her voice took on an authoritarian tone that Elizabeth and Mary were used to hearing. Then she held her hand out. "We need to get a better look at that knee. Give me your pants."

John's face, already reddened by the cold, turned darker. "Sorry," he said, "but that's not gonna happen."

"Martha!" Elizabeth said, her cheeks hot with embarrassment.

Mary didn't say anything, but it didn't help Elizabeth to see her holding her hands over her mouth, trying not to giggle. Seconds later, she lost the battle and burst out laughing.

Martha put her hands on her hips and glared at her sisters. "You people need to grow up. You know what I meant. I can't treat this leg while he's wearing pants."

"How about this?" John suggested. "You give me whatever I need to clean up my knee, and I'll take care of it."

Martha stared at him for a moment but finally nodded. "I guess that will be all right." She pointed a finger at Elizabeth. "Why don't you get some bandages and hydrogen peroxide from under the bathroom sink? Give them to John so he can take care of that cut." She frowned at John. "Somehow I need those pants so I can mend them." She looked over at Mary. "Do you still have those sweatpants Michael left here?"

Mary nodded, her mouth twitching. It was clear to Elizabeth she was still tickled by Martha's treatment of John. "Yes, they're upstairs."

"Good," Martha said. "Give them to John. He can change into those so I can see if his pants can be mended."

Elizabeth was pretty sure the slacks were shot, but it seemed John was too mortified to argue with Martha.

Mary left to get the sweatpants while Elizabeth led John to the bathroom. She knelt down and got out the bandages and peroxide. She also got a clean washcloth from the linen closet. She put everything on the counter next to the sink. Mary came up behind them and handed John a pair of black sweatpants.

"Are you sure it's all right with Michael for me to wear these?"

Mary nodded. "I'm sure. Michael has lots of sweatpants. He won't miss these."

"I'm so sorry about what Martha said," Elizabeth started to tell John, but she made the mistake of looking at Mary, who was barely holding on. Although she tried to hold it back, Elizabeth started laughing. Mary joined her, and to her surprise so did John.

"I...I shouldn't laugh...," Elizabeth tried to get out, "but... but if you could have seen...your face."

That set the three of them off again. Elizabeth hadn't laughed this hard in a long time. It felt good. At first she was horrified to react that way in front of John, but he had clearly seen the humor in the situation himself.

"Boy," he said finally, "I hate to say it, but Martha scares me a little."

Elizabeth grinned at the idea that a big, strapping police officer would be afraid of a little woman like Martha. Yet she knew what he meant.

"Martha is very self-assured," she said, chuckling. "Most of the time it's best to just go along with her."

"Well, this wasn't one of those times," John said ruefully. "I had no intention of just handing her my pants. I'm glad we worked it out. Thanks for the sweats, Mary."

"No problem," Mary said, actually wiping tears from her eyes. "And thanks for the laugh."

"Uh, you're welcome, I guess."

Elizabeth pulled Mary away from the bathroom. "Let's leave the man alone for a few minutes," she said.

"Okay. But how about some pie and coffee, John?"

Elizabeth smiled at her sister. "I already offered him just that."

Mary put her arm around Elizabeth's waist and gave her a hug. "Great minds think alike, don't they?" She gazed into Elizabeth's eyes. "I'm so glad you're okay." All hints of humor were gone.

Elizabeth was touched by the sincerity in Mary's eyes. "I love you too, Sis," she said softly. "Now, back to the kitchen."

She and Mary left John to repair his injured leg, along with his wounded pride. When they got to the kitchen they found Martha cutting one of Mary's pies.

"You finally get to try my pie," Mary said. "Which one did you pick, Martha?"

"I decided on the Dutch apple because it smells so good. But it was a hard choice between that and the cherry. They both look absolutely delicious."

Mary smiled happily at Martha's praise. Martha started a pot of coffee while Elizabeth set the table. By the time the coffee was brewed, John came into the kitchen. The sweatpants fit him perfectly. He handed his slacks to Martha.

"I tried to wash out the blood," he said. "Not sure I got it all out though."

"Not a problem," Martha said. "Have a seat."

John sat down while Martha put the knee of John's slacks under the kitchen faucet. If anyone could get the blood out, it was Martha. She was a whiz at getting rid of stains.

Elizabeth put the slices of pie that Martha had already cut onto the dessert plates she'd set out. Then she poured coffee into everyone's cup.

Martha left to put John's pants in the dryer. "They need to dry before I mend them," she said when she came back. "Or they won't turn out right."

"Thank you for trying to fix them," John said. "They're one of my favorite pairs. I'd hate to lose them."

"It's lucky they ripped on the seam," Martha said. "I should be able to easily mend them."

"You shouldn't have tried to help me out of the car," Elizabeth said. "If you hadn't done that you wouldn't have slipped."

"But you might have," John reminded her. "I wear my wounds as a badge of honor," he said, bowing his head.

His silly antics made Elizabeth and Mary giggle. Even Martha smiled.

John took a big bite of Mary's pie, and his eyes widened. "This is delicious," he said. "This might be the best Dutch apple pie I've ever tasted."

Mary's cheeks flushed. "Thank you," she said. "It took me several attempts before I reached *delicious*."

Martha nodded after taking her first bite. "It's wonderful, Mary. You did a great job."

Elizabeth agreed. It really was good.

"I've been meaning to ask you something," John said, "ever since you told me about the pictures, Elizabeth. Why aren't there copies?"

"The thief took the pictures and the negatives," she answered.

"Where did you have the pictures developed?"

She explained about the old film and how Todd had agreed to develop it in his darkroom.

"He didn't scan the film?" he asked.

Elizabeth looked at him blankly. "I don't understand what you mean."

"A lot of people scan the negatives in case something happens to the originals. That way the pictures won't be lost."

Elizabeth looked at Mary. "Did Todd say anything about scanning the negatives?"

She shook her head. "No, but I'm going to call him right now and find out." She walked over to the kitchen counter where her phone was being charged. She picked it up and scrolled through her numbers. Then she hit an entry. A few seconds later she was talking to Todd. When she hung up she came back to the table.

"We're in business," she said with a smile. "He's going to make another set of prints and get them to us as soon as he can."

Elizabeth was overjoyed. Not only could she return the pictures to Lauren, but now they could look at them and try to figure out why someone had stolen the first set from Secondhand Blessings.

CHAPTER FOURTEEN

Elizabeth woke early, while it was still dark. She'd become accustomed to most of the sounds associated with the farm. Reddy, the rooster, crowing at daybreak. The dogs snuffling at the door to be let out. Martha—and lately, Mary—rising early to bake. But the noise that had shaken her from sleep this morning was different. Definitely a sound she'd never heard before. Like someone cutting down trees or working machinery, like a chain saw.

She looked through the window but couldn't see anything. Maybe someone was outside, cutting up fallen tree limbs? The heavy winds during last night's snowstorm had likely knocked a few branches down. She made a mental note to check the property and clear the yard of debris after she got ready for the day.

Maybe she could find the source of the noise if she went out on the front porch. She pulled on a thick, woolly robe and some slippers before heading down the hall. Tink greeted her, though she kept her tail tucked between her legs. She was obviously troubled by the unfamiliar noise too.

"Good dog," Elizabeth said as she gave the dachshund a gentle pat. "It's okay, girl. Probably just someone working outside." As she said the words, a thought struck her. If it was someone working outside, why would they be doing it so early?

The sun hadn't even risen yet. Whoever it was had to know they'd be waking people. Could it be an emergency? A person in a car trapped under a fallen tree?

She moved a little faster toward the stairs. Maybe someone needed help. Tink waddled loyally after her.

Both Martha's and Mary's bedroom doors were closed, which told Elizabeth they were still sleeping. Where was the sound coming from? She headed down the stairs and stopped still, nearly bursting into laughter.

"I found the source of our disturbance," she whispered to Tink, who perked up and wagged her tail.

The chain saw–like noise was John. Snoring louder than anyone she'd ever heard before. He was sprawled across the couch, a blanket tangled around his legs. His hair was bunched up like a rooster's comb.

The storm had continued through the night, and the roads had worsened, so he had stayed the night downstairs. He had protested quite a bit at first, until Martha got stern with him.

"One car wreck is quite enough for today," she'd said with her hands on her hips.

"Arthur Graves was the one who flipped his truck. We weren't in an accident," Elizabeth tried to tell her, but Martha cut her off.

"I won't hear any more of it. He's staying here until the roads are cleared, and that's that."

John looked sheepish but finally agreed to stay if the sisters would let him shovel the walkway for them in the morning.

Elizabeth chuckled as she remembered the events of the previous night. As embarrassed as John had been about the pants situation with Martha, she imagined he'd be mortified if he caught her spying on him now through the banisters. It was early, anyway. Best to let everyone sleep for a few more minutes.

She snuck back upstairs. She was too wide awake to go back to bed, so she got ready for the day. Then she peeked out the window again. The sun was starting to rise, faint glimmers showing through the window, but the rest of the house was still asleep. Elizabeth decided to take advantage of the opportunity to soak in the quiet and read her Bible. After a few minutes she looked up when she heard faint rustling from the hall and peeked out. Martha was fully dressed and getting ready to head downstairs.

"Sleep well?" she asked when she saw Elizabeth.

"I slept all right. I've actually been awake for a while." Elizabeth smiled, thinking of John's earth-shattering snores. How on earth had her sisters slumbered through that noise? "You?"

"Slept like a rock, as I always do." Elizabeth believed it. Martha was sensible and steadfast even when she was sleeping. She noticed her sister was sporting her heavy-duty snow boots.

"If you're getting ready to take care of the animals, you can skip it this morning," Elizabeth offered. "You and Mary have taken on so much with the house and store while I've been looking for Lauren's pictures. I'm happy to take on my share of the chores this morning."

Martha looked relieved. "That would be very nice. I'll start breakfast. At least I know I'll start with a clean kitchen this morning. Mary didn't do any sunrise baking today, thank goodness. I wish she'd stick to the things she does best. It would save me a lot of trouble."

"I agree that the messy kitchen is an annoyance, but it does seem like it bothers you more than it should. Mary's only trying something new."

"I'll just be happy when she tires of this new hobby, and I can get my kitchen—and my peace of mind—back," Martha grumbled.

The two sisters headed downstairs, and Mary soon joined them. John had woken too and had neatly folded his bedding on the couch. When he saw Elizabeth pull her coat on, he offered to walk her out.

"There are likely still icy patches," he said, "and you don't want to take a spill like I did last night." He rubbed his leg and grimaced.

"Poor John. How is your leg this morning?"

"It's pretty sore, but I'll survive." He grinned at her, and Elizabeth smiled back.

"Well, that's a relief."

"Shall we?" He held out his arm, and she accepted. She would have felt flustered, but John immediately put her at ease.

"I'm holding on to you as much for me as for you," he joked. "I'm apparently a bit of a klutz." Once they got off the slippery parts of the drive, Elizabeth waded through the snow to check on the three goats—Wynken, Blynken, and Nod—and the chickens. She carefully slipped the eggs into her coat pockets. They'd been going through eggs like water lately, with Martha and Mary both baking so much. Her sisters would be happy to get them.

True to his word, John shoveled the walk while she was completing the chores. They headed back inside together, where the mouthwatering aroma of bacon greeted them. Martha was sitting at the kitchen table, finishing up the repairs to John's pants.

"Mmm, smells good in here," said John.

"Here, take these," Martha said as she shoved his pants toward him and tucked her thread, needle, thimble, and scissors into her sewing kit. "They should be fixed now." She moved to the stove to flip the sizzling bacon.

John turned the fabric over in his hands. "Martha, you did an amazing job on these. I can't even see where the tear was."

"I'm glad they meet your standards. Can't have our police officers looking shabby, can we?"

John folded the pants into thirds and stuck them under his arm. "Ladies, thanks for letting me intrude on your hospitality, but I'd better be going."

Martha shook a clean spatula, this one hovering over a skillet of pancakes, at John. She had her schoolmarm look on again, so Elizabeth knew she meant business. "You're not going anywhere just yet. The snowplow hasn't been by yet this morning, and from what I can tell from the PennDOT website, the roads are still rough. You're staying right here and filling up with a hearty breakfast before the plow comes through."

John didn't even protest this time. He just plopped down in a chair. "The bacon does smell good."

"Men and bacon." Mary laughed. "I have my eyes on those pancakes."

The phone rang, and Mary got up to answer. After a brief conversation, she hung up. "That was Rachel Fischer. She's canceled the quilting circle this morning because of the weather."

"I expected it," Elizabeth said, "but it was nice of her to call."

Rachel was an Amish woman who led a weekly quilting circle. They usually met on Thursday mornings at Secondhand
Blessings. Elizabeth was learning to quilt with Rachel's help,
and she really enjoyed it. Rachel also helped out in the shop
from time to time.

After Martha finished cooking and dished up the food,
they said grace and began eating. The pancakes, topped with
plump, juicy blueberries and maple syrup, were delicious, and
the bacon was a perfect savory complement to the sweetness.
Elizabeth sighed with contentment and stretched. "Now I feel
like taking a nap, not going to work."

Martha scooped up her last bite of pancake. "I'm not sure we
should even bother with opening the shop today. I can't imagine
we'd have many customers, if any, after that snowstorm—"

Her comment was interrupted by a sound outside. Mary
peered out the window. "I don't know, Martha. It looks like
there's at least one person out in this mess." She squinted at the
4×4 truck crunching into the driveway, and gasped. "It's
Todd!"

Elizabeth's heart leapt. She hadn't expected to see Todd
today, but it was thrilling to think they'd finally have copies of
Lauren's pictures in hand. How wonderful it would be to call
her with some good news for a change. It would help put
Elizabeth's mind at ease to see the photos for herself. Maybe
they would provide a clue as to why someone left them that
menacing note a few days ago. *Forget the pictures.*

Todd parked his vehicle and carefully navigated up the
porch stairs. Mary greeted him at the door. "Todd! We didn't
expect to see you today."

He shrugged and knocked his boots against the side of the porch to clean them of snow before stepping inside. "I get cabin fever. Besides, I've got four-wheel drive."

"Are the roads any better?" Mary asked.

"Still covered right now. The plows are starting to go through though. I'd imagine they'll have your roads cleared by the afternoon."

Elizabeth smiled at John. "Looks like you might be stuck with us a little while longer."

His blue eyes twinkled. "Don't mind in the slightest."

"So, were you able to reprint the photos?" Mary asked Todd eagerly.

"Got them right here. They turned out great." Todd reached into an inner pocket of his coat and pulled out a large envelope. He handed it to Elizabeth, who opened the envelope and spread the photos out on the cleared table. The first photos in the pack all seemed to be taken at the same location: an Amish farmstead. Some pictures were of the sweeping fields outside, others were of various outbuildings, and a couple of them looked to be taken inside a farmhouse and featured a striking young man with a dark-colored suit and straw hat and a clean-shaven face. The rest of the pictures seemed to be battleground shots.

"What a dashing gentleman," Martha said, referring to the Amish man. "When do you think these photos were taken, Todd?"

"It's tough to tell. The Amish farmsteads of today haven't changed much through the years, so that doesn't help to date it. But the camera you all brought me that contained the film was a make and model common for a certain time period. The grain of the photographs is consistent with that too, so it stands to reason the photos were taken in the early 1940s."

"These war photos are really powerful," John said. "It looks like some of the pictures were taken before the camera was carried into the battlefield."

They continued studying the collection for a few minutes, and Elizabeth offered Todd a cup of hot coffee. After he'd finished it, he handed her the empty mug and moved toward the front door. "Better get going. Hope you all enjoy the photos."

"Goodbye, Todd. And thanks again." Elizabeth smiled at him, and he waved before heading back to his truck and pulling away.

Mary stood still, staring at the photos. "It was nice of him to bring these by," she said, but she sounded distracted.

"Everything okay?" John asked.

"I think so," said Mary slowly. "I can't quite put my finger on it, but that man—the Amish one, I mean—looks so familiar. It doesn't make sense if these pictures were taken seventy years ago like Todd said, but I feel as if I've seen this man before."

"I don't know why you'd recognize him," said Martha. "Everyone associated with these photos is either long gone or pretty advanced in years. For that reason alone, it doesn't make sense why someone would steal them. Or leave us a threatening note, for that matter."

"What threatening note?" John asked.

Elizabeth told him about the note they'd found.

"I'd like to see that."

She got up and went to a drawer in the kitchen where she'd put the note. Then she handed it to him.

"I don't know…," said Elizabeth when she sat down again, scanning the photos for more clues. Then her eyes lit on a detail she'd missed. One of the photos of the Amish man was taken inside a house, in what looked to be a parlor. "Wait, look at this."

"What?" Mary squinted to see, and Martha peered over Elizabeth's shoulder. John leaned across the table.

"I missed it at first because it's so obscure, but look to the left of the man. What do you see?"

"A beautiful pie safe that would fetch thousands of dollars in an antique shop today?"

"Yes, but look closer. The cabinet doesn't have the normal punched-tin doors. It has glass ones."

Mary gasped. "Glass doors that show the reflection of the photographer."

"Exactly. You can't see his face, but look at what he's wearing. An army uniform. Todd was right about World War II."

Martha looked perplexed. "The Amish are pacifists and not too keen on having their picture taken. Why would an outsider, a soldier at that, be snapping photos of an Amish farmstead during the war?"

"I don't know," said Elizabeth. "But I think our mystery runs deeper than missing pictures."

CHAPTER FIFTEEN

John spent the morning with the sisters, looking over the pictures. Elizabeth took out her phone and snapped shots of each photo so they could try to figure out why they were so important to someone. She called Lauren to let her know they had the copies, but she only got her voice mail.

Even though the roads were being cleared, the sisters decided to keep the shop closed.

Martha fixed grilled cheese sandwiches with ham for lunch along with homemade potato salad. For dessert she served a plate of fudge brownies.

"I couldn't hang around here a lot," John said after his second brownie. He patted his trim stomach. "I'd weigh five hundred pounds." He shook his head. "You're an amazing cook, Martha."

Martha blushed. "Thank you. My husband used to compliment my cooking. I loved cooking for him, and I enjoy baking for the shop. It means a lot to me when people go out of their way to buy my pastries, breads, and cakes."

"I'm sure it means a lot to the people who enjoy your efforts." John sighed. "I will not eat a third brownie. If I do, I'll need a nap. I think it's time I headed out."

"Do you have to go to the station?" Elizabeth asked.

John shook his head. "No, I'm off today. My schedule changes from week to week. This week I have Wednesday and

Thursday off." He hesitated a moment, then nodded at the pile of pictures. "I have an idea. Since I'm off, and the shop is closed, why don't I call my professor friend at the Pennsylvania College of Art and Design? See if he's there today. We could find out a little more about this Grant..."

"Slavick," Elizabeth finished for him.

"Yeah, Slavick. Just to make sure he didn't take the photos."

"Rosie Gittrich told me Grant was having a pretty intense conversation with Arthur Graves the day the pictures went missing," Mary said. "You might want to ask him about that as well."

"If we decide Grant is innocent, I'd like to show him the pictures," Elizabeth said. "See if he notices anything unusual."

John nodded. "Well, let me see if Russ is in before we get too carried away. They may have canceled classes today." He got up from the table, took his phone out of his pocket, and walked into the living room. A few seconds later, the sisters could hear him talking to someone.

"Well, let's tidy up from lunch," Martha said. "We don't need to be listening to John's telephone conversation."

The sisters set about cleaning up the kitchen, although Elizabeth couldn't help trying to overhear John in the other room. A few minutes later he came back.

"He's in, and so is Grant. They canceled morning classes but opened this afternoon for students who weren't snowed in." He smiled at Elizabeth. "He's happy to talk to us. Had a lot of good things to say about Grant. He hasn't shown up with any World War II pictures. I think that probably lets him off the hook."

"Maybe," Elizabeth said. "But I also want to find out what he and Arthur Graves were talking about."

"While you guys are gone, I can do some baking," Mary said. "It's nice to have a day off once in a while."

"When is the Helping Hands benefit?" John asked.

"This weekend," Mary replied. "I hope you'll come."

John smiled. "Wouldn't miss it. I'll be on duty, so I won't be able to stay long. Not unless some pies go missing or some of the cooks get in a fistfight."

Mary laughed. "Not much chance of that. But I'll be happy to see you there no matter how long you can hang around."

"I'll see you there," John said with a smile. He turned to Elizabeth. "Are you ready to go?"

"Just let me get my coat and purse."

While John waited, Elizabeth checked her hair and makeup. Then she slid on her coat and scarf, got her purse, and went back into the kitchen. Martha had put some brownies in a plastic container for John to take with him. Elizabeth was glad her sisters liked John. Not that there was anything romantic going on, but maybe someday... He was in Elizabeth's prayers. She hoped that someday he would realize how much God loved him and that his faith would grow.

Elizabeth had wanted to get Lauren's permission to show the photos to John's friend, but she hadn't been able to reach her. However, she was certain Lauren would approve, since she wanted to find out all she could about her family. To keep the new photos safe, Elizabeth decided to take her phone and show Russ those shots.

After saying goodbye to Martha and Mary, Elizabeth and John stepped outside. The cold was like a slap in the face. As they walked toward the car, Elizabeth held on to John's arm.

Even though he'd shoveled the walk, there were still slick spots here and there.

It took them a little over thirty minutes to reach the Pennsylvania College of Art and Design. The college, founded in 1982, was small, but it had a wonderful reputation. It was primarily created for students who wanted to pursue art as their life's work. Besides graphic arts, illustration, and other conventional forms of art, the college also offered classes for photography.

John helped Elizabeth out of the car and again held on to her as they made their way to the front door.

Once they were inside, John led Elizabeth to Russ's classroom. There were several students inside, including the young man Elizabeth had met the day the photos went missing. Grant saw them and smiled. Then he said something to an older man with reddish hair and a beard who turned around and grinned at John. He came over and put his hand out. John took it.

"So happy to see you," he told John. "It's been too long."

John smiled. "Chasing down criminals keeps me busy."

Russ laughed. "More likely you're chasing down speeders and people who don't use their turn signals."

John chuckled good-naturedly. It was obvious these two friends liked to tease each other.

"Good to see you again," Grant said to Elizabeth.

"Nice to see you too, Grant."

Russ pointed toward an office connected to the larger room where the students worked. "Let's go into my office so we won't bother anyone," he said. "I'd like to see these infamous photos. Grant told me about them."

Grant followed them into the office and closed the door behind them. Russ sat down in a chair behind the desk.

"Have a seat," he said to Elizabeth and John, gesturing to several metal chairs pushed up against the wall. John pulled a couple of them up next to Russ's desk. Elizabeth and John sat down while Grant stood behind them.

Elizabeth took her phone out of her purse, pulled up the photos, and handed her phone to Russ. He scrolled through them slowly. Sometimes stopping to stare at a particular picture. Finally, he handed the phone back to Elizabeth.

"Those are incredible," Russ said. "I can understand why Grant raved about them. There are some shots from the battlefield that are incredibly moving. Faces of World War II troops. The pictures of the Amish man are also interesting. Especially since pictures of the Amish were rare due to their beliefs. They were a lot stricter about it back then. I'm surprised to see these."

"Do you mind if I look at them?" Grant asked. "I only got a quick look the other day."

"I guess so," Elizabeth said. "I wanted to ask the owner of the photographs if it's all right to share them, but I couldn't get hold of her this morning."

"If you think she'd be upset about it…"

Elizabeth shook her head. "I honestly don't think she'd mind. I'll just tell her I showed them to you. I'm sure it will be all right."

"Thank you."

Grant took the phone and scrolled through the photos. "These really are cool," he said. "It's amazing they showed up after all this time."

Elizabeth smiled. "A friend at church was able to develop the film. Thankfully, he scanned the negatives. That's the only reason we still have them."

Grant handed the phone back to Elizabeth. "I can't believe someone would steal these. As interesting as they are, they're not very valuable. Why would anyone want them?"

"That's the question, isn't it?" Elizabeth put the phone back in her purse. "You didn't notice anyone take them, I gather."

Grant shook his head. "No, but there was this older guy. He kept asking me questions about them. He seemed really engrossed. I left before he did, so I have no idea if he might be your culprit."

"What kind of questions was he asking?" John said.

Grant was quiet for a moment. "I'm trying to remember. He wanted to know who took the photos. I told him I had no idea. Then he asked who the owner was. I remembered your sister saying they belonged to a Lauren Collier." He frowned. "I'm sorry if I shouldn't have repeated her name. I hope that wasn't a mistake."

"Don't worry about it, Grant," Elizabeth said. "You didn't do anything wrong."

"Sorry I couldn't help more." Grant looked at Russ. "I need to get back to work."

Russ nodded at him. "I'll see you in a minute."

Grant said goodbye and left the office. Elizabeth stood to her feet. "Thank you for taking time to see us, Russ. I appreciate it."

"I just wish I could have helped you more. Now that you've made another set, do you mind if I ask why you're still trying to find the person who took them?"

Elizabeth smiled. "I guess I feel I have a duty to find out why someone thought it was okay to steal something from one of my customers. It upsets me to think we've lost some trust because of what happened."

Russ stood up. "I can understand that," he said. "You have a heightened sense of justice. Something we don't see a lot of nowadays." He held out his hand, and Elizabeth took it. "Good luck, Elizabeth. And keep an eye on this guy. He cheats at cards."

"You wish. You know I win fair and square," John said, laughing. "You just can't deal with failure."

"But you cleaned me out," Russ said. "You should have had pity on me."

"I think you can recover from losing a dollar twenty-nine."

Russ sighed dramatically. "That's what all you high rollers say."

John grinned. "Let's go, Elizabeth, before he tells you something about me that will make you decide you don't want to spend time with me anymore."

He led her out the door and back to the car. When they got inside, Elizabeth said, "Thank you for taking me to see your friend. Not sure it did any good."

"I'm sorry." He sighed. "I still can't figure out why anyone would want the pictures enough to steal them."

"Me neither. You know, I'd completely forgotten that Mary mentioned Lauren's name when she brought the pictures into the shop. Anyone could have overheard her—or Grant."

"And found out where Lauren lived," John said. "Then tried to break into her house."

Elizabeth nodded. This new revelation worried her. Was Lauren in danger?

A short time later they were pulling off the main road into the farm's long driveway. As they came around the curve, Elizabeth gasped.

An ambulance was parked in front of her house.

CHAPTER SIXTEEN

Elizabeth hurried around the vehicle toward the front door but stopped when she saw two EMT workers hoisting Martha onto a stretcher. Her younger sister was conscious but looked pale. Her face was tight with pain. Mary bustled out the door behind her with two purses—one hers, one Martha's—looped over her arm.

"What happened?" Elizabeth asked.

"There were still some slick spots on the drive," Mary said. "Tink ran out the door and wouldn't come back in, so Martha went out to get her. She was wearing those silly house slippers that don't have any traction, and she wiped out when she hit the ice. Hurt her ankle pretty badly. She couldn't get up. I was baking in the kitchen when I heard her yelling."

Elizabeth glanced toward the house. It seemed like a silly thing to worry about with Martha injured, but she hoped Mary hadn't gotten distracted and left her pies to burn in the oven again.

As if reading her thoughts, Mary said, "Don't worry. I made sure to turn off the oven this time. Thankfully, the pies were already done. They're cooling on the drainboard now."

"Excuse me, are you going to ride with her?" one of the EMTs, an olive-skinned man with spiky hair, asked Mary.

"Yes," Mary answered briskly. She climbed into the ambulance and took Martha's hand. "I'll call and update you as soon as we know something at the hospital. The techs said earlier they don't think she broke anything, but they want to get X-rays to make certain."

Elizabeth watched as the doors shut and the vehicle sped away, lights flashing and sirens blaring. She was thankful the roads were cleared at least. One less thing to worry about.

Mary seemed to have things well in hand. She'd always had a delightful, sunny personality, but the downside of that was that she also tended to be scattered and disorganized. Yet here she'd been in a tough situation, and though it must have been frightening to see strong, capable Martha injured, Mary had handled the situation just fine. She'd sounded so calm, so authoritative when Elizabeth had arrived. She knew just what to do.

"I hope Martha's all right," John said. "Do you want to ride with me to go to the hospital?"

"No, that's okay. You've shuttled me around enough lately. I'll take my own vehicle. You're welcome to follow me, if you'd like, though. I'd appreciate the company, if you have the time."

"Don't have any other plans. We've had quite a bit of excitement the last few days. It'll be a relief to go back to the police department tomorrow. Might be a little more relaxing."

Elizabeth made a face at him. "Not exactly the kind of excitement I tend to want in my life, but we'll manage."

They drove the few miles to Lancaster General Hospital. Elizabeth shuddered as she thought of John and her ill-timed meeting yesterday with Arthur Graves. She only hoped they didn't run into him again, since it was possible he'd been kept overnight for observation. She had a feeling he wouldn't be too keen on the idea of crossing paths with her again either.

She and John sat in the waiting room for about half an hour before Mary met them, supporting a limping Martha with her ankle wrapped in an elastic bandage.

Martha motioned toward the cluster of chairs where John and Elizabeth sat. "I need to rest for a minute before we head out to the car." She grimaced as Mary helped her sit down.

"So, what did the doctor say?" Elizabeth asked. "You're walking, so I guess that means nothing's broken."

Martha shifted position in her chair. "No, I'm thankful to say it's just a bad sprain. They're letting me go home, and I'm glad. I don't want to leave you down a person in the store."

Mary jumped in. "You're not working tomorrow. You need to take it easy. Remember what the doctor said? Rest, ice, compression, elevation."

"I'm sure it's not that serious. I can sit at the register."

"With your ankle elevated above your heart? Our patrons will think you've joined the circus. You need to stay on the couch. Elizabeth and I will cover the store."

Elizabeth agreed. "Mary's right. I haven't been doing my share lately. I'd be happy to mind the store. Maybe Rachel can help us out if we get in a pinch."

Martha reached down to rub her injured ankle. "I don't intend to push my work off on poor Rachel. She has enough to do managing her own home."

Mary's voice was firm. "She's always been happy to help out in an emergency, and that's what this is. An emergency. If you don't rest your foot, you're likely to develop a more serious injury that won't heal as easily." Mary put her hands on her hips, a classic Martha stance. "I won't take no for an answer."

Mary also sounded just like Martha. Elizabeth had to chuckle at the role reversal of her two sisters.

"I have it all figured out," Mary continued. "We'll turn the living room into a sickroom for a few days. You'll be close to the bathroom and the kitchen, which are easy enough to walk to unassisted. One of us will check in on you periodically. And if we're not around and you need us, you can give us a call."

Martha was silent for a moment, seemingly at a loss for words. Mary had ready answers for all of her protests. "It sounds like you have it all figured out, then."

Mary smiled. "I do."

"Well then." Martha reached into her handbag, which was resting on a low table in front of them. She pulled out a notepad and an ink pen. After a few minutes of scribbling, she flipped through the pages. "That should take care of it."

"Take care of what?" Mary asked.

"You two running things without me." Martha tore off the top page and handed it to Mary. "Here are instructions for the store. Several customers have orders on reserve. I want to make sure you know where their items are being kept."

Elizabeth fought a smile. "Aren't they in the storeroom? Where we always keep them?"

She glanced at John, who was wisely staying out of their conversation. He looked amused.

"It's not a laughing matter, Elizabeth." Martha raised an eyebrow at her two sisters. "You two don't know how I pick up the slack."

"I feel confident we can manage. Don't worry," Elizabeth said, trying her best to reassure her younger sister. "In fact, I think Mary could probably handle it on her own if she had to. She's been juggling multiple jobs lately and doing so well."

"Perhaps," Martha said. She looked thoughtful and then addressed Mary. "I do have to admit, you've surprised me. You've really stuck with your baking. You haven't gotten frustrated or given up on it. I think you can apply that to anything else you try as well."

Mary looked touched. "Thank you, Martha."

Content with having dispensed her instructions, Martha got to her feet with difficulty. "Why don't we go to the car now? I'm ready to get home."

As the group headed for the exit, a person caught Elizabeth's eye. Her heart sank. The last person in the world she wanted to see was fast approaching. She tried to hide her face, but it was too late.

Arthur Graves had already seen her and was marching toward her like a man on a mission.

CHAPTER SEVENTEEN

Elizabeth ignored the urge to run the other way and waited until Arthur stood in front of her, his face only a few inches away.

"Hello, Arthur," she said with a forced smile. "How nice to see you. I'm happy you're up and around."

"Well, you won't be happy by the time I'm done with you."

"What do you mean?"

"I'm talking about my truck. About the bill for the hospital. You caused that wreck. You're going to have to pay my bills and buy me a new truck."

Elizabeth's mouth dropped open in surprise. "I have no idea what you're talking about."

"If you hadn't chased me, I wouldn't have gone off the road. This is all your fault."

Elizabeth looked to John for help. Were they really responsible for Arthur's troubles?

John walked over and got between Elizabeth and Arthur, which took some effort because of how close the upset man was to her.

"First of all, I was driving, not Elizabeth," John said, his voice steady but firm. "And secondly, no one told you to speed in dangerous conditions. The only fault here lies completely with you."

Arthur sputtered several times, making noises that didn't sound like any words Elizabeth had ever heard. Finally, he said, "I'm not finished with this. I'll go to your superiors."

"You have every right to do that. I'll even help you with the paperwork."

Graves's face turned dark red.

He didn't say another word. He just turned on his heel and hurried toward the large automatic doors that led to the parking lot.

"If no one minds, I need to get going," Martha grumbled. "My foot hurts."

As if she'd been listening to their conversation, a nurse came up next to them with a wheelchair. "You left your room before I had a chance to bring this."

Martha waved her away. "I don't need a wheelchair," she said curtly.

"You need to keep off your foot as much as possible, and you should have it elevated. Let me wheel you out there. This isn't a time for you to don your superhero costume."

Elizabeth fought hard to suppress a giggle. She was certain the nurse was doing the same thing Graves had just tried to do. Except this attempt at manipulation was for Martha's own good.

Martha grumbled under her breath, but she sat down and allowed the nurse to push her out to the parking lot.

By the time they got home, Martha had calmed down. Elizabeth had to wonder what kind of patient her sister was going to be. She was pretty sure Martha wasn't going to allow them to look after her without some complaints.

Elizabeth got on one side of Martha and Mary got on the other, making sure she got safely from the car to the front door. At first she fought them, saying she could get up the steps by herself.

"Martha, there could still be some slippery spots," Elizabeth said firmly. "We are going to help you into the house, so you might as well quit griping."

Probably aware that she wasn't going to win this argument, Martha clamped her lips into a thin line and allowed her sisters to assist her.

When they finally got her inside, Martha wrestled away from them and clumped into the living room, where she plopped down on the couch. Elizabeth was surprised. Martha had been fighting the idea of staying on the couch. A look at her face told the story. She was in pain.

"Let's get you settled in," Elizabeth said. She turned to Mary. "Will you get Martha some water and her pills?" Elizabeth didn't call them pain pills, since Martha didn't like to admit when she was hurting. Best to just refer to them as *the pills*.

While Mary went to get Martha's prescription, Elizabeth helped Martha get her feet up on the couch. She put a pillow underneath the sore foot, elevating it, and two pillows behind Martha's back. Then she took the quilt from the arm of the couch and pulled it over her sister.

"Would you rather have your pillow from upstairs?" Elizabeth asked.

Martha shook her head. "No, this is fine. Thank you. I'm sorry for being so cranky. I guess I see myself as a caretaker, not as someone who needs to be taken care of."

"I know that, but for a little while, you have to let us help you. You'll be up and around soon. The next few days will go by quickly." Elizabeth smiled at her. "Just think. You can watch some TV and read those books you say you've had no time to enjoy. Why don't I get Mama's crutches out of the closet? They might come in handy."

Martha nodded. "Yeah, I guess so." She frowned at Elizabeth. "You need to call Rachel and see if she can help out."

"Doctor Cartwright said you need to stay off that foot for at least a week."

Martha was quiet for a moment. "Okay, maybe through Wednesday." She pointed her finger at Elizabeth. "You let me decide when I'm ready to get back to the shop. Don't try to *handle* me, Elizabeth. I mean it."

Before she could respond, Mary came into the room with a glass of water and the bottle of pills they'd picked up on the way home. She didn't say anything as she put them on the coffee table. Obviously, she was thinking the same thing as Elizabeth.

"Mary and I are going to start supper. Do you need anything?"

Martha shook her head. "I'm just fine, thanks."

"Okay," Elizabeth said. "Just holler if you need us."

Mary turned and headed toward the kitchen with Elizabeth right behind her. When they were out of Martha's hearing, Elizabeth whispered, "Best not to mention those pills are for pain. I don't want her to decide she needs to be heroic and do without them."

Mary nodded. "I know. That's why I didn't say anything." She sighed. "I have a feeling that taking care of Martha is going to be more work than we might imagine. Most of it is acting as if we're not *really* taking care of her."

Elizabeth put a hand to her mouth to cover a giggle. "You're right," she said when she put her fingers down. "This will definitely be a challenge." She grinned at Mary. "Okay, so what do we fix for supper?"

Mary went to the refrigerator and opened it. "We have some of that tuna casserole Martha made. How about that? I'll make a salad to go with it. We've got some rolls. Should make a decent dinner."

"Sounds great," Elizabeth said. "I'll make roast in the slow cooker tomorrow."

"After I get the pies done for Saturday, I'll be glad to help out more with the cooking. I used to make a pretty good taco casserole. The kids loved it."

"That sounds great. But like you said, focus on those pies for now. Why don't you let Rachel and me handle the store tomorrow while you bake and keep an eye on Martha?" Elizabeth hesitated a moment before saying, "You might want to keep the kitchen as clean as you can. I don't want Martha getting too concerned about what's going on in here."

Mary chuckled. "Yeah, I understand. I'll clean as I go. And if I get in trouble, I'll hide the dirty dishes in the laundry room."

Elizabeth laughed before lowering her voice. "Sounds like a perfect idea. Now, let's get supper going before Martha storms in here asking what's taking so long. You get the tuna casserole heated up, and I'll try calling Rachel about working tomorrow. I'm really not sure if the Fischers can hear the phone ring from that shed at the end of their driveway. In the winter all the windows will be closed against the cold. If no one answers, I'll walk over."

While Mary got the casserole into the oven, Elizabeth tried calling the Fischers. Thankfully, Rachel's husband, Silas, answered. He assured her that Rachel would be happy to help out and would be there in the morning.

"Elizabeth," Mary said slowly when she came back into the kitchen, "you haven't said a word about that awful man at the hospital. Are you worried about it at all?"

Elizabeth had been trying to ignore Arthur Graves's accusations, but quite honestly, she was having a hard time getting them out of her mind.

"I'm not responsible for his decision to drive too fast on unsafe roads," she replied, "but I have to admit that I wonder if the crash would have happened if we hadn't been chasing him."

"But were you actually chasing him? Or were you just following him? Those are two different things."

Elizabeth smiled at her sister. "You're right. John said the same thing. Thanks, Mary. Knowing you feel the same way makes me feel a little better. Now let's get this meal made."

As the sisters scurried around the kitchen fixing supper, Elizabeth honestly did feel some relief after Mary's comments. Yet there was something about Arthur Graves that continued to bother her. Was he going to drop his threats? Even if he did, Elizabeth couldn't help feeling that they hadn't seen the end of him.

CHAPTER EIGHTEEN

Martha spent a restless night on the couch. Although her bed was certainly more comfortable, Elizabeth and Mary had made sure she had everything she needed to sleep as well as she could. Truthfully, it wasn't the couch that bothered her—it was knowing she had to depend on other people to take care of her. So far, her sisters had done a wonderful job. Supper was good, and they told her the kitchen was spotless. Tomorrow Rachel would be helping Elizabeth in the store while Mary finished the pies for the fund-raiser on Saturday. Martha had already decided to stay away from the kitchen while Mary baked her final goodies. She didn't want to discourage her sister. Wanting to raise money for a fine organization that helped foster children was admirable.

Martha was aware that she was too rigid. She liked things done a certain way and didn't have much patience when others didn't live up to her expectations. She'd been too harsh with her baby sister ever since they all moved in together. Yes, Mary was somewhat scatterbrained, but there were worse personality traits. Mary was also kind, warmhearted, and willing to take a risk to help others. After what she'd been through, it was amazing she wasn't closed off and suspicious of everyone. Actually, Martha was amazed by Mary.

She'd finally fallen asleep a little after one in the morning. When she woke up, she smelled bacon cooking and coffee brewing. Elizabeth must have started breakfast. Martha pulled herself up to a sitting position, still careful to keep her ankle propped up by the small pillow. She had just smoothed out her covers when Elizabeth came down the stairs and saw her.

"Do you need any help?" she asked.

Martha shook her head. "I'm fine." She frowned at Elizabeth. "I thought you were making breakfast."

"No, it's not me. Must be Mary."

"Oh, Lizzie. Maybe you should—"

"Maybe I should let her do this on her own?" Elizabeth said. "Yeah, you're right. Think I'll go back upstairs and get dressed. Be back soon."

Martha fought an urge to call her back. Ask her to check to see how Mary was doing. Instead, she lay back on her pillows and waited. Elizabeth was right. Mary could do this. And even if she messed up, it was okay. She'd get it right the next time. Martha took a deep breath and let it out slowly. She was surprised when someone touched her shoulder.

"Sorry to wake you up," Mary said. "Are you hungry, or do you want to sleep a little longer?"

Martha sat up. "I thought I was awake. I must have dozed off again." She looked down at the coffee table and saw a plate of bacon, scrambled eggs, hash browns, and toast that looked absolutely perfect. "Oh, Mary. This looks delicious. Thank you. I really am hungry."

She let Mary help her swing her legs off the couch and sit up straight. Mary got a small stool and propped up Martha's foot.

"Is that comfortable?" she asked.

"That's great," Martha said with a smile. "Thank you, Mary. I really appreciate it."

"You're welcome. I'll get your coffee and be right back."

Elizabeth came out of the kitchen holding her own coffee cup. She smiled at Martha. "Good for you, Sis."

"I just have one question," Martha whispered. "Is this her first attempt?"

Elizabeth shook her head. "I think it would be better if you let it go."

Martha laughed softly. "Okay. Never mind."

"The animals are all fed, and I'm heading out to the shop. Rachel should arrive any minute. Mary will be here if you need anything." Elizabeth sought Martha's gaze. "I want you to relax, watch TV, or just read. I brought down several of the books you had on your nightstand. Just take it easy, okay?"

Martha noticed the stack of books on the end of the table for the first time. She held her hand up. "I promise to do my best. Change doesn't always happen overnight, but I'm working on it."

Elizabeth smiled at her. "That's all I can ask. I'll check back with you at lunch."

Martha nodded. "Sounds good. Thanks, Lizzie."

Elizabeth headed out just as Mary walked in with Martha's coffee. She set it down on the table next to the plate.

"What else can I get you?" Mary asked.

Martha could tell her sister was nervous. That she wanted to please her. Martha felt even worse about her past critical attitude.

"Mary, this is lovely. I can't think of anything else I need. Thank you so much."

Mary's face beamed with happiness. She had obviously worked hard to make this meal a success. "I'm glad you like it," she said. "Call me when you're done. I'll come and get the dishes. I'm going to start working on those pies for tomorrow." She cleared her throat. "I'll try hard to keep the kitchen clean."

"Don't worry about it," Martha said. "Just do the best you can. That's all any of us can do. Try to clean as you go, but don't let the pies suffer. The kitchen will get clean, trust me."

"Okay." Mary drew the word out some, looking rather suspiciously at her older sister. Did she think Martha was up to something? This new attitude might take some getting used to on both sides.

Mary left the room, and Martha began eating. Everything was perfect. After a few bites, she decided to watch some TV. She picked up the remote and clicked it. When the television came on, it was already on Martha's favorite channel, one that only played old movies. Martha wasn't impressed with Hollywood's newer pictures. Give her a musical with Gene Kelly or a movie with Jimmy Stewart. She also loved Audrey Hepburn and Grace Kelly. Martha firmly believed the older movies were the best.

The movie that was playing now was *Wings of Love*. Martha hadn't seen it in years. It was about a pilot whose plane crashed in snow-covered mountains. He was flying a rich woman and her staff to some big shindig. The pilot and the woman were the only people who survived. At first they hated each other, but as they fought to survive, love blossomed. It was rather corny, but Martha really enjoyed it. She and Chuck had watched it together more than once. Thinking of him made her heart ache. Oh, how she missed him.

Martha had finished her breakfast when Mary walked into the room. She gathered the dishes onto a tray. "Do you want another cup of coffee?" she asked.

"I would love that," Martha said. "Everything was great. You're an excellent cook."

Mary didn't say anything, but her cheeks turned pink. Martha's praise had clearly made her happy. Mary had just turned to leave when she stopped and stared at the TV. "It's him," she said.

"Him who?" Martha asked.

"The actor Rosie has a crush on. Evan Masters."

"Rosie has a crush on Evan Masters?" Martha was confused.

"Remember? I told you about the special room she has in her house? With pictures of an actor? It's him."

"I guess I can see that. He was terribly handsome, wasn't he? Died a few years ago."

Mary shrugged. "I guess we all have that one crush on someone famous."

"Who do you have a crush on, Mary?" Martha asked.

Mary laughed. "Actually, there are several. I think I'll keep that to myself. I don't want to give you and Elizabeth fodder to tease me."

Martha grinned. "That might be wise."

As Mary walked out with the tray, Martha laughed to herself. She'd always had a crush on Sean Connery, but she had no intention of telling anyone else about it.

As Martha watched, she realized that there was something about Evan Masters that had bugged her ever since she'd started watching the movie. What was it? Try as she might, she couldn't figure it out. It was like she'd seen him somewhere else. Somewhere he didn't belong. But that didn't make any sense. She tried to dismiss the nagging feeling that tugged at her, but it wasn't easily dismissed. She picked up her bottle of pills. They must be making her loopy. Still, even as she blamed the pills for her odd reaction to the handsome actor, she still felt unsettled. Whatever is was that bothered her felt important, but for the life of her, she couldn't figure out why.

CHAPTER NINETEEN

After hours of standing on her feet, Mary's back ached. She sank into a kitchen chair to ease the pain and surveyed the beautiful line of pies running the length of the kitchen counter. Dutch apple, blueberry, and boysenberry. She had to admit, she was quite proud of her efforts. She'd learned to make decent versions of three different pies. Maybe she'd take up baking as a legitimate hobby after this. Who could have imagined?

The kitchen smelled wonderful. The sweet smell of pies lingered in the air, and Mary's stomach growled. She glanced at the clock and was surprised to see it was after two.

Martha had slept most of the morning and into the afternoon, apparently skipping lunch, which was just fine with Mary. She had tried to clean up the kitchen as she went, but there was still plenty to do before things were back to normal. Rubbing her lower back to further dispel the ache, she rose reluctantly to her feet. She didn't relish the idea of cleaning up when she was already tired, but she'd promised Martha. Maybe she could cobble together some soup and sandwiches for Martha when she woke up.

She dropped some cracked eggshells into the trash can and used a wet dishrag to swipe at the flour-covered counter. She put the lids back on the flour and sugar containers and started a sink of hot, soapy water to scrub the dirty bowls, spoons, and measuring cups. She'd just put a few things in to soak when she heard Martha calling her from the living room.

"Mary?" Her sister was awake. Her voice sounded scratchy. Mary heard Martha clear her throat. "Mary? More water, please?"

Mary rushed to fill a glass and took it to Martha, who slowly drank it. When she finished, she smiled gratefully at Mary.

"The house smells great," she said. "I'm guessing your pies turned out well?"

Mary beamed. "I think they did. Just in time too, with the fund-raiser tomorrow." She wiggled her fingers at Martha. "And I'm positive there aren't any fake fingernails in them this time, either."

Martha guffawed. "I'm sure everyone will appreciate that."

"I can see the humor in it now," Mary said. "But at the time, I was pretty mortified. Thank goodness it didn't happen in front of a huge crowd." She was pretty sure the image of Emily Miller scooping the Scarlett Sensation-colored nail from her blueberry pie would stick with her forever, though.

Martha groaned. "I sure hope I feel up to the fund-raiser tomorrow. What horrible timing. I really want to be there to support you and the Lancaster County Helping Hands." She gave Mary a small smile. "I really am proud of you."

Tears stung Mary's eyes. She could see that Martha was being genuine.

"Thank you," she said. She reached over the couch to give Martha a hug. "I hope you can be there tomorrow. Rest is the best medicine, though, I'm sure."

"I have no plans of going anywhere today," Martha said, settling back into the cushion and readjusting her leg on its pillow.

"Me either. We should have a pretty quiet day."

Just then there was a knock at the door. Mary jumped. "Who could that be?" She wasn't expecting company. Maybe it was Rachel with a question from the store.

She hurried to the door and was surprised to see Lauren Collier standing on the porch, a pretty polka-dotted scarf wrapped around her neck.

"Hi," Lauren said, almost apologetically. Noticing Mary's flour-dusted apron, she took a step backward. "I'm sorry. It looks like you're busy. I should've called first. I just heard your voice mail message about the pictures."

"No, no," Mary said, waving her inside. She untied her apron and looped it over one arm. "You're fine. I just finished baking some pies for a fund-raiser we're going to tomorrow."

Lauren stepped into the warm house and unwound her scarf. "It smells great in here." She shook her head in amazement. "How do you ladies find time to do all the things you do? Run the store, bake pies, attend fund-raisers. You make me feel pretty lazy."

Mary smiled. "Well, we're not cleaning out decades-old homes by ourselves. That's a pretty big job."

"I'm not by myself," Lauren said. "Peter's helping out too. And you ladies, of course." She followed Mary into the living room and gasped when she saw Martha stretched out on the couch with her injured leg propped up. "What happened to you?"

"Fell on the ice. Winter weather can be hazardous to your health, apparently." Martha motioned to a chair next to the couch. "Why don't you have a seat?"

Lauren looked reluctant. "Are you sure?"

Martha laughed. "I hardly think I'm going anywhere. I'd appreciate the company."

Lauren glanced at Mary, as if for confirmation, and Mary nodded. "We'd love to visit with you for a while. And I'm guessing you're anxious to see your pictures?"

Lauren perched on the edge of the chair like a bird lighting on a tree branch. "I would love that. Going through all of my grandfather's stuff makes me sad, but it also helps me feel closer to him."

Mary swallowed. She remembered how difficult it had been when their mother had passed away. No matter how old you got, your parents and grandparents were special, and losing them shifted everything around in your world. "Let me get them." She found the envelope with the prints and handed it to Lauren.

As Lauren flipped through the photos, the look on her face was one of wonder. "These are really wonderful." She swiped her fingers under her eyes. "I just wish there were more photos of Grandfather."

"Well, actually, we wanted to talk to you about that. We particularly noticed this one." Mary pulled out the photo that featured the photographer's reflection in the glass of the pie safe. "We were wondering if this was your grandfather. Or someone else?"

Lauren squinted at the photo. "I...I think it's him. It's hard to tell because the reflection is faint, but it looks like his height, his build." She wrinkled her brow. "Who's the Amish man he's taking a photo of, though? Half of these pictures are of the same Amish farmstead. The fields, the house, inside and out. It's almost like he was documenting something."

"Maybe he was," Martha said. She swung her leg down off the couch as she leaned forward. Mary gave her a disapproving look. To her utter surprise, Martha looked like a scolded child and immediately planted her foot back on the pillow.

"What do you mean, 'maybe he was'?" Lauren asked.

"Well," Martha continued, "maybe your grandfather knew this place well. Knew the young Amish man. You said he was ex-Amish, right?"

"He was." Lauren looked thoughtful. "Granddad could have been a member of this community before he left the Plain way of life. He never admitted to it though. You all know the Amish families around here, don't you?"

"I don't know about all of them," Martha said. "But we know a few."

Mary perked up. Lauren seemed to be stoking a kindling hope. Rachel was working with Elizabeth in the store. Maybe she would recognize the Amish man in the photo. "In fact, we know someone you could talk to right now."

"Really?" Lauren stood to her feet, clutching the photos to her chest.

"One of our friends, Rachel Fischer, is helping run the shop today. I know she'd love to talk with you if Elizabeth and she aren't too swamped."

"That would be absolutely wonderful," said Lauren, looping her scarf around her neck again.

"Don't mind me if I don't see you to the door," Martha said drily, but she gave Lauren a little smile and wave.

"We'll be right back," Mary assured her sister.

"Take your time," Martha said. "I might watch another old movie. I'm afraid I could get fat and sassy being spoiled like this."

"No chance of that, I'm sure," Mary said with a grin as she headed out the door.

"So, does he look familiar to you?" Mary slid the photo of the Amish man across the counter to Rachel.

Rachel studied the photo. Then she touched her fingers to her lips. "Where did you get this, if I may ask?"

Lauren told her about cleaning out her grandfather's home and about the vintage camera. "Do you think you can help me?" she asked.

Rachel nodded solemnly and continued to stare at the photo. "This man resembles the members of a family I know."

"What are you thinking?" Elizabeth leaned over the counter, gingerly lifting one foot to flex it, then the other. Mary wondered if her arches were bothering her. It certainly could happen on a busy day at the store when the chances to sit down were scarce.

"I do not like to believe in coincidences. Providence is more often at play," said Rachel slowly. She tapped the photo with a finger. "If this is who I think it is, I can introduce you to his family. They still live in this area."

"Great," said Lauren. She practically bounced on the tips of her toes, she was so excited. "When do you think we could meet up?"

"They are going to be at the foster family fund-raiser tomorrow, I believe." Rachel said the words hesitantly, as if she was trying to decide if she wanted to take them back or not. Mary's heart beat fast at Rachel's sidestepping. She was usually so forthright and open.

"I'm free tomorrow," said Lauren. "I'd love to support you all at the event."

"We'd love to have you there," said Elizabeth. "The more the merrier."

Rachel continued slowly. "It may be a delicate situation, though. I feel the need to warn you."

"Why is that?" Mary asked. Something must be wrong if Rachel was walking on eggshells.

"The man in this photo? I believe his name is Joshua. He is one of the biggest mysteries to ever happen in Bird-in-Hand. He disappeared without a trace over seventy-five years ago."

CHAPTER TWENTY

Elizabeth woke the next morning to aching feet. The store had been unusually busy the day before. She guessed it had something to do with the bad weather from a few days ago. Any time the temperature perked up a few degrees in winter, people liked to get out of the house. Not that that was a bad thing. The fund-raiser would likely have great attendance if the good weather continued.

A quick peek out the window showed brilliant blue skies and plenty of winter-white sunshine. Not a cloud in sight, and for that, she was grateful. Mary had been putting so much effort into getting everything ready for today's event, Elizabeth hoped everything would go off without a hitch.

She got dressed and headed downstairs. She tiptoed through the living room so as not to wake Martha, who lay lightly snoring on the couch. Mary, as Elizabeth had expected, was already in the kitchen, sorting the pies she'd made the day before and putting them into boxes. "I thought you'd never wake up," she said when she saw Elizabeth.

Elizabeth laughed. "It's only seven thirty."

Mary glanced at the clock with a look of surprise. "I've been up for a while. I guess I'm excited. Or nervous. Something like that."

"You don't have any reason to be nervous. Your pies are incredible. The last batch I taste tested were delicious, and I bet these are even better. What a good cause they're going for too."

Mary smiled. "I'm so happy to be helping out. When I think about all those children looking for a family...Well, my heart just breaks. Yet God still brings good out of it somehow. Knits people together. I'm sure Emily and her family have been a blessing to Timmy."

"And I'm sure he has been to her as well."

"Water, please," Martha croaked from the living room. Elizabeth rushed to take her a glass. Martha swallowed her pills, then reached for her crutches. "I'll need you two to help me get into the car."

"Oh, no," Mary said, crossing her arms. "You're not going to the fund-raiser. You're staying home to rest."

"I've sat around long enough," Martha said. "I want to be there to support you. You've worked so hard."

Mary shook her head. "I won't hear of it. If you push your-self too fast, you'll never recover." Martha argued with her for a few more minutes, but finally, her protests grew weak, and she settled back into the couch with the TV remote and the cordless phone.

"Well, I've certainly learned a lesson over the past week," she said to Elizabeth, readjusting the pillow under her foot.

"What's that?"

"Sometimes you just have to go with the flow and let some-body else be in charge." The way she said it made Elizabeth think this was about more than Martha handing over the reins to her little sister when it came to making pies. It was a heart issue between her and God. There was nothing wrong with plans and preparation, but sometimes you simply couldn't control what life threw at you. And in those unsteady moments, you had no choice but to lean on Him.

Mary pulled on her coat. "Call us if you need us."

"I will. Promise," Martha said. "Now shoo. Go show off your beautiful pies."

Mary beamed so brightly at their middle sister's praise that it made Elizabeth smile too. They left the house and got into Elizabeth's SUV.

"Don't forget we have to drop by Rosie's house first to pick up the Italian cream cake she made," Mary said.

"She isn't going to the fund-raiser?" Elizabeth asked.

Mary sighed. "You know Rosie. She's a bit of a homebody."

"Maybe we could ask her if she'd like to ride with us."

"I don't think she'll accept, if my last visit with her is any indication," Mary said. "We were actually getting along pretty well until I made the mistake of noticing pictures of her celebrity crush pasted all over the walls. I guess it embarrassed her. Martha knows all about it."

"Tell me you weren't snooping."

Mary shook her head vehemently. "No, I wasn't, I promise. The door to her back bedroom was open just a crack, and I glanced in as I was standing in the living room."

"That's odd. Why would she care about something like that?" Elizabeth couldn't help but be amused. The thought of elderly Rosie Gittrich nursing a schoolgirl crush on some far-off film star was funny. "Who's her crush?"

Mary snapped her fingers. "Oh, what's his name? He was in that movie about the airplane crash that Martha was watching yesterday. Eric...no, Evan! That's it. Evan Masters."

The name rang a bell with Elizabeth, but she couldn't immediately recall his face.

The sisters stopped by Rosie's house, but as expected, she didn't want to attend the fund-raiser, so Mary thanked her for her Italian cream cake and left her alone. The car was warm and toasty by the time the sisters pulled into the already-packed parking lot of their church, Mount Zion Mennonite. Families straggled past them, toting boxes and baking dishes.

"Looks like there will be plenty of pies," said Mary nervously. Elizabeth wondered if she was feeling intimidated by the other entries.

"You know how church people are about making sure there's an abundance of food," she said. "Even Pastor Nagle said he was planning to try his hand at a pumpkin pie."

"Really?" Mary hid a giggle with her fist. Elizabeth had to admit, the thought of their burly pastor standing in front of an oven with flowered mitts made her chuckle, but a humble leader was a good one, in her opinion.

"Why don't we go inside? If you're ready?"

Mary took a deep breath. "Let's do this." They carefully unloaded the pies. Elizabeth gasped as she entered the basement of the church. It was a fairly large, open space, most often used for after-church dinners or baby showers for new moms in the congregation, but the space brimmed with people now. It was as full as she'd ever seen it. The room buzzed with conversation, and long tables lined the perimeter of the room, filled with an assortment of pies, cakes, and other baked goods.

Elizabeth and Mary checked in their pies and got their numbered paddles for the auction. Mary glanced at her watch. "We have a few minutes before they start," she said. "Why don't we check out the competition?" Her tone was casual but edged with nervousness. Elizabeth felt for her. It was like practicing your heart out for a piano recital and then getting stage fright the day of the performance. At least Mary didn't have to be up on the block with her pies.

They walked down the first row of tables. Paper tents behind each item listed the name of the baker and the type of baked good. "Cherry, strawberry-rhubarb, plum, peach," she read off the placards. "And here's Pastor's pumpkin pie." While Pastor Nagle's contribution was simple, it made her feel proud to know the man leading their church was willing to step out of his comfort zone for a good cause.

"Look at that beautiful German Black Forest cake, Elizabeth. Doesn't that look mouthwatering?" Mary pointed at a lavish dessert a few spaces down. It was a work of art, complete with swirled frosting, chocolate shavings, and bright cherries dotting its surface. Elizabeth could practically taste the sweet, rich filling.

"It looks delicious," she agreed with Mary. "Who made that one?"

Mary leaned closer to glance at the placard and then smiled. "No surprise here. Rachel Fischer." Mary sighed. "She's such a wonderful cook. This makes my pies look positively homely in comparison."

"Oh, Mary." Elizabeth quelled the urge to laugh. "Stop fussing. Rachel has been baking since she was a little girl. You've only just learned."

"I suppose so."

"Maybe you and Rachel could get together sometime, and she could teach you what she knows. As long as it's not a secret family recipe, I'm sure she'd be happy to share her knowledge."

Mary brightened. "That's a great idea." She looked around the room. "Where is Rachel anyway? Did you see her when we came in?"

Elizabeth scanned the busy room then pointed toward the arrangement of chairs before the auction block. "She's over there, talking to Sarah Kauffman."

Mary smiled. "Oh, I see her. And look at Timmy. How nicely he's playing with Rachel's children. Emily has made such a difference in his life. That's why this fund-raiser means so much to me."

They started to head her way but were stopped by a booming announcement. "Ladies and gentlemen, could we find our seats, please?" The auctioneer, a tall man with a rust-colored beard, stood at a podium at the front of the room.

"I guess we'll have to catch her after the auction," said Mary as they settled into a row of chairs. As the bidding started, John showed up and slipped into a seat beside Elizabeth. She smiled at him, and he grinned back.

The multitude of baked goods went quickly, thanks to the seasoned auctioneer's smoothness and the ready bidders on the floor. The pies were up first, so Mary didn't have long to wait. Beside her, Elizabeth saw Mary clench her fists in her lap. Her sister's worries were unfounded, though. As soon as the bidding started, a man at the back of the room immediately threw up his paddle.

Elizabeth swiveled around in her seat to see who had put such a quick bid on her sister's baking. She wasn't surprised to see it was Bill Richmond, Mary's childhood friend. Elizabeth knew he was sweet on her. Mary's cheeks stained red, but she didn't say a word.

John bought the next pie that belonged to Mary, but no one needed to have worried that the rest of her donations wouldn't sell. Her blueberry crumble and Dutch apple went in a flash, and for a nice price too. Elizabeth nudged Mary with her foot. "Rachel Fischer couldn't have done better," she whispered, and Mary smiled.

After the pies were finished, the cakes—more difficult to make and fewer in number—went up on the block. Rachel's Black Forest cake caused quite a flurry of activity, and Rachel's husband, Silas, got into a good-natured bidding war with Uriah Barnhart, though Silas eventually won, amid cheers and lots of clapping.

"I bet that's the most expensive cake anyone's ever bought at one of these fund-raisers," John whispered beside Elizabeth. She couldn't help but laugh.

"I wonder what Rachel thinks of all this fuss," Mary said. Elizabeth glanced toward the row of chairs where Rachel had been sitting with her brood of children. But her seat was empty.

"Where did she go?" asked Mary. "We have to ask her about Joshua. Find out if he knew Lauren's grandfather."

"I'm sure she hasn't left," Elizabeth said. A moment later, Rachel came back into the room with her twin boys and six-year-old Dorcas.

"I'm going to go ask her what she's found out," Mary said. "Be right back." She squeezed down their row and rushed toward Rachel. In her haste, she tripped on a chair leg. It wouldn't have been a big deal if Silas Fischer hadn't been returning to his seat at the exact same moment with his wife's prized Black Forest cake in his grip.

Caught off balance, Mary bumped into him. The beautiful cake tumbled out of his hands and smashed to pieces on the concrete floor of the basement.

CHAPTER TWENTY-ONE

Elizabeth got up and hurried over to Mary's side. She seemed frozen in place, staring at the remnants of the beautiful cake that lay in pieces on the floor. Silas was also gazing at the ruined dessert, but when he looked up, Elizabeth was surprised to see a smile on his face.

"My wife has been after me to watch what I eat," he said. "You have just saved me many, many calories. I am grateful." He followed up his words with a hearty laugh.

Elizabeth looked at Mary, who seemed shocked at his reaction, but the relief in her expression was clear.

"Please let me pay you for the cake," she said to Silas.

"Absolutely not," he replied. "Remember that the money made today goes to Helping Hands. I do not care about the cake. I only care that they raise a good amount of money so they can help foster children." He grinned at her. "My wife will make many more cakes just like this. Please, do not concern yourself."

Before Elizabeth had a chance to do anything about the mess, several Amish women came over and began cleaning up what was left of Rachel's efforts.

"Oh no," Mary said to them. "Let me do that."

One of the ladies, an older Amish woman Elizabeth didn't know, waved her comment away. "Ach, now. Do not upset yourself." She smiled at Mary. "This is not the first cake to end up this way, and it will not be the last. We are used to cleaning up the results of slippery hands or accidental collisions. Please, do not think another thing about it."

Sure enough, within minutes the floor looked as good as new. Elizabeth grabbed Mary's arm and led her back to her seat.

"Oh, Lizzie," Mary said once they were seated. "I'm such a klutz."

"It was an accident. That's all. Let it go, Mary. That kind woman was correct. It will probably happen again. Maybe you can help the next person who has a mishap."

"I...I guess so."

"Your sister is right," John said. "No one is upset about the cake except you. Your efforts have made money for Helping Hands. Concentrate on that."

Mary finally smiled. Elizabeth hoped she would put the incident behind her and enjoy the rest of the auction. As John said, her pies had sold well.

As the auction continued, the items changed from baked goods to craft items and the beautiful Amish quilts many of the people in the room had been waiting for. They would sell for quite a bit. People loved them, and the workmanship was incredible.

When a large Prairie Star quilt came up for bidding, Elizabeth felt a tug on her arm. She turned to see Rachel, who slid into the seat Mary had vacated so she could fetch them glasses of lemonade.

"The family you wanted to meet is over there," Rachel whispered, pointing toward a family seated near the front. "The

Derksens. They are the relatives of Joshua. Although his mother and father are deceased, his younger sister, Hilda, is the woman with the gray hair. The man and woman on her left are her son, Albrecht, and his wife. On her right are her grandson, Ezra, and her granddaughter, Amity."

"So I should talk to the sister?" Elizabeth asked quietly.

Rachel nodded. "She will be your best chance to find out what happened to Joshua."

"But do I show her the pictures? Will she be offended?"

Rachel shrugged. "I cannot answer for another, but I believe she will not fault you for having the images."

"I…I guess so. But I can only show her the photos on my phone."

Rachel laughed softly. "Elizabeth, you know that our community is acquainted with cell phones. Hilda will not have a fit if you show her your phone."

Elizabeth sighed. "You're right. Sorry. Things have changed over the last decade. I don't know why I can't seem to remember that."

Rachel patted her arm. "Not your fault. Just give Hilda a chance, ja? You might be surprised."

"I will."

Rachel got up just as Mary came back with their lemonade. She handed one to Elizabeth and took several sips from her own glass. "Mmm. This is really good. You know it was made from fresh-squeezed lemons. Not the concentrated stuff we buy."

Elizabeth grinned at her. "Well, if you want to squeeze lemons, you go ahead. I think I'll pass." She glanced around the room. "Have you seen Lauren? She said she was going to bring another box of her grandfather's belongings for us to go through. I'm surprised she isn't here yet."

Mary shook her head. "No, I haven't noticed her."

Just then, a quilt came up for auction that made Elizabeth gasp. It was a Star of Bethlehem quilt with a large star-shaped image in the middle. It was an extraordinary quilt made up of purple hues and cornflower-blue accents on a cream-colored background. One of the most beautiful Elizabeth had ever seen. When the bidding began, it gathered a lot of attention. The bid amount grew and grew, more than any of the previous quilts offered. The bidding had almost stopped when John suddenly lifted his paddle. Elizabeth started to grab his arm. Did he know what he was doing? No one else bid after him, so the auctioneer pounded the podium with his gavel and pointed at John. Elizabeth's jaw dropped.

"Do you realize how much you just spent on that quilt?" she whispered to him.

He smiled at her and nodded. "I planned to just write a check as a donation, but when I saw that quilt. I mean, you liked it. I thought... Well, I thought maybe you'd accept it as a gift."

Elizabeth was so surprised she couldn't speak. She tried to gather her thoughts. She couldn't accept something so expensive from John...or could she? She really wasn't certain. If it wasn't for charity, she would have turned him down immediately. Was this different? She looked at Mary, hoping to see her reaction, but she didn't seem to be shocked by the offer. For now, Elizabeth refocused her attention on the auction.

It wrapped up about thirty minutes later. The contributions added up to a rather large amount for Helping Hands. The director was wiping tears of joy from her face, as were her two assistants. Elizabeth smiled. Obviously, they were happy with the results.

People began to stand up. Before Elizabeth could say anything to John, Rachel came over and grabbed her arm. "Let me introduce you to Hilda."

Elizabeth followed her over to the family she'd pointed out earlier. Hilda was a tall, thin woman with sharp features. She was quiet as Rachel pulled Elizabeth over to stand in front of her.

"Hilda, this is a friend of mine, Elizabeth Classen. She and her sisters run Secondhand Blessings. I believe you knew their maam."

Hilda's stoic expression cracked with a small smile. "Ja, I liked your mother very much. She was a *goot* woman."

"Yes, she was," Elizabeth said. "I…I asked Rachel to introduce me to you because of some pictures that showed up in an old camera given to our store. I was told you might be interested in some of the images."

The old woman's smile slipped away, and a wariness took over her features. "I do not understand. Why would I have an interest in worldly photos? You have made a mistake."

"Now, Hilda," Rachel said softly. "There is nothing wrong with looking at these old pictures. We must not be judgmental."

Ignoring Rachel's gentle admonishment, Hilda turned to walk away. Before she really thought about what she was doing, Elizabeth reached out and took hold of the woman's sleeve.

"Please," she said. "I know I'm asking you to step out of your comfort zone, but this is important. Someone has been trying to keep these images from being seen. The original photos were stolen. Our friend, Lauren, had her house broken into. We need to know why. Although I'm not certain the photo I want to show you is the reason these things have happened, I do wonder about it. If you'll just look quickly and tell me if you can think of some reason these photos are so important, I won't bother you again. You have my word."

Hilda hesitated just long enough to give Elizabeth the encouragement she needed. She quickly took out her phone and pulled up the pictures. First she showed the woman the photo of the Amish man taken by Lauren's grandfather. "I was told this man's name is Joshua and that he might be a member of your family. I was also informed that he disappeared from your community many years ago. Is this true?"

Hilda's face turned white, and her eyes widened. Elizabeth was shocked to see tears fill her eyes. She looked up at Elizabeth.

"I cannot help you. You promised you would leave this alone if I looked at your photos. I will expect you to do as you have said."

With that, she turned and strode quickly toward the back entrance. Her son and his wife followed in her wake. But the younger couple stayed behind. Although the granddaughter seemed uncomfortable, Elizabeth could tell the grandson wanted to say something. She kept quiet and waited.

Finally he said, "My name is Ezra Derksen. Please forgive my grandmother. This is very hard for her."

"Will you help me?" Elizabeth asked.

"Perhaps. I must pray about it. I know where your shop is. If I can help you, I will." He nodded at his sister, and the pair walked away.

Elizabeth stood staring after him. Would he really show up? The family certainly knew something about the man in the photo. Although Elizabeth had wanted to show Hilda all the photos, it seemed the picture of Joshua was the one that was the most important. What in the world had happened to him? Why wouldn't anyone talk about him? Was he dead? The possibilities in Elizabeth's mind ranged from innocent reasons for the young man's absence to ones that made her blood run cold.

Mary came up next to her. "Doesn't look like things went well."

Elizabeth sighed. "No, not well at all." She told Mary about the elderly woman's reaction to the picture as well as her grandson's promise to pray about talking to her.

"Something is definitely wrong, Elizabeth," Mary said, frowning. "The more we try to find answers, the stranger things get."

Elizabeth nodded. "I agree." Her eyes swept the room. "Where is Lauren? I'm getting a little concerned. She's always so reliable. If she couldn't come, she would have called."

"We still haven't gone through the first box she brought us," Mary said. "Now that I'm through baking pies for a while, I'll start on it."

Elizabeth had just started to dial Lauren's number when John came rushing up to them. "I just got a call from the station," he said. "Someone tried to break into Lauren Collier's house again last night. She confronted the intruder and was attacked."

Elizabeth gasped. "Attacked? Is she okay?"

John nodded. "She was struck on the head. Knocked out. She's at the hospital getting checked out, but I hear she'll be fine."

Elizabeth grabbed John's arm. "Did the prowler get away?"

"Unfortunately, yes. When Lauren regained consciousness, he was gone."

Elizabeth shook her head. "I'm getting frightened, John. We have to figure out what's going on. Before someone gets really hurt—or worse."

CHAPTER TWENTY-TWO

As the sisters drove back home, Elizabeth called Lauren and was relieved when she picked up the call on the second ring. "Lauren! Thank goodness you're okay," Elizabeth said. "We just heard about the break-in at your house last night. What happened?"

Lauren's voice sounded thin on the other end of the line. "I don't know. I was in the back room, going through some more of Grandfather's things, when I heard a sound like glass breaking."

"Oh, Lauren, how frightening."

"It was. I didn't have a clear path out of the house, and there was nowhere to hide in the back room. I didn't even have my cell phone. It was plugged into a charger in the living room."

"Why would someone break in your house while you were there? Don't burglars try to make sure homes are empty?"

"I don't know. Maybe he thought I was gone. The evening had snuck up on me, and I hadn't turned any lights on yet, except for a lamp where I was working."

"What did you do? John said the intruder attacked you?"

"Oh, Elizabeth, it was awful. Luckily, there was a baseball bat in one of the boxes, so I grabbed that and snuck out into the hall. Then I saw someone going through items in the living room."

"Did you see who it was?"

"No, it was dark, and I couldn't see his face clearly. I know it was a man, though, and about how tall he was."

"Then what happened?"

"Well, he heard me come around the corner and lunged at me," Lauren said, her voice shaky. "I swung the bat, and the next thing I knew, something hit me on the head and I blacked out. When I woke up, he was gone. I called the police right away." She sighed. "I'm at the hospital, but I'm okay. I'll be leaving here soon. I'm just waiting to see the doctor so he can release me."

Elizabeth couldn't imagine what poor Lauren had gone through. Secondhand Blessings had been broken into before. Both times had been nerve-racking experiences that left her feeling vulnerable and unprotected. To actually run into the intruder and be attacked, though, was an entirely different situation. Much worse.

"Lauren, I know this might be an inconvenience for you, but would you be interested in staying with me and my sisters? Just for a little while, so you're not alone at your house?" She glanced at Mary for confirmation, and Mary quickly nodded her agreement.

"Really?" Lauren sounded close to tears. "That would be such a comfort. I've been dreading nighttime. This person has already broken in twice. What's to keep him from trying again?" She paused for a moment and took a deep, shuddering breath. "You know, I really believe Grandfather has something valuable somewhere in his possessions. I have a feeling that whoever keeps breaking in knows what it is." She sighed. "Boy, I certainly wish he'd share the information with me."

"Don't worry about it now. Just pack up whatever you need," said Elizabeth. "Our spare room is already set up. I can pick you up."

"Thanks, Elizabeth, but the doctor cleared me to drive. I feel fine. I'll be over as soon as I get out of here and can throw some stuff in my overnight bag. Is it okay if I bring more boxes? We need to sort through it all anyway, and I'd like to get as much out of there as I can so it won't be stolen."

"Of course." Elizabeth ended her call with Lauren as the sisters pulled up in front of Secondhand Blessings.

Though they had closed for the morning in order to attend the fund-raiser, the sisters opened the shop for the afternoon.

"I'm not sure it was worth it to open today," said Mary, wiping down the counter by the register, even though it was perfectly clean. They'd had few customers so far, and the afternoon was already growing late.

"I'm just happy to be off the couch for a while," Martha said as she propped her leg up on a stool.

"You shouldn't be out here," Mary said, frowning.

"I won't stay much longer," said Martha. Her jaw was set. Mary and Elizabeth had grown tired of arguing with her and finally agreed that she could come out to the shop for a short while. As long as she was careful and kept her foot elevated.

Elizabeth broke in before things could get argumentative. "Lauren should be here soon."

Her tactic of distraction worked. Martha pivoted toward her. "I can't believe someone tried to break into her home again. She really does need to get a security system if she's going to be staying there."

"What do you think they're looking for?" Mary asked.

Elizabeth started to respond when a customer came in the door. Actually, two customers. Elizabeth was excited to see the young man and woman from the fund-raiser. Hilda's grandson and granddaughter.

Elizabeth hurried over to them. "Welcome to Secondhand Blessings. I'm so happy to see you here." She was sure they weren't just here to browse the wares. They were here to talk about Joshua.

The young man, Ezra, didn't respond to her greeting. He stepped forward hesitantly. "*Grossmammi* does not know that we are here. Our grandmother would be very upset if she knew we were speaking with you."

"Why?" asked Mary, coming up behind Elizabeth. "What have we done?"

"You have not done anything wrong," Amity replied. "It is what somebody else did."

"Is this about the Amish man in the old photos we tried to show your grandmother?" Elizabeth asked.

"Joshua Derksen," Ezra said. "That was his name. Our great-uncle. He was a member of the Bird-in-Hand community until World War II."

"He went missing after that?" Martha hobbled over on her crutches.

"Yes. No one knows what happened to him. He disappeared without so much as a goodbye." Ezra lowered his voice to a whisper. "He was never found. It was a great tragedy."

Elizabeth held her breath. "Does your grandmother think that Lauren's grandfather had anything to do with Joshua's... disappearance?" That would explain Hilda's cold reception and her reluctance to talk with the sisters.

Amity glanced at her brother. "They think that might be the case," she said.

"Lauren mentioned her grandfather used to be Amish. Was he part of the community here? Did he know Joshua well?"

"Amity, I fear we have said too much." Ezra reached for his sister's arm and turned toward the door.

Amity gently pulled away. "They are only trying to help. I love our grandmother very much, but it is not doing her any good to ignore the truth. You see how it hurts her. How she fears the truth. That should not be."

She turned to the sisters. "Joshua and Lauren's grandfather, Josiah, were brothers, you see. That is why my grandmother does not want to know what happened to her brother Joshua. Josiah left the community to support the war effort." Elizabeth thought of the soldier's reflection in the pie safe glass. That had been Lauren's grandfather, taking pictures of his brother and their family home. But why? As a keepsake before he left for a war that might kill him?

"But Lauren's grandfather's last name was Collier. He went by Joe Collier."

Ezra nodded. "He changed his name when he came back to Bird-in-Hand after the war. He did not want to bring further shame to his family. It was also a way to avoid questions about his past ties to our community."

"Does your grandmother think Joshua became a soldier too?"

"I think she suspects that Josiah talked him into it, yes," Amity said. "But as I said, she does not want to know the truth. It was bad enough for one of her siblings to leave in a cloud of disgrace, but for two? For now, the disappearance of Joshua is a mystery. But it is known that Josiah left to aid the war effort. That is cause enough for embarrassment. Our grandmother is not interested in adding to her humiliation."

Ezra chimed in. "Even though the general attitude of those in leadership is less strict now, our grandmother still feels it is better to leave things as they are."

"Even if that means they're unresolved?" asked Martha.

Ezra's voice held a note of pleading. "She only wants to hold on to Joshua's memory in a pleasant way. She wants to remember him as her brother. Not as an outsider."

"I understand," said Elizabeth. "We certainly aren't trying to stir the waters. But our friend, Lauren, is in real trouble right now, and we wonder if it's related in some way to the mystery of Joshua's disappearance. Do you know of anyone else who would know what really happened?"

"I am afraid I do not," said Amity. "I am sorry."

Ezra walked toward the front entrance. "I pray you have a goot evening," he said. "Please, keep what we have told you to yourselves. It would greatly upset our grandmother for the story to get out. And do not tell her we were here. She would be angry with us." With that, Amity and Ezra headed back out into the cold afternoon.

Elizabeth stared at her sisters. "Joshua and Joe Collier were brothers. Lauren has a family."

"What are we going to do?" Mary asked. "Ezra and Amity asked us not to tell anyone."

"We have to tell Lauren," Martha said. "Don't we?"

Elizabeth just shook her head. What should they do? At that moment, she just wasn't certain. They still didn't know what had happened to Joshua. Had he joined the army like his brother? Why hadn't Joe Collier told his family the truth? Was the answer something more sinister than anyone had considered?

CHAPTER TWENTY-THREE

The sisters were quiet as they contemplated the news they'd just learned. Elizabeth was torn. Her loyalty was with Lauren, yet was she prepared to take a step that might cause pain to the Derksen family?

"There's something that bothers me," Martha said. "Joe Collier knew he had family in Bird-in-Hand. Lauren's family. But he never told anyone. And when he passed away, they didn't bother to acknowledge his death or reach out to his granddaughter." She shook her head. "I think that's awful."

Mary shrugged. "We've seen it before. Families cut ties with certain members and never try to mend the past. The Amish aren't quite as strict as they used to be, but people are people. You don't have to be Amish to shun your family." She took a deep breath. "Brian and I had friends who wanted nothing to do with me after the divorce. Even though he cheated on me."

"I'm so sorry, Mary," Elizabeth said. "But you're right." She went over and sat down on the chair by the cash register. She looked back and forth at her sisters. "So now what? Do we tell Lauren she has family she didn't know anything about?"

Martha sighed. "If they shunned her grandfather, I doubt they'll want anything to do with her."

"Not necessarily," Elizabeth said. "Remember that her grandfather left the community. Lauren hasn't done anything wrong."

Martha seemed to consider Elizabeth's point. "You might be right." She groaned. "Okay, you may also be right about something else. My ankle is screaming at me. Maybe I pushed myself too hard."

Elizabeth clucked her tongue. "I told you to stay inside. Why don't you listen?"

"Maybe because I have my own mind," Martha huffed.

"Let's close up and get Martha inside," Mary said. "Lauren could be here soon, and we need to decide what to do."

Elizabeth stood up. "You're right. Sorry, Martha. I just worry about you. Remember what the doctor said. If you don't take care of your ankle, you could delay your recovery."

"I know," Martha grumbled. "Sorry. I'm just so bored on that couch."

"Stay off your foot tomorrow," Mary said. "Maybe you'll be doing better by Monday."

"Or Wednesday," Elizabeth said under her breath.

"I heard that."

Elizabeth had to laugh. "Mary, you help our stubborn sister inside. I'll close up."

Mary went over to Martha, who was struggling to get to her feet. She put her arm around Mary. Pal, who had been especially solicitous of Martha since her injury, came up to her other side and walked next to her as if also trying to support her. Elizabeth smiled at the trio as they slowly made their way toward the house.

As she straightened up the store and counted the money in the register, all Elizabeth could think about was the shocking revelation delivered by Ezra and Amity. At least it answered the question about the photo. It had always seemed odd that an

Amish man had allowed someone to take his picture, but a brother wanting a keepsake of a sibling that he loved? Made perfect sense. So Lauren's grandfather had left the community as had his brother, Joshua. Then Joshua had disappeared. Elizabeth wondered just how involved Joe Collier had been in Joshua's departure. She figured he probably knew what happened to his brother. So why had he kept his family in the dark all these years? Now that Joe was gone, had the truth about Joshua died with him?

Elizabeth made her way to the storeroom in the back of the barn to see if they had any more handmade aprons. They were made by a local Amish woman and seemed to fly off the shelves. Sure enough, there were a couple more. As she retrieved them, Elizabeth noticed the box of items Lauren had brought them. She needed to go through it soon. With Martha's injury, the box had been on the back burner. Now Lauren was bringing more of Joe's possessions for them to go through. Elizabeth would have to sort through this first box soon. Right now, she needed to look after Martha.

She left the storeroom, locking the door behind her. Then she laid the aprons out for the next week. After putting out the fire in the small cast-iron stove, she pulled on her coat and left the shop, locking the door behind her. As she walked toward the house, a car she didn't recognize came barreling up the drive. Elizabeth waited for the car to stop. They'd closed up a little early, but if this was a customer, she'd open up again.

The car door swung open, and Peter jumped out. He hurried over to where Elizabeth stood. His face was pale, and he was breathing heavily. "I just heard about Lauren," he said.

"I've been trying to call her, but it keeps going to voice mail. Do you know if she's okay?"

Elizabeth reached out and put her hand on his arm. "She's fine, Peter. Just a bump on the head."

He let out a long breath, obviously relieved by the news. "I should have been there. I had a church event. I...I help the youth pastor, and the kids had a party last night."

"Oh, Peter. There wasn't any way for you to know that Lauren would be assaulted. You can't blame yourself."

"Maybe, but I still wish I'd been able to help her. I heard the news from a friend at church. He knows Officer Marks. But no one seems to know where she is right now."

Elizabeth smiled. "She's probably on her way over here. We asked her to stay with us for a while. Until the house can be more safely secured."

"Should she be driving? I could go get her."

"I offered, but she turned me down. She says the doctor cleared her to drive."

"That's great news." He hesitated a moment. "Could... could I wait around for a bit? I'd just like to see her. Find out if there's anything I can do for her."

Elizabeth pulled her coat tighter. "It's really cold. Let's go inside. Why don't you stay for supper? We'd love to have you, and you could spend some time with Lauren."

For the first time since he'd arrived, Peter smiled. His dark blue eyes met Elizabeth's. "Thank you. That'd be great."

"Good. Follow me."

The two of them went into the house. Mary was standing at the stove, taking a teakettle off the burner. She was probably making tea for Martha. Elizabeth glanced into the living room. Sure enough, Martha was back on the couch, her foot elevated. Good.

Elizabeth introduced Peter to Mary and Martha. Although Elizabeth was happy to have Peter with them, she realized she and her sisters would have to wait to talk about their discussion with Ezra and Amity. Elizabeth was still concerned about the situation, but she'd come to the conclusion that they would have to tell Lauren. There was no way around it. She had the right to know she had a family. She would have to decide what to do with the information. It wasn't up to Elizabeth or her sisters to make that decision. Nor was it Ezra and Amity's business.

Elizabeth hung up her coat while Mary talked to Peter, who sat down at the kitchen table. Elizabeth had put a roast in the slow cooker before they'd left for the fund-raiser. She was relieved to know she had enough food to feed two extra people. That wasn't true every day.

Peter took out his cell phone and tapped on it. He listened and then shook his head. "Still no answer. Why won't she pick up?"

"Lauren may have turned it off at the hospital," Elizabeth said. "She was waiting to talk to a doctor when I spoke to her. I know I've done that before and then forgotten to turn my phone back on. Or she could be on her way over here already."

"Yeah, maybe."

Even though he'd agreed with Elizabeth's explanation, it was clear he was still worried. "What can we do to make her house more secure?" she asked. "Do you have any ideas?"

Peter nodded. "My uncle owns a home security firm. I called him before I drove over here. He's offered to put up some cameras and motion sensor lights. If anyone shows up at the house, Lauren will be alerted. She can see what's going on by looking at her phone."

"That's amazing," Elizabeth said. "But isn't that rather expensive? Lauren doesn't have much money."

Peter shook his head. "No. He's doing it for free. We all go to the same church. He wants to help her."

"That's really generous," Mary said. She'd taken Martha her tea and had come back into the kitchen.

"He's a great guy," Peter said. "My dad died when I was young, and my uncle has tried to help me out as much as he can. He's been a great support."

"That's wonderful," Elizabeth said. "I'm glad you've had someone like him in your life."

"Thanks. Me too."

Elizabeth heard a car drive up outside and went to the window. "It's Lauren," she said.

Peter stood up. "I'll go out and see if she needs help with her bags."

Elizabeth stayed by the window and watched as Peter went out to the car. When Lauren got out and saw him, she immediately put her arms around him. Elizabeth smiled. Maybe Lauren wouldn't feel alone much longer.

As the young couple carried Lauren's bags toward the house, Elizabeth worried about how the news of a family she never knew about would affect Lauren. Would it be a blessing...or a curse?

CHAPTER TWENTY-FOUR

Mary showed Lauren to the guest bedroom, where she plopped down her bags. "Oh, Mary, this is just beautiful." She took in her surroundings, and Mary had to admit, the space did look nice. Though the sisters had changed little in the main rooms of the house, including the kitchen with its original enamel stove, they had spruced up most of the bedrooms a few months back.

Elizabeth had decided to keep her room the same, with the exception of a fresh coat of paint to brighten the walls. The guest room Lauren was staying in had been given a nice treatment: new floral sheets, bedspread, and shams, with delicate lace curtains hung at the windows. Hand-braided rugs warmed up the floor, and an antique washbasin and bowl graced the top of the dresser. The room was cozy but not too fussy.

"What do you have in here, rocks?" Peter joked as he followed on Lauren's heels, a sealed cardboard box in his hands.

"Ha, very funny," said Lauren. "I don't even remember what's in that one. I didn't realize you'd grabbed it. It goes to the shop. All the other boxes do too. Those are items from the house that the sisters are going to help me sort through."

"Hopefully we'll find something worth more than rocks." Mary smiled, and Peter smiled back at her.

"I just hope no one tries to break into the house again," said Lauren with a shudder. Her fingers drifted to the cut on her forehead. "I tried to pull out everything I thought the robber might have been after, but it's tough to know. I feel like one of those people on *Antiques Roadshow* who finds out the junky old lampshade they've stored in the attic is worth a fortune. Problem is, I have no idea what I'm looking for."

Peter laughed and ran his hands through his hair. He pointed to the box he'd just set with a thump on the floor. "That is definitely not a lampshade."

"Probably not," said Lauren, giving him an amused look. She used the jagged edge of one of her keys to slit open the packing tape securing the top of the box. She pushed the flaps out of the way. "I don't even know what this is, to be honest with you. But it looked old and like it might be worth something."

Mary peeked around Lauren's shoulder to peer into the box. It contained a dusty item that reminded her a little bit of a typewriter, but it wasn't like any version she'd ever seen. "That's an unusual piece."

"Oh?" asked Lauren. "I was hoping you'd know what it was."

"Hmm…" Mary searched her memory. They'd certainly never had anything pass through the shop like it. It did seem somewhat familiar, though. "Maybe it's some kind of dictation machine?" she offered.

"Like the kind court reporters do shorthand on?" asked Peter. "Aren't those smaller? I thought they were small portable machines."

"That's what they use now," said Mary. "But maybe when they started out they were chunkier. Think about computers.

The first versions took up an entire room. Maybe this was an early type of transcription machine."

"Could be." Lauren looked thoughtful. "Do you think your sisters would be able to shed any more light on what it is?"

"Maybe," said Mary. "We could ask them." A lump grew in her throat as she thought of Elizabeth and Martha waiting to spill the beans to Lauren about Joshua—and the possible new family members she stood to gain as a result. "Why don't we go downstairs now?"

"Sure, sure," Lauren quickly agreed. She headed out the door. Peter hefted the heavy box to his shoulder again and muscled his way down the stairs after her.

"Do you need any help carrying boxes?" Elizabeth asked Peter, rising to her feet. Martha was set up on the couch again, though she'd mentioned she was ready to move into her old bedroom to sleep for the night. Mary wasn't sure how she felt about that, with the room being upstairs and Martha still learning to navigate on her crutches.

"I think I can manage the rest of them," said Peter.

"I'll help you," said Lauren, but he waved her off.

"You take it easy. You've had a rough day. I'll take care of unloading the car."

Peter headed outside, and Lauren sank into an armchair beside Martha with a grateful smile. "I wanted to ask you about something in one of the boxes," she said.

Elizabeth took a deep breath. "Before we do that, we have something we need to talk to you about." She cleared her throat and hesitated.

Mary knew how difficult this was for Elizabeth. How would Lauren take the news?

"We spoke with an Amish family who is related to Joshua, the Amish man in the photo...and to you," Elizabeth said finally.

A puzzled look crossed Lauren's face. "What do you mean, related to me?"

Martha leaned forward. "Joshua wasn't just someone your grandfather knew. He was his brother."

Lauren's eyes widened. "His brother?" Her hand flew to her mouth as she took in the information. "I just assumed that Joshua was a friend. Grandfather told me he didn't have family living here anymore. But if taking those pictures... They were important because it *was* his family. I should have realized..."

"Hindsight is always clearer," offered Elizabeth. "We were a bit surprised to learn the news as well."

Lauren's eyes misted. "So if Joshua is alive somewhere...it means I'm not alone. If he has family..."

"There's more," Martha said. "Joshua's family...your family... still lives in Bird-in-Hand."

"I don't understand," Lauren said, frowning. "Grandfather said—"

"He and his family parted ways many years ago, Lauren," Elizabeth said. "When your grandfather decided to join the army. Your grandfather believed they wanted nothing to do with him. That's probably why he never mentioned them."

Mary was worried. Would Lauren be angry with her grandfather?

"I can't believe this!" Lauren said, her expression joyful. "This is wonderful. I'm not alone. I've had tons of relatives, right here in front of me this whole time."

The sisters exchanged glances. As elated as Lauren was to find lost family members, they weren't sure her Amish family was so eager to reconnect. Mary hoped Lauren wasn't going to face more heartache and loss.

"I have to meet them," she said. "They're my relatives. I have to talk with them. They must have stories of my grandfather when he was a kid, a young man." Tears streamed down her face. "Is Joshua still living? Does anybody know what happened to him?"

Mary shook her head. "No, that's the great mystery in all of this. Joshua disappeared from the area years ago, not long after your grandfather left the community. No one has seen or heard from him since. I wonder if he stayed in touch with your grandfather after he left."

"I haven't found anything from him," Lauren said. "Not a trace." She sighed. "It really is like he disappeared into thin air."

CHAPTER TWENTY-FIVE

Elizabeth whipped up some mashed potatoes and made gravy to go with the roast in the slow cooker. Then she added sweet corn with butter and biscuits. Her biscuits weren't as good as Martha's, but they would do in a pinch. After they all sat down to supper, Elizabeth asked Peter to say grace. His prayer was bold and expressed his heartfelt love for God. Elizabeth was impressed with the young man. She didn't need to wonder if Lauren saw how special he was. As they began to eat, she caught Lauren's glances at him. She seemed smitten.

After everyone had been served, Lauren asked about her family. "I'd like to know more about them," she said. "Can I visit them? Talk to them?"

The sisters were silent. Finally, Elizabeth said, "It might be a little difficult." She cleared her throat and prayed that God would give her the right words to say to Lauren, whose face displayed her eagerness to hear about the family she hadn't been aware of. "Your grandfather's sister, your great-aunt, doesn't want to talk about him," she said slowly. "He left the community, like your grandfather. It seems his sister shunned your grandfather even though he came back here to live. So ignoring her other brother isn't too hard, since she's not sure where he is."

Lauren's expression fell. "So she doesn't know what happened to him?"

"No," Elizabeth said. "And she doesn't want to."

"What can I do?" Lauren asked. "I need to talk to her. Try to change her mind."

"I'm not sure it's wise," Martha said. "Her grandchildren came to us and told us the truth. Begged us not to tell their grandmother what they shared with us."

Lauren was quiet for a moment. Then she shook her head. "So they don't want me?"

"It isn't that," Elizabeth said. "The grandchildren, Ezra and Amity, believe their grandmother doesn't want to deal with the situation. I guess she's more comfortable ignoring it."

Lauren pushed her chair back and stood up. "I'm not hungry anymore. I think I'll go to my room." She walked out of the kitchen and headed upstairs. The door to the guest room closed with more force than necessary.

"I'm sorry," Peter said. "Lauren has felt alone since her grandfather died. Give her some time to deal with this new development. She's strong. She'll be okay."

Elizabeth said with a sigh, "I would feel the same way if I were her."

"But Lauren doesn't owe Ezra and Amity anything," Mary said. "She can do whatever she wants."

"Yes, she can." Although Elizabeth recognized the validity behind Mary's words, she felt bad thinking that Hilda's grandchildren would regret sharing the truth about Joshua with them. It was a courageous thing to do, and Elizabeth appreciated it. Still, Lauren had the right to confront her own family. If her great-aunt didn't like it, too bad.

"Well, we can't do anything about it now," Martha said matter-of-factly. "Let's finish this fine supper Elizabeth made for us. We all need to pray for Lauren and her family. God is the repairer of the breach. What's impossible for us is child's play for Him."

"You're right, Martha," Elizabeth said. "God is the only One who can fix this. I'll keep Lauren and her situation in my prayers."

"Me too," Mary said with a smile.

"And I'll do the same," Peter added. After finishing his second helping of mashed potatoes, he stood up. "I'd like to check on Lauren, if that's okay with you all."

"We have peach cobbler for dessert," Elizabeth said. "Martha made it. It's delicious."

"Then I'll definitely be back soon," he said with a smile. "Peach cobbler's one of my favorites." He hesitated. "Would it be all right if I took some up to Lauren? She must be hungry. But maybe you'd rather not have food upstairs."

Elizabeth got to her feet. "I think it will be fine in this instance. I'll get her some cobbler with ice cream." It only took her a few minutes to put the cobbler and ice cream in a bowl. Then she stuck a spoon in the yummy dessert. "Lauren barely touched her coffee," she said. She handed the cobbler to Peter and poured a fresh cup. "Okay, let's go," she said. "I'll give her this and leave so you can talk in private."

"Thanks," Peter said with a grin. "Not sure if I want to tackle the situation about her family just yet. I just want to let her know I'll pick her up for church in the morning." He frowned at Elizabeth. "What about those boxes? Can I help you go through them?"

"Sure," Elizabeth said. "But we won't tackle that until Monday."

"Okay. I have to work, but I could come by in the afternoon. Would that be okay?"

Elizabeth smiled at him. "That would be perfect. If we have a busy day on Monday, it will take us a while to get to them."

"Okay. Are you ready for this strategic advance on our target?"

Elizabeth laughed. "Ready, sir," she said, trying to look serious. "I'm right behind you."

"Good. Let's do this."

The two of them headed up the stairs. When they reached Lauren's room, Peter knocked, and Lauren opened the door. Peter handed her the bowl of ice cream and cobbler. "We thought you might be hungry," he said.

Elizabeth could see the tears on Lauren's face. She held out the cup of coffee. "You didn't finish your coffee," she said softly.

"Thanks," Lauren said, reaching out for the coffee. "Sorry to make such a scene."

Elizabeth smiled at her. "Not a problem. The situation would upset anyone. We totally understand."

"You're too kind," Lauren said. "I'm so glad you're in my life."

"We feel the same way." She patted Peter on the back. "This young man wants to talk to you for a few minutes. I'll be downstairs."

She turned and headed back down the stairs. Martha and Mary were quiet as they waited to hear if Lauren was all right.

"Everything will be okay," Elizabeth told them. "I think she's sorry she made a fuss. She just needs some time. Tomorrow she'll be fine."

"I hope so," Mary said with a sigh.

"We'll just have to put it in God's hands," Martha said matter-of-factly. She pointed toward the cobbler sitting on the counter. "Can I get some of that?"

Elizabeth had to chuckle over Martha's no-nonsense reminder of not worrying about things you can't fix. It really was an exercise in futility. She got up and made a bowl of cobbler and ice cream for herself and some for Martha and Mary. She'd just handed Martha her serving when Peter came downstairs. She fixed another serving for him.

"How is she?" she asked as she handed him a bowl.

"She's fine," he said as he sat down. "Just a little embarrassed she got so upset. She appreciates everything you've all done for her." He stuck his spoon in the cobbler. "She really wants a family. It's awful to feel so alone in the world."

"Well, she has you," Elizabeth said.

Peter swallowed the big bite of cobbler he'd stuck in his mouth. His cheeks turned red, and he looked down at the table. "I...I like her a lot, but I'm not sure she likes me in *that* way. Right now, we're just friends."

Elizabeth thought about the glances Lauren had been tossing toward Peter. She started to say something encouraging, but she quickly clamped her lips together. Getting into Lauren's business had already caused trouble. Maybe it was time to mind her own business.

"Well, no matter what happens, she has a good friend in you," Mary said. "If God has other plans for you two, you'll know when the timing is right."

Elizabeth nodded. Mary had handled it just right, and Elizabeth was relieved she hadn't jumped in with something inappropriate. Trying to interpret a look wasn't always accurate. She might have completely misinterpreted Lauren's actions. Better to let the two young people work it out themselves.

After Peter finished his cobbler, he left, promising to pick Lauren up for church in the morning. Martha went back to her spot on the couch. Elizabeth was relieved. She really wasn't certain how she and Mary could get her upstairs without aggravating her ankle.

Mary helped Elizabeth clean the kitchen. She was glad to see how happy Mary was about the results of the fund-raiser.

"Are you through baking for a while?" Elizabeth asked her.

Mary sighed. "I don't know. I don't want to lose what I learned. I'll bake again, but to be honest, I need a break. I think it's best to leave most of the baking to Martha. She's got a natural talent for it."

"I know I've said this before," Elizabeth said, "but I'm proud of you."

Mary smiled at her sister. "I'm kind of proud of myself. Brian used to tell me I was pretty but useless. Maybe he was wrong."

Elizabeth put down the dish she was wiping. She reached over and took Mary's arm. "He was absolutely wrong, Mary.

You're smart and talented. And you're a fighter. You never gave up. You learned to bake better than I ever have. You matched Martha, and that's remarkable. I truly believe you can do anything."

Mary wiped her eyes. "I'm so glad we're all together again. I really don't know what I would do without you and Martha."

"I feel the same way." Elizabeth gave her sister a hug, and then they finished the dishes. When Mary went upstairs, Elizabeth stayed behind. She turned off the lights in the kitchen so the only glow was from the porch light.

Then she lowered her head and prayed.

CHAPTER TWENTY-SIX

"Where do these go?" Lauren approached Elizabeth with a stack of delicately embroidered pillowcases Beulah Amstadt had recently brought in to sell. It was Monday afternoon, and Lauren seemed fine. She obviously enjoyed helping out in the shop and worked hard to assist their customers. Elizabeth was praying that God would soften Hilda Derksen's heart and that somehow Lauren would finally have the family she'd hoped for.

Pastor Nagle had delivered a wonderful sermon on Sunday that had spoken directly to Elizabeth's heart. The worries she carried lightened, and she'd left the church feeling buoyed, optimistic that God was working on the situation. She'd started the week with a fresh attitude, and it looked like Lauren felt the same.

Elizabeth smiled and pointed across the room. "You can set them on the shelf over there," she said. "I think Martha's already tagged them, so they should be ready."

Lauren turned to go, but Elizabeth stopped her. "I'm really sorry about the situation with Joshua's family. And you were right. If you want to approach the Derksens, you should. Ezra and Amity don't have the right to ask you to keep your relationship secret just so Hilda won't get upset."

"I appreciate that." Lauren stood there for a moment. "I'm sorry too. I shouldn't have huffed off like I did. It was childish of me."

"You were hurt. It was human of you."

"Maybe. Realizing I had family, only to have the door slammed shut again, was hard to deal with."

"I know," Elizabeth said. "I'm praying everything will work out, and I believe it will. You may have to be patient for a while."

"Thank you for praying. I haven't decided what to do yet, but thank you for being here for me. It means more than I can say."

"You're welcome. We enjoy helping you. We don't want to overstep our boundaries, though. Just tell us if we begin to interfere."

Lauren reached over and gave Elizabeth a quick hug. "I'm not worried about that. It's nice to have people who care about me." She turned away and placed the pillowcases on the shelf Elizabeth had indicated.

Elizabeth heard a car pull up outside. Mary had a clear view of the window from her perch at the register. "It's Peter," she said. The doors slid open as the young man approached, and Lauren ran to greet him, throwing her arms around him for a quick hello hug. Peter blushed but looked pleased at the attention.

"What can I help with?" asked Peter.

Elizabeth led him and Lauren toward the house. "Mary's going to stay at the store to wait on customers, so we can work without interruption for a few hours," she explained. As they entered the living room, she pointed at a neat collection of boxes stacked on the floor. "We moved all the boxes that we had in the storeroom to the house so we could sort through them privately. I wouldn't want anything to get mixed up with our other inventory, especially if there is a really valuable item hidden somewhere."

Martha, as usual, had a game plan ready. "Why don't we each take a box, and if we see anything unusual, we can set it aside to assess it."

Everyone agreed and started sorting through the items. "What about this?" asked Peter, holding up a vintage comic book. "Superman's popular among collectors. Could this be worth anything?"

Elizabeth took it from him and turned it over in her hands. "It's in pretty shabby shape. Most collectibles like that have to be in near-mint condition to fetch any serious money."

Peter set the comic book aside, and everyone continued searching. Elizabeth opened the box nearest to her, which held the cumbersome machine that looked like a typewriter. "Let's take a closer look at this," she said. She turned to Lauren. "I remember seeing this at your grandfather's house. Do you have any idea what it is?"

"We noticed it the other night," said Peter. "Mary wasn't sure what it was and wondered if you or Martha might have an idea. Could it be some kind of early dictation machine?"

"Hmm," said Elizabeth. "It could be, but it seems pretty complex for dictation." She swiveled around to face Martha. "Did you ever call Loretta at Sweetbrier Antiques to see what she thought about that Tiffany-style lamp we found at Lauren's?" Loretta Morris had recently moved to Bird-in-Hand

and was an expert on antiques. The sisters were beginning to rely on her more and more for her expertise.

Martha nodded. "I did, but I don't think I told you about it. It turns out the lamp isn't really antique. It's made in the style of a Tiffany, but it's clearly a reproduction. She said she could tell by the glass seams."

"Oh," said Lauren, looking crestfallen. "That's too bad."

"Chin up," said Elizabeth with a smile. "That makes it more likely that we have something worthwhile just waiting for us in one of these boxes."

"I guess you're right," said Lauren. "I'm just getting so stressed out about how I'm going to pay the bills. I need to find something soon."

"Martha," Elizabeth said, "why don't you call Loretta and see if she'd be interested in appraising"—she cast a look at the mystery item at her feet—"whatever *this* is."

"Sure," agreed Martha. She hobbled over to the phone, took it in the other room, and returned a few minutes later.

"Well?" asked Lauren. "Did it ring a bell for her?"

Martha shook her head. "She has an idea of what it might be, but she said she needs a visual to confirm." She pulled out her cell phone and snapped a quick photo. "I'm going to text her a picture, and she'll get back to us."

They continued sorting through the items and pulled out a few more pieces to ask Loretta about, including a sterling silver soup tureen, a figurine that looked like a Hummel, and a set of dog-eared baseball cards. Martha snapped more pictures and texted them all to Loretta. Lauren and Peter seemed to be having a nice time as they huddled close together, pulling various items out of the boxes. It made Elizabeth smile to watch them.

A few minutes before five o'clock, the group headed back over to Secondhand Blessings to help Mary close up the shop for the evening. Martha stayed behind, taking her place on the couch. Elizabeth could tell she was tired.

After they'd finished closing up, they started across the lawn for the house. Peter climbed into his car and waved. "See you ladies later."

"Wait," said Lauren eagerly. "Don't go. Why don't you stay for dinner?"

Peter grinned. "I guess I should wait and see if the Classens have enough food for me. I've already tested their hospitality once. Not sure I want to push my luck."

"Oh, right." Lauren blushed. "I'm sorry," she said to Elizabeth. "My words ran away with me."

Elizabeth smiled. "I don't know if I can speak for Mary, since she's the one preparing dinner tonight, but as far as I'm concerned, you're welcome to stay, Peter."

Mary drew her lips together as she thought. "I actually hadn't thought about what we'd eat tonight. I suppose we could always have a *yoyo* meal."

Peter looked confused. "A what?"

Mary laughed. "Haven't you heard that term before?" Peter and Lauren both shook their heads.

Elizabeth explained. "Our mother used to have yoyo meals all the time. The letters stand for 'you're on your own.' It was the one night through the week that was a free-for-all."

"We all loved it," Mary said with a smile. "Even though our mother was a fantastic cook, on yoyo nights, we all got to choose exactly what leftovers we wanted out of the fridge. Even if it was a few helpings of dessert and a serving of mashed potatoes."

"Her mashed potatoes were even better the next day," Elizabeth said. "I'm practically drooling thinking of them now." She held the screen door open for Peter. "Come on in. I'm sure we have enough leftovers to make a pretty impressive spread."

"All right," said Peter, shutting his car door and walking up the steps to the porch. "I won't turn you down. I was planning on going home to a nice bowl of cold cereal."

"Cold cereal for dinner?" asked Martha. "You're an absolute bachelor, through and through."

"I don't know about that." Peter snuck a glance at Lauren and then quickly ducked his head. "Ladies first, though." He gestured for the sisters to go into the house before him, and he lingered back with Lauren. As Elizabeth turned to let the screen door ease shut behind her, she saw Lauren lean her head on Peter's shoulder.

"I'm glad you're staying," she said, and the wistfulness in her voice made Elizabeth's heart twinge. Lauren had been through so much. Elizabeth felt, in her heart, that they were getting close to redeeming some of the losses the young woman had dealt with recently.

She said a quick prayer as she stepped across the threshold into her family home.

Please let things be well with Lauren, Lord. Please let her heart find what it's looking for.

CHAPTER TWENTY-SEVEN

Supper was a great success. Mary pulled several storage containers out of the refrigerator and put them on the counter. There was lasagna, roast beef, mashed potatoes, two kinds of gravy, green beans with ham, and some hamburger casserole. Mary also took a package of rolls out of the bread box.

"Come and pick out what you want," she announced with a smile. "Guests first. Lauren and Peter, what appeals to you?"

The young couple got up from the table and surveyed the offerings. Peter picked roast beef, green beans with ham, and mashed potatoes with chicken gravy.

"Wouldn't you rather have beef gravy with roast?" Elizabeth asked.

Peter smiled. "No, I love mashed potatoes with chicken gravy. You said I was on my own. This is what I choose." He turned to look at the sisters. "Unless someone else wants it."

Elizabeth laughed at him. "It's your choice. If you want chicken gravy with pot roast, so be it."

"And what do you want, Lauren?" Mary asked.

"I love hamburger casserole. That and a roll is plenty for me."

Mary nodded. "Okay, you two sit down. I'll heat it up for you." She laughed. "I may not be the best cook around, but I'm pretty good at warming food up." She scooped the selected items onto plates and stuck them in the microwave with a splatter cover. A few minutes later Lauren and Peter were eating.

Martha asked for lasagna and green beans. Elizabeth decided to finish the last of the hamburger casserole, knowing the dish wasn't Mary's favorite. That left the rest of the roast and mashed potatoes with beef gravy. Mary scooped the items onto her plate and was soon sitting at the table with everyone else. There was still some roast beef remaining, but it would make great sandwiches during the week.

Lauren was asking some questions about Secondhand Blessings when Elizabeth's cell phone rang. She'd meant to turn it off during supper but had forgotten. It was Loretta. Elizabeth got up from the table and carried the phone into the living room so her discussion with the antiques dealer wouldn't disturb anyone else.

When she answered, Loretta's voice sounded strange. "The figurine you thought might be a Hummel isn't. Not worth anything. The soup tureen might fetch a few hundred dollars. The baseball cards and the comic book would be worth a few dollars if they were in better shape." She hesitated. "I need to see the…machine in person, Elizabeth. Will you bring it into the shop tomorrow?"

"Sure. Do you think it's valuable?"

Again, silence. What was going on? "I don't want to say anything more until I see it. Just bring it in. And please, carry it in a box. Be very, very careful with it, and don't show it to anyone else."

"Loretta, what are you not telling me?"

Loretta, who was usually restrained, seemed a little rattled. Her manner worried Elizabeth.

"I don't want to say anything else until I can examine it closely. It just wouldn't be right. Bring it in tomorrow, first thing. I'm open at eight."

With that, she hung up. Elizabeth stared at the phone, trying to figure out what had just happened. She put her phone in her pocket. What should she do? She gazed toward the kitchen. The last thing she wanted was to see Lauren disappointed again. She decided not to mention Loretta's strange reaction. No sense in stirring things up.

When she entered the kitchen Martha asked, "Anything important?"

Elizabeth slid back into her chair. "That was Loretta. Good news, bad news. The comic and the cards aren't valuable. The Hummel is a knockoff. But the silver soup tureen could be worth something. Maybe a few hundred dollars. Oh, and she needs to see that...that machine thingy...in person. She can't tell much about it from the pictures."

Lauren sighed. "Well, the soup tureen will help. But I need a lot more than a couple hundred dollars."

"We'll find something," Mary said. "I feel it in my bones."

Lauren's expression lightened, and she laughed. "I hope your bones are accurate, Mary."

Elizabeth smiled. "Her bones are almost always right." She looked at Peter. "I wonder if you could drop the tureen and the machine off at Loretta's on your way to work in the morning?"

Peter was an IT specialist who worked for the city of Lancaster. He drove right past Sweetbrier Antiques every day on his way into the office. He nodded. "Be happy to. Don't let me forget to load them up before I leave."

Before Elizabeth could respond, there was a knock at the door. She frowned as she got up. Who could it be this late? When she opened the door, she was surprised to see John standing there in his uniform.

"Sorry to bother you," he said. "But there's something important I need to discuss."

Elizabeth held the door open, and John stepped inside. He removed his hat and nodded at the people sitting at the table.

"We were just finishing supper, John," Elizabeth said. "Can I get you something? How about a roast beef sandwich?"

"Thanks," John said with a smile, "but I've already eaten."

"At least sit down. How about a cup of coffee?"

"That would be great. It's pretty cold out there. Warming up a bit would be wonderful."

Elizabeth poured him a cup of coffee as he sat down next to Peter. After handing it to him, she slipped back into her own chair. "You said you had something to tell us?"

He took a sip of coffee and then put the cup down. "I'm glad you're here, Lauren," he said. "We just arrested someone trying to break into your house again."

Lauren's mouth dropped open. "He tried it again? Why? What is he looking for?"

John shook his head. "He won't say."

"Who is it, John?" Martha asked.

John took a deep breath. "Arthur Graves. He's your burglar."

Elizabeth was certain she looked as surprised as everyone else at the table, but somehow, she wasn't really shocked. It was almost if she'd known it was him.

"So he took the pictures," she said slowly. "There's something in those photos he's after."

"He insists he didn't steal the pictures," John said, frowning. "Look, I know he's a thief and a liar, but my gut tells me he's telling the truth about the pictures."

"But it's the only thing that makes sense," Mary said. "He took the photos because he saw something in them that he wanted. That he thought was valuable."

"I agree that seems to follow," John said after taking another sip of coffee. He reached into his pocket. "I shouldn't show this to you, but I made a copy of his booking paperwork. Does his handwriting look familiar?"

Elizabeth picked up the sheet of folded paper John pushed toward the middle of the table. She opened it. "It looks similar to that threatening note."

"It does look similar, but again, we can't prove it."

"But doesn't that mean he had to be the one who took the photos?" Peter asked. "I'm not trying to be argumentative, but he seems like the most likely culprit."

"Not necessarily," Elizabeth said slowly. "He saw the pictures in the shop the day they went missing. He could have noticed something then. He didn't really need to steal them."

"So is he in jail?" Lauren asked.

"No. He was charged with breaking and entering. He didn't have any stolen merchandise in his possession. He posted bail, but we'll keep an eye on him."

Martha grunted. "But if he's convicted, he'll go to prison, right?"

John shook his head. "Not necessarily. He could be fined. Put on probation. Jail is possible, but it would depend on previous crimes. It will take a while for us to sort it all out."

"And what about conking Lauren on the head?" Peter asked, anger coloring his tone.

John shrugged. "Unless Lauren can identify him, there's nothing we can do. We have no evidence he was the one who attacked her. If we can prove it, he would have a much greater chance of going to jail." He looked at Lauren. "We'd like to go inside the house and check for fingerprints. See if we can find evidence that Arthur Graves was in your house."

Lauren nodded. "Of course. I'm sorry I can't be more helpful, but I didn't see who hit me. There's no way I can say it was him."

"I realize that," John said. "For now, he's under surveillance and will have to appear before a judge. I hope that will put the fear of God in him. You and your property should be safe."

"I still think he took those pictures," Mary said. "No disrespect to your gut, John."

John chuckled. "My gut appreciates that."

"I brought the pictures with me," Lauren said. "Should we go through them again? Maybe another look will help us see something we missed before?"

Everyone around the table agreed it was a good idea. John was on a supper break, so he had some time to go over the photos. Elizabeth was willing to try again, but frankly, she'd stared at the pictures so many times she felt as if she'd memorized them. There was no way to tell what Graves was after. Still, several heads were better than one. Maybe they'd turn up something. She got up and put on another pot of coffee. Everyone at the table accepted her offer of pie. As she scooped the pie onto plates, she couldn't help but wonder what in the world was so valuable at Lauren's house that Arthur Graves was willing to physically attack an innocent woman and risk jail time. She wasn't comforted to know he was free. Would he really stay away from Lauren? Or was he willing to do anything to get his hands on the item he had his eye on? Could Lauren be in more danger than John realized?

CHAPTER TWENTY-EIGHT

Elizabeth took a small sip of steaming coffee and let its comforting warmth spread through her. She really shouldn't be drinking coffee this late in the evening. The sisters had run out of decaf, and any time she drank caffeinated beverages in the late afternoon, she slept fitfully. Coffee or no, though, she had a feeling rest would elude her tonight. The fact that Arthur Graves was so determined to acquire whatever valuable object Lauren owned, combined with knowing he was now out on bail, unnerved her. Not that she needed to worry. They had a full house tonight with a police officer in their number.

They'd moved to the living room so Martha could lie on the couch yet not feel isolated from the group.

"Were all of these photos taken before World War II?" asked John as he flipped through the pictures.

"I don't think so," said Elizabeth. She set her coffee down on a coaster. "The majority of them seem to have been taken prior to the war, but Lauren's grandfather must have taken the camera with him when he left. There are several photos of the battlefield." She fanned out a few pictures from the middle of the stack that showed a tank sitting in a scrubby battlefield and another of rubble in a bombed-out street. "There are also some shots that were taken later, once he was back in Bird-in-Hand. Not too many of those, though."

"Let me see the pictures taken during the war," Martha said as she leaned over from her reclined position on the couch. She pointed to the photos showing the debris-lined streets. "This is England. See, there's Big Ben in the background."

"I wonder when they were taken," said Lauren. "I mean, specifically, what year. Do you think this was after the Blitz?"

"Must have been," said Elizabeth. "US troops didn't get dispatched to England until '42. If your grandfather took these, which seems the likeliest scenario, he wouldn't have been overseas before then."

"What about the photos at the end of the roll?" asked Mary. She reached down to scratch Butterscotch behind the ears. The cat purred and rubbed up against the legs of the chair. "What do you think about those? Are those taken in Europe too?"

Elizabeth handed the wartime photos down the line so everyone else could examine them, then spread out the remaining photos on the coffee table. The last pictures were of the interior of a home, generic photos of a living room. "I don't think so. This looks like a house you'd find...well, around here, to be honest."

Martha took a final bite of pie and scooted her plate to one side. "It's definitely not the Amish farmstead from the first pictures. The furniture's more modern."

Elizabeth leaned close over the pictures, studying them for any semblance of familiarity. Then an idea dawned on her. "If anybody disagrees with me, please jump in...but don't they look like they were taken at Lauren's grandfather's home? It would make sense."

Lauren picked up the photos and squinted at them. "I don't know..."

The idea had taken hold, though, and Elizabeth could see it now. "I'm serious. Adjust the couch so it's facing the entry. Put paneling up on the walls. Add a cuckoo clock before the hallway. Do you see it?"

Lauren caught on. "Oh my goodness. I think you're right." She paused and scratched her head. "Why would my grandfather take photos of an empty room, though? Doesn't that seem odd to you? The other photos are of people, meaningful events. These are...pictures of furniture."

Mary snapped her fingers. "Maybe he wasn't taking photos of anything."

Lauren shook her head. "I don't follow."

"I'll bet he was using up the roll. Haven't you ever done that with film? Just squeezed in a few extra shots so you could hurry to develop?"

"My dad used to do that, but he wouldn't let me touch his camera when I was a kid," Peter said. Lauren just shrugged.

Martha harrumphed. "Kids. Both of you. Babies born in the digital age."

Mary smiled and gave Butterscotch a half-hearted pat on the head. Bored with Mary's divided attention, the cat meowed loudly and jumped into Lauren's lap. Lauren studied the pictures for a while, then drew in a quick breath. "I see something I missed before. Look in the background."

Elizabeth zeroed in on the item Lauren highlighted. An item that looked like a typewriter sat on a shelf at the back of the room. The same item she'd seen in Lauren's grandfather's house last week. "That's the machine. The one we just called Loretta about." The box holding the mysterious-looking type-writer sat at Elizabeth's feet. She nudged open the box flaps to stare at the device. "Could that be what Arthur Graves was after?"

"You mean, *is* after," said Mary with a shudder. "That man gives me the creeps."

"Maybe that's why Loretta mentioned being careful with it," said Elizabeth. "It's probably worth something, and Arthur knows it."

She tried to organize her thoughts. Something was bother-ing her. Why had Arthur denied stealing the photos? He obvi-ously had seen the machine in them and had single-mindedly pursued the object. The first time he'd broken into Lauren's house had been in broad daylight, and the second time had escalated to physical violence. He wanted the item badly enough that consequences weren't a deterrent, and he didn't seem particularly secretive in his motives.

Mary heaved a sigh. "Does anyone want more coffee?"

"I'll take some," Peter said.

"Half a cup for me, please," said John.

Mary moved to the kitchen and returned with the coffeepot. She topped off Peter's coffee. "Sugar or creamer?" she asked.

Peter started to answer when Lauren pressed a finger to her lips. "Hush." Her wide-eyed look immediately silenced his answer. She jerked a thumb toward the front window, its cur-tains pulled against the dark outside. "Do you hear that?"

Now that everything was quiet, Pal's frantic barks from outside could be heard clearly. Wordlessly, John rose to his feet and crossed to the window. "There's another car out there. You all expecting company?"

"Not tonight," said Elizabeth. "We hardly ever get visitors this late."

John set his lips in a line. "I think I know who it is." To Elizabeth's surprise, he stepped out onto the porch to confront the visitor. She heard him mutter under his breath, "Thick-headed rascal…"

She stepped onto the porch with him. "Who is it?" she asked. She didn't recognize the vehicle, but the driver's face was all too familiar. Before she had time to respond, Arthur Graves flicked his lights to bright and gunned backward out of the driveway fast. If the ground hadn't been frozen solid, she was sure he would've torn ruts in their yard.

"That man has some kind of nerve showing up here," said John, pacing back and forth in the hallway.

"John, it's fine. Really." Elizabeth tried to reassure him, but she understood his protective instinct after the whole frightening situation that had happened with Lauren. She had to coax Pal back inside with a dog biscuit.

"Why would he come to our house?" Mary asked.

"Maybe he wanted to talk with us," Martha said.

"I can't imagine what he'd want to talk about," Elizabeth said, remembering Arthur's hostility at the hospital. "Unless he was going to try to convince me to pay for the damages to his truck again."

"If he wanted to talk to you, why did he peel out like that?" Peter asked.

"Maybe he wanted to talk, but he thought it was just going to be us. All the cars out front scared him off," offered Mary. "We do have a full house tonight."

"Hogwash," said Martha. "Arthur's not a timid man. My guess is he wasn't expecting to see a police officer staring him down from the front step." She crossed her arms over her chest. "Serves him right, though. He has no business running around terrorizing innocent people because they might have something he covets."

Lauren looked worried. "What if he was spying on you? Maybe he knew I brought stuff from my grandfather's house with me. You don't think he would've tried to break in here, do you?"

"I'm sure he wouldn't have," said Elizabeth with more confidence than she felt. "Not with all of us here."

"The way Pal was barking, I don't think he would've gotten very far even if he tried." Mary raised her eyebrows. Pal was a big baby doll with the sisters, but it was good to know he'd turn into a watchdog in a pinch if he sensed his home was being threatened.

John rubbed his forehead. "I have to go into the station tonight, but I want to make sure you all are taken care of. Would it be all right if I have someone keep an eye on the house until the morning?" Elizabeth nodded, and he put a call in. "I'm going to stay until the officers get here. Just in case."

Elizabeth swallowed. "Thank you, John." Her stomach fluttered with nerves. Would Arthur return, and what would happen if he did? She busied herself helping Mary clear away empty coffee cups and pie plates.

"I can always stay if you need me to," offered Peter.

Lauren shook her head. "You have work in the morning. We'll be fine."

"All right. If you're sure." Peter didn't look convinced, but Lauren finally persuaded him to head home and get a good night's sleep. He loaded up the items he'd promised to drop by Sweetbriar in the morning and told them all goodbye.

Not long after he left, a police cruiser pulled into the driveway. "Thanks for the pie," John said. "And the coffee. That'll keep me awake tonight. I want to talk to the officer outside. Make sure he knows what to do." He shrugged into his coat and opened the door. "I'm curious to see what you find out from the antiques dealer about that piece Arthur seems so fixated on. Let me know, okay?"

"We will," Elizabeth said as John headed out into the cold. Tomorrow they'd talk to Loretta and finally get some answers.

CHAPTER TWENTY-NINE

The sisters awoke to the sound of the wind shrieking with fury, shaking the windows of the old house. Elizabeth went downstairs and found Mary in the kitchen, starting the coffeepot.

"Will you finish getting breakfast ready?" she asked Elizabeth. "I want to check the goats and the chickens. Make sure they're all right."

John had added a generator to the small shed where the goats could shelter down when the weather was bad, but it hadn't been tested in this kind of weather. The chickens also had heating in their roost, but for safety's sake, it wasn't very powerful. For the most part, chickens were pretty resilient when it came to the cold. However, Elizabeth understood Mary's concerns.

"Of course. Go on."

Elizabeth was amused to see Pal waiting at the door. But Tink was nowhere to be seen. She didn't like cold weather or rain. Tink would wait until the last minute to go outside. And when she did, her business would be done in record time. Once she was done, she wanted nothing more than to find a spot in the kitchen where she could curl up and stay warm. Mary had put a small bed in the corner of the room, near the heating vent. That was Tink's favorite spot on a chilly day.

Once Mary put on her coat, gloves, and scarf, she and Pal ventured outside. Elizabeth turned on the small radio tucked into the far corner of the kitchen counter and tuned to a station that regularly broadcast the weather. As she took out the waffle maker and prepared the batter, she kept an ear tuned. Sure enough, a few minutes later the forecast came on. High winds, blowing snow, but only a couple of inches. Elizabeth breathed a sigh of relief. The way the wind shrieked outside, she'd worried they were in for a major storm.

As she waited for the waffle iron to heat up, Elizabeth sat down. The pictures they'd looked at last night were still on the kitchen table. As she sorted through them, she focused on the shot of a room with the odd machine in the background. She could hardly wait to find out what it was.

As she moved the photos around, she wondered once again what had happened to Joshua. How could someone just disappear off the face of the earth? "Where are you?" she whispered to the man in the photo.

She finally got up, started cooking sausage patties in a pan on the stove, and then poured the batter into the waffle iron. Just about the time everything was ready, Mary came inside, Pal running in behind her, almost knocking her down.

"Boy, he's not too crazy about that wind," Mary said, laughing. Even though she'd covered part of her face with her scarf and pulled her hood over her head, her face was bright red.

Pal slid up next to Tink, who was snuggled up in her small bed. If he thought he could, Pal probably would have shoved her over and tried to join her. However, Tink wasn't too amenable about sharing her things. Especially her bed.

"You'll have to go out eventually, you know," Mary said to the small dog. "No two ways about it." Tink turned her head as if she hadn't heard Mary. Elizabeth laughed.

"What's so funny?"

Elizabeth turned to see Martha limping into the kitchen.

While Mary explained, Elizabeth poured Martha a cup of coffee and a glass of orange juice. Then she put a waffle and some bacon on a plate and set it on the table. Martha carefully lowered herself into her chair.

"Thanks, Lizzie. This looks great." She smiled at her sister. "I think I can help out in the store today. I'm feeling a lot better."

Elizabeth shook her head. "It's supposed to snow today. Not much, but it's horribly cold out there. The sidewalks are liable to be really slippery. Let's wait a bit. I'll lay down some ice melt later. If it's better tomorrow, and you feel like it, maybe you can go out then, okay?"

Martha grumbled a bit but eventually nodded. "All right. But if I don't get back to work soon, I may go nuts and start talking to myself."

"You do that anyway," Mary said as she put the basket of eggs on the counter and took off her coat.

Martha sighed. "I started doing that after Chuck died. Couldn't stand the quiet. Now it's hard to stop."

"I understand," Mary said. "I had conversations with myself after Brian left. I'm afraid they weren't anything I'd want anyone else to overhear."

"Well, now you can both have conversations with me." Elizabeth put Mary's plate down on the table. Then she poured her a cup of coffee. She was preparing her own plate when the phone rang. She spoke briefly then hung up.

"That was Peter. He dropped the machine and the soup tureen off at Loretta's." Another huge gust of wind shook the house. "Boy, I'm glad he offered to do that this morning. I wouldn't have wanted to venture out in this weather."

"Our customers may feel the same way," Mary said.

"Well, it hasn't started snowing yet," Elizabeth replied. "Let's open and see what happens."

Just then Lauren came down the stairs wearing sweats and a T-shirt. "Boy, it's awful out there," she said. "I was so nice and warm in bed, but the smells coming from this kitchen forced me downstairs."

Butterscotch padded behind her, going straight for her bowl of food that Mary had filled before going outside.

"Did he sleep with you?" Martha asked. "I wondered why he never showed up last night."

Lauren laughed. "Yeah, he did. I guess he thinks the entire bed is his. I tried to move him a couple of times, but he wasn't having any of it."

"I hope he didn't bother you too much," Elizabeth said.

Lauren shook her head. "Nope. I finally snuggled up next to him, and we did great. I enjoyed it. I think it's time for me to look for a pet. Might help me to not feel so alone."

"That sounds like a good idea," Mary said. "Lots of animals out there need homes."

Elizabeth handed Lauren a plate and put another on the table for herself. After making sure everyone had what they needed, she sat down and started eating. She told Lauren about Peter's call.

"Not sure when we'll hear from Loretta, but I assume it will be sometime today. Once in a while she has to do additional research when it comes to certain antiques. This...machine might be one of those items."

"I'm really interested to see what it is," said Lauren.

Elizabeth had to admit that it was a mystery to her as well. She had a lot of knowledge about antiques, but this item was in a class all by itself.

After breakfast Elizabeth and Mary made sure Martha was comfortable on the couch. Although she didn't look happy about staying inside another day, Elizabeth was certain she realized she wasn't ready to take on the wind and the snow that was on its way.

Elizabeth, Mary, and Lauren made their way to the shop, although Elizabeth kept wondering if they should even open today. Two inches of snow wasn't so bad, but the blasts of icy wind were more than uncomfortable. Pal, who always wanted to go with them to the shop, elected to stay indoors. It had taken a while to get Tink outside. She quickly did what she needed to do and ran to the front door. Elizabeth would have liked to join her. This certainly wasn't a day to lollygag outside.

The women spent the morning cleaning and straightening the shop. A little before noon, Elizabeth made the decision to shut down the rest of the day. The snow had reached them and was blowing sideways. She couldn't imagine that anyone would want to venture out in this. She had just announced her decision to Mary and Lauren when the door to the shop slid open.

The wind blew snow inside, and the icy cold made Mary gasp. Elizabeth looked over and saw Loretta standing there just inside the doors.

"Sorry," she said, as the door slowly closed behind her. "The wind is fierce. Snow's blowing everywhere. It's really nasty out there."

"It's okay," Elizabeth said. "It's just a little snow. What in the world are you doing here? You should have just called us."

Loretta's cheeks were flushed, and her hair was going every which way. At first Elizabeth thought her elevated color was from the wind, but it didn't take long to find out it nothing to do with the weather.

"I know what the machine is," she said breathlessly. "You won't believe it. You just won't believe it." She walked over to Lauren and took her hands. "Unless I miss my guess, young lady, you're going to make a great deal of money."

CHAPTER THIRTY

"Then I'm guessing it's more than a typewriter?" Lauren asked, looking hopeful.

"Let's go into the house, and I'll explain everything," Loretta said.

"Perfect timing," said Elizabeth. "We were getting ready to close anyway."

"Great," said Loretta. "Because you're all going to want to hear this. You have quite a find, Lauren."

Mary headed back to the house with Loretta while Elizabeth and Lauren finished closing up. "I'm so excited, I'm shaking," said Lauren, holding a hand out in front of Elizabeth to demonstrate. "I wasn't sure if we'd really find anything. I was starting to think this was all a wild-goose chase."

Elizabeth shut the register and turned to face her friend. "If Loretta is right, it sounds like you have a golden goose, not a wild one."

Lauren smiled. "It would be such a relief to know I won't lose Grandfather's house. I know it's just a place, but I have so many memories of him attached to it. What a dream it would be to live there."

"And you'd feel comfortable staying there alone after the break-ins?"

Lauren finished tidying one of the shelves in front of her. "It does bother me a little. But Peter's uncle offered to set up an alarm system for the house. And like I was saying earlier, a dog wouldn't hurt either. For company or defense."

"As long as it's bigger than Tink," said Elizabeth with a grin. "You need a large dog."

"Agreed. A large, territorial one."

"Why don't we go meet up with Loretta and get her take on things before we get ahead of ourselves?" asked Elizabeth. Lauren nodded, and the two women headed toward the house. The temperature was still frigid. They wrapped their coats tightly around themselves and kept their heads down to stave off the brisk wind. Even though the trek across the yard was short, Elizabeth still felt a palpable sense of relief when they reached the warmth and light of the front door.

Loretta, Martha, and Mary huddled around steaming coffee cups in the living room. "Took you long enough to get here," said Martha. "We're chomping at the bit."

Elizabeth ignored Martha's grumbling and squeezed into a spot on the couch next to Mary. "We're here now. Did you bring the machine with you, Loretta, or did you leave it at your shop?"

"I left it in the safe at the store," said Loretta. "I figured it would be secure there, and once I found out what it was, I didn't want to risk damaging it by carting it back and forth any more than necessary."

Loretta pulled her cell phone out of her back pocket and retrieved the photos of the machine Martha had sent her a few days ago. "I was taken by this piece as soon as you contacted me. I had an inkling right away of what it was, but I felt I needed to research a bit more to get solid information for you."

"So?" asked Lauren, breathlessly. "What is it?"

"This," said Loretta, passing her phone around the group so everyone could see the photos, "is an Enigma machine."

Mary laughed. "That's fitting. It's certainly been a mystery to us."

Martha plowed forward. "So, we know what it's called." She set her half-full coffee cup on the table. "What was it used for?"

"The history is fascinating, really." Her eyes shone, and Elizabeth could see why Loretta had taken up the occupation she had. She clearly had a passion for antiques and the stories behind them. "The first Enigma machine was created in Germany and used to encode messages between Axis powers. Then the Allies got their hands on some codebooks in 1942, when they assumed control of a German U-boat. Bletchley Park, in England, became a cryptography headquarters, and once the code was broken, the British were able to decipher confidential messages from the enemy for weeks. It was a heroic effort. Some people estimate that the work the mathematicians did at Bletchley helped shorten the war by several years."

Lauren leaned forward, clearly transfixed by the information Loretta was sharing. "Grandfather served in the war, and we know he was in England. Do you think he was involved in working to suppress Nazi activity?"

Loretta shook her head. "I have no way of knowing if he was involved or not. If he wasn't, though, it's likely he was connected to someone who was moving in those circles. Otherwise,

I don't think he could have gotten his hands on a machine like this, in such pristine condition."

"Tell us more about this Enigma machine," said Martha. "How does it work?"

"Happy to," said Loretta. "You all were partially right in thinking that the item was similar to a typewriter." She pointed to the configuration of lettered punch keys on the device. "But there are some significant differences. Like the keyboard."

Martha squinted at the screen. "Right. There are two keyboards, one above the other. It almost reminds me of an organ, with the double sets of keys."

"That's it," said Loretta. "The first set of keys are for typing. The second set, located directly above the first, are for ciphering. When you press a key, the rotors"—she pointed to three dials positioned at the top of the device—"turn and encrypt the letter into a new letter, which lights up on the second keyboard, called the lampboard. Depending on how you set up the rotors, there are hundreds of millions of combinations that could be conveyed from the keyboard through the rotors to the lampboard, making the code multilayered and very difficult to break."

"Why is the keyboard layout different?" asked Elizabeth. She wasn't a tech wiz, but she'd typed enough to know which letters belonged where. The keyboard on the Enigma machine was almost identical to her modern computer keyboard, but with a few small differences. Several of the letters, like *Y*, *P*, and *L*, were in different spots.

"Ah, you're noticing that the keyboard isn't set up in the traditional QWERTY arrangement?" asked Loretta. "The layout you're seeing on this machine is called the QWERTZ layout, and it's commonly used in central Europe. Remember, I mentioned this machine first originated in Germany? It makes sense they would follow a European model."

"So that verifies its origin even more, right?" asked Lauren. "And you said the Enigma machine was in good condition? Not to rush into money talk, but what does that mean, if I choose to sell it?"

"Well, if my instincts are right, you're looking at a bundle of money."

"How much would you estimate?" asked Lauren. "Just ballpark? I don't mean to seem overeager, but any amount of money would solve an awful lot of problems with my grandfather's estate."

Loretta readjusted her glasses on her nose and chewed her lip thoughtfully. "If I were to venture an educated guess...I'd say it's worth at least fifty thousand dollars at auction. Maybe more. Maybe a lot more. A machine like this just sold for an incredible amount at a well-publicized auction." She frowned at them. "I don't want to tell you what it fetched. I don't want to get your hopes up. Let's just take one step at a time."

Lauren sucked in a deep breath, and from the stunned looks on Martha's and Mary's faces, Elizabeth guessed they were all sharing the same sensation of shock. Lauren fanned herself with her hands. "Are you serious? Are you *serious?*"

"I'm serious," said Loretta. "You're sitting on a piece of war memorabilia any collector would give his eyeteeth for."

"Or one particular collector," Elizabeth said. "This is definitely what Arthur Graves was so desperate to find."

"Who's Arthur Graves?" asked Loretta, confusion creasing her features.

"Never mind," said Elizabeth. "Thanks for all your help, Loretta. What you said just confirms our suspicions that this piece is uniquely valuable. I'm glad you have it under lock and key."

Loretta directed her attention to Lauren. "I know a man who collects war memorabilia. Is it all right with you if I contact him? You might do better at auction, but that would take a long time. This man is the one person who could be interested in snatching the machine up before it goes to auction."

Lauren nodded. "Sure. I guess. If he makes an offer, I can turn it down if it's not enough?"

Loretta nodded. "Absolutely. You're in charge here. It will be your decision."

"Then contact him," Lauren said. "My grandfather's creditors don't seem willing to wait much longer for payment. I'm on the verge of losing his house."

Loretta smiled. "Okay. If he's interested, I'll let you know right away."

Later, after Loretta left, Lauren and the sisters gathered in the kitchen. Outside, the wind continued to howl fiercely and rattle the windows in their frames.

"I can't believe it," Lauren kept saying. "It's just surreal. Not only was my grandfather right when he said he had a valuable item in his possession, but he may have also been a real hero during the war. All this time, he's had this secret life I never knew about, and it's amazing to feel like I'm getting to know him in a different way. Usually when people harbor secrets, it's because they're hiding something bad. My grandfather was hiding something good."

"He knew his family wouldn't approve of his wartime efforts, though, no matter how laudable they might appear in hindsight," said Martha, resting her hand on Lauren's shoulder.

"I just hope that his family…" Lauren paused. "I mean, my family, can see past all that now. I really want to meet them. I'm discovering things about my grandfather I never would have dreamed a month ago. They hold a missing piece to the puzzle too."

"I'm sure things will turn out all right in the end," Elizabeth said. She said the words with confidence, but inside, felt a tremor of doubt. She only hoped, for Lauren's sake, her prediction was right.

CHAPTER THIRTY-ONE

For supper, Mary, Elizabeth, and Lauren joined Martha in the living room. Since it was to be her last night on the couch, they had decided to make an occasion out of it. Elizabeth made lasagna, one of Martha's favorite foods, and Mary baked a Dutch apple pie. Elizabeth went downstairs and brought up a set of TV trays they rarely used. After cleaning them off, she set them up in the living room. She was headed back to the kitchen when the phone rang. It was John checking up on Lauren. Elizabeth told him about the Enigma machine.

"That's amazing," he said. "Arthur Graves must have known it was there."

"I think so too."

After promising to keep them updated on anything their investigation might uncover, John said goodbye, and Elizabeth hung up.

"Since it's Martha's night, she gets to pick our movie," Mary said after they were all seated. The wind shrieked outside, making the house feel extra cozy and warm. Everyone was still buzzing about the Enigma machine. Lauren hadn't stopped smiling since she'd gotten Loretta's news.

Martha was silent for a moment. Let's check that old movie channel, you know the one," she said. "I think *Rendezvous with Destiny* is on tonight."

"I love that movie," Elizabeth said.

Mary frowned at her. "I've never heard of it. You two and your old movies."

"I remember you watching a few of them," Elizabeth said with a smile. "Anything with Cary Grant."

Mary snorted. "Well, that's different. Cary Grant was...dreamy."

The women laughed while Elizabeth checked the channel Martha had asked for. Sure enough, *Rendezvous with Destiny* was on at seven. Since they had about thirty minutes to wait for the movie to start, the women spent some time talking about the Enigma machine. It was such an exciting find.

"I would love to know how it ended up with Grandfather," Lauren said. "I'll bet that's an interesting story."

Something Lauren had said earlier popped into Elizabeth's head. "You said you found some letters in the basement," she said to Lauren. "Have you had time to go through them?"

"I looked real quickly through them," she said. "Most of them were from people I never heard of or companies Grandfather had business with. I haven't had time to look at them closely." She paused a moment. "You're thinking there might be something in that pile of old letters that explains the machine?"

"Not necessarily," Elizabeth said, "but it's possible, isn't it? Maybe one of the letters was from the person who gave your grandfather the machine."

Everyone stopped eating and stared at Lauren, who grinned. "You want me to get the letters and go through them now, don't you?"

"What do you think?" Martha blurted. "I'd rather do that than watch the movie."

"Me too," Mary said, laughing.

"Did you leave the letters in one of those boxes we took to the shop?" Elizabeth asked. "I don't think any of us want to brave this weather to hunt for a pack of letters, no matter how exciting it might be."

"Well, actually, I'd do it," Lauren said, smiling, "but I don't have to. I took the letters out of the box. They're upstairs in my room. I'll be back in a minute."

Lauren took the last bite of her lasagna and ran up the stairs. Elizabeth had to wonder if Lauren's grandfather really was involved in decoding operations during the war. Was it possible he kept it secret? Maybe Lauren would find something that would help to explain more about his involvement. Elizabeth found his service fascinating because of his upbringing. Although she'd known who he was, she'd never gotten to meet him. He'd kept to himself. Now she understood why. Probably didn't want to run into his family or have to explain his past life to anyone.

A couple of minutes later Lauren came down the stairs holding a pack of letters tied with a red ribbon in her hands. She picked up her plate and took it to the kitchen. Then she came back and put the letters on her tray. She untied the ribbon and began to look through them.

"Maybe it would go faster if we helped," Mary offered.

Lauren gave each sister a stack of letters. Elizabeth looked carefully through hers. One was a letter from Joe's insurance company about a claim. She put that one aside. Another had to do with a refund to a local store. There was a letter from a fellow soldier, but it had to do with the death of one of their comrades. Elizabeth put her pile down.

"Nothing here," she said.

"Or here," Martha said.

Mary gasped. "This might be it," she said. She handed a letter to Lauren, who put hers down and took the pages from Mary's hands.

She read the first page quickly and smiled. "I think Mary's right. I'll read it out loud."

> Dear Joe,
>
> I so enjoyed seeing you last night. You have grown to mean a great deal to me. I pray we will have more time together now that this war has ended. Perhaps we will find the happiness so many have lost during this terrible conflict.
>
> Thank you for agreeing to accept the item I brought to you. As I said, it is important to me as I spent so much time working with it. Although my official assignment has ended, the memories of my service will stay with me forever.
>
> I must go home and see if my family has survived. The bombing has stopped, so I should return safely to you. But if anything should happen to me, please keep the item. It may be worth something someday, since our work was so secretive. Few people have seen this wonderful machine.
>
> Your prayers for me and for my family are appreciated.
>
> Love, Cecilia

"Something must have happened to her," Mary said. "Oh, how sad."

"There's another letter here," Lauren said. "Attached to Cecilia's." She pulled it out and began to read.

> Dear Mr. Collier,
>
> I hope this reaches you. I found a letter from you in my cousin Cecilia's suitcase. I am sad to tell you that Cecilia and her sister, Ardys, were searching through the ruins of our parents' apartment, hoping to find some of their belongings, when the building collapsed. Neither of them survived.
>
> I am so sorry to bring you this news. It seems from your letter that you and my cousin were very close.
>
> You will be in our thoughts and prayers,
> Oliver Beecham

There was silence for a moment. Finally, Mary said, "Oh, how awful." She blinked back tears. "Sounds like they might have gotten married if she'd lived."

"Of course, if they had gotten married, I wouldn't be here," Lauren said softly. A tear rolled down her face. "My grandfather faced more tragedy than anyone should. Losing my grandmother and my parents. Now I find out he suffered another loss. One that he never talked about."

"How did your parents die, Lauren?" Mary asked.

"A car accident when I was sixteen. My grandmother had just died, and my grandfather was alone. He wanted me to live with him, but I ended up moving in with my best friend's family in Youngstown. In the end, it was a better fit. I didn't have to change schools. But my grandfather visited me frequently and did everything he could to be there for me. That's why coming here when he was ill was a no-brainer."

"I think your grandfather and Cecilia would both be pleased to know that the machine ended up with you," Elizabeth said gently. "Something good coming out of tragedy."

Lauren nodded. "I hope so. I do wish Cecilia hadn't died though."

"I know," Martha said. "But at least now you know where the machine came from."

Mary stood and picked up her empty plate as well as Martha's. "Why don't you help me with the pie, Elizabeth?" she suggested. "The movie is about to start."

Elizabeth picked up her plate and followed Mary into the kitchen.

"Wow, that's really something, isn't it?" Mary asked. "I'm happy for Lauren's good fortune but sad for her grandfather and Cecilia."

"I know. I feel the same way," Elizabeth said as she rinsed the dinner plates in the sink. "Lauren has gone through so much. Seeing the way she turned out is…inspiring."

Mary nodded. "I was thinking the same thing."

"Well, at least now we know Arthur Graves has failed. He tried to get the machine, but he didn't. I'm so relieved it's safe from his clutches now."

"It makes me so angry to think he'll get away with attacking Lauren. Can we do anything? He needs to go to jail."

Elizabeth shrugged. "If Lauren didn't see who hit her, there's no way to charge him."

Mary cut four pieces of pie while Elizabeth got some vanilla ice cream out of the freezer. A few minutes later everyone had pie and either coffee or tea. As they watched the movie,

Elizabeth began to feel unsettled. As if she'd missed something. But what was it?

"That's Evan Masters," Mary blurted out. "You didn't mention he was in this movie."

"Why would I?" Martha asked sharply. "Now hush."

Mary sighed. "But that's Evan Masters, the actor Rosie
Gittrich has such a crush on. Remember, I told you. She has a
whole room set aside with his pictures, interviews, newspaper
articles.... It's weird."

Martha shook her head. "Seriously, Mary. You need to be
quiet...." Her voice trailed off, and she frowned. "You know,
now that you mention it, I feel like I've seen him somewhere
else, but I certainly haven't been to Rosie's house."

Elizabeth stood up. "Oh my," she said. "It's been staring us
all in the face, but we didn't see it."

"What are you talking about?" Lauren asked.

Elizabeth hurried out of the living room and into the
kitchen where she quickly went through Lauren's pictures. She
found the one she wanted and went back into the living room.
She grabbed the remote and paused the movie.

"Well, I give up," Martha groused. "I guess we're never
going to see this movie."

"I don't know about that," Elizabeth said. "But I know why
you felt as if you'd seen Evan Masters before." She held out one
of the pictures from Lauren's pile, the one with the young
Amish man.

"It's Evan Masters," she said, her voice trembling with emotion.

"What are you talking about?" Mary asked.

"Don't you see it? It's Joshua. He's Evan Masters."

CHAPTER THIRTY-TWO

Mary's mouth fell open, but she couldn't help it. Evan and Joshua were the same person? It seemed unbelievable. If it was true, it meant that Evan—the dreamy actor from the golden era of stage and screen—had grown up in the same Amish community that consisted of their neighbors and friends. She took the photo from Elizabeth and squinted at it. There he stood, fresh-faced, in Amish summer garb. Then she stared at the image of Evan Masters, decked out in a pirate costume, frozen on the TV screen in front of her. This older version of him sported an Errol Flynn-like mustache. Though the two men seemed different as night and day, she saw some similarities now. The same deep-set eyes. The same build. How old would Joshua have to be now? Eighty? Ninety? That was assuming he was still alive.

Lauren gazed at the screen as though a ghost had appeared in front of her. "That's my grandfather's brother?"

Mary handed her the photo she'd been looking at. "I know it's a stretch, but the pieces all fit. I can see the resemblance now that I'm expecting it."

Lauren studied the picture with intensity, sneaking looks at the screen as she browsed for information on her cell phone. "This is absolutely unbelievable. How wild. I'm still recovering from Loretta's news about the Enigma machine, and now this?"

Martha un-paused the movie, and as the action sprang to life on the screen, the sisters and Lauren gathered around the television again. The movie was mesmerizing. Evan Masters played the part of a nefarious brigand, who learned to give up his criminal ways after falling in love with the admiral's daughter. As he leapt and sword-fought his way across the set, the women stared at his image.

"Well, I understand now why Joshua disappeared into thin air," said Elizabeth. "Moving out to Hollywood might sound glamorous, but it's not exactly following the Amish model."

"That's a diplomatic way to put it," said Martha. "It's considered a pretty seedy culture—the polar opposite of what most Amish would hope for their children."

"Judge not lest ye be judged," countered Mary. "We don't know anyone's heart for certain, only God does. The fifties were a less sensational time in the media than now, anyway." She turned to look at Martha. "Have you ever seen an Evan Masters film that was crude?"

"No," admitted Martha. "And I've watched all of them over and over again. They were mostly swashbuckling adventures about crashed airplanes or ships. Survival stories. A little bit of romance, but very tame."

"Well then," said Mary. "We all have unique talents. If we're using them for positive things, I wouldn't think anyone should get upset."

Elizabeth set the photos down on the coffee table. "Still, tradition is an important part of most religious denominations—and most communities, for that matter. People like to create structure. It makes them feel safe and helps them handle complicated situations."

Lauren took a deep breath. She gestured toward her phone. "I looked Evan Masters up. I'm still not totally convinced that *that man*"—she pointed a finger at the TV and Evan Masters, who was scaling the ship's mast—"is my great-uncle. Assuming he is, though, do we tell his Amish family?" She gulped. "*My* Amish family?"

Mary felt bad for Lauren. She'd had enough shocks to last her a lifetime the past few weeks, and the hits just kept on coming.

"Don't you think Joshua's family would appreciate some closure?" asked Martha. "What if he's still alive?"

"He's not," said Lauren. "I checked."

"If he was," Mary said, "he'd probably be about the same age as…" She gasped as a thought flew into her head. Rosie Gittrich. The elderly woman could have been a friend of Joshua's, a contemporary.

"What?" asked Lauren. "Are you all right?"

"I'm fine," said Mary. "But I just realized who would know what happened to Joshua. Rosie. She had all those pictures plastered in that little room of hers. Evan Masters during his acting years. It's too big a coincidence to think that she didn't know who he was. She probably grew up in the community with him."

"She's Mennonite, though," said Martha. "I wouldn't think she would have been a close friend of his."

"I don't know," said Elizabeth. "Think about us and Rachel. She's been such a dear friend to us. The community barriers haven't seemed to divide us."

"Yes, but we're all women," said Martha. "You don't think an Amish man and a Mennonite woman would run in the same circles, do you?"

Elizabeth looked thoughtful. "During *rumspringa*, they might. Lots of the Amish teens get together with Mennonite church groups for social mixers during that time. Rosie and Joshua could have easily met then."

"But why would Rosie know that Joshua became an actor, when his own family doesn't even know what happened to him? Doesn't that strike you as odd?"

Martha's musing was cut short by the telephone. Elizabeth answered the call. "Hello?" She pressed the phone to her ear, and a worried look crossed her face. "John, why are you calling so late? Is everything all right?"

"Don't tell me it's something to do with sticky-fingered Arthur Graves again," muttered Lauren, and Mary gave her a sympathetic look. Martha just appeared pained.

"Well, that's wonderful news," said Elizabeth. Her anxious expression dissolved, and she finished the phone call.

"What?" asked Martha, sounding as impatient as Mary felt. "What's wonderful news?"

Elizabeth set the phone down triumphantly. "You're never going to guess."

"And I don't want to," said Martha dryly. "Just tell us."

Elizabeth made a good-natured face at her younger sister and then turned toward Lauren. "Arthur Graves has confessed to breaking and entering at your grandfather's house. He's also confessed to attacking you, so he's being held now."

Lauren didn't take her eyes off Elizabeth, and Mary noticed her fingers were clenched tightly in her lap. "With or without bail?"

"Without bail," Elizabeth said with a smile, "and awaiting trial."

Lauren blew out a sigh that sounded as if she'd been holding her breath a while. "You don't know how relieved that makes me feel. That will definitely help me sleep better tonight."

"Why did he confess?" Mary was shocked. Arthur had seemed so adamant about denying involvement in the break-ins and the assault on Lauren.

"A neighbor of Lauren's came forward. Gretchen Davis? She said she saw Arthur coming out of Lauren's house the night he hit her. The police brought him back to the station, and she positively identified him from a lineup. This time, as soon as the officers began to question him again, he broke down and confessed."

"Thank goodness for neighbors," said Lauren. "I should take Gretchen Davis a pie for all her trouble." She grinned at Mary, who put her hands up in a surrender pose.

"Don't look at me. I've baked myself out with the foster care fund-raiser. I'll leave it to Martha from now on." She ventured a grin at Martha. "Mostly."

"Humph," Martha grunted, but she looked pleased. "At least my kitchen will stay clean."

"Now, don't you two get into it again," said Elizabeth, but her tone was teasing.

Lauren continued. "I wonder why Gretchen didn't say anything the night of the attack?"

Elizabeth shook her head. "I don't know. John didn't say. Maybe she didn't realize what she'd seen was important at first? A lot of times witnesses come out of the woodwork later on, for any number of reasons."

"Maybe." Lauren looked thoughtful. "Either way, I'm beyond grateful."

Mary stifled a yawn and glanced at the clock. "Gals, do you know what time it is?"

Elizabeth's eyes flew wide. "Oh my! It's almost midnight. We're regular night owls."

"Time flies when you're solving decades-old mysteries," said Lauren with a grin.

Mary helped Martha to her feet, since she was headed to her room. "First night's sleep I've had in my bed since I fell," Martha said. "It'll feel good to get a proper sleep. That couch is too lumpy."

"Well, you'd better get some good R&R," said Mary, "because we have plans tomorrow morning."

"We do?" asked Martha with a frown.

"Other than the store?" asked Elizabeth.

"Yes," said Mary. She raised her eyebrows. "We're going to pay a visit to Rosie Gittrich."

CHAPTER THIRTY-THREE

Bright and early the next morning, a knock sounded on the door. The house was quiet as Elizabeth quickly threw some clothes on and rushed to the entry.

She opened the door to John's smiling face. Too late, she realized her hair must be wild after sleeping on it all night, and she tried to discreetly smooth it down with her fingers. If John noticed her disheveled appearance, though, he didn't mention it, and smiled as warmly at her as he ever had.

"I'm sorry to be dropping by so early," he said. "I hope I didn't wake anyone up."

Elizabeth adjusted the blouse she'd thrown on and tried to look more awake than she felt. "You're fine. You know we usually get up early to check on the animals anyway." As if on cue, Reddy the rooster blared a scratchy crow from the backyard.

"Good. I'm glad I didn't disturb you. I have to get to the station for a shift in a few minutes, and I wanted to stop by before I was on the clock so I could let you know that we recovered some stolen items Arthur Graves had taken. He stole antiques from several area stores, and it turns out that even though he couldn't lift the Enigma machine from Lauren's grandfather's house, he did steal some war medals. They're in perfect condition though. We'll call her in to retrieve them sometime this afternoon."

"I'm sure she'll be grateful. I don't think she realized anything was gone."

"There was a lot of stuff in that house. I don't wonder that she didn't miss them, especially since they were small items."

"What about the photos?" Elizabeth asked. "Did he have those? The ones of Lauren's that were stolen from the shop?"

"No, I'm afraid not. He still insists he didn't take them."

"That's so odd." Elizabeth crossed her arms to shield herself from a cold breeze drifting in the door. "What about that note? Did he say anything about it?"

"I asked him, but he was through talking. We didn't get much else out of him."

"I still think it was his handwriting," Elizabeth said. "Of course, I can't be sure."

John scratched his chin. "Sorry, I'm up a creek on this one." He tapped his watch. "I'll let you know if I get any more information. It's time for me to head in to the station."

"Of course." Elizabeth told him goodbye and started doing chores for the day. Although Mary normally took care of the goats, fed and watered the chickens, and gathered eggs, Elizabeth decided to let her sleep. She went out in the bitter cold and took care of the animals. She had to laugh at the goats, pushing against her in their excitement to be fed. She stayed with them a bit and petted each one. They were such friendly little creatures.

When she was done, she returned to the welcome warmth of the house and went back upstairs to get ready for the day. As she was finishing up, she heard stirring from her sisters' rooms. Martha made for the bathroom and began splashing cold water on her face, while Mary padded sleepily down the hall to Elizabeth, a robe hanging loose over her flowered pajamas.

"You're up earlier than usual. Did I hear the door, or was I dreaming?"

"John stopped by. He had some more news about Arthur."

"Anything interesting?"

"He mentioned Arthur had confessed to several other robberies around town. He also said the police found out Arthur had nicked a few items from Lauren's house. Some war medals."

Mary pulled her robe around herself and cinched the belt at her waist. "I bet Lauren will be glad to get those back."

"I'm sure she will. And I'm glad to know Arthur won't be hassling anyone else anytime soon. It sounds like they'll have him on several counts."

Martha finished freshening up and moved to her room to get changed. Mary headed down the stairs in her robe and slippers. "Why don't we go to the kitchen? I know I'm still in my robe, but it's only you girls around anyway. I thought I might fix something simple for breakfast this morning, so we can figure out our game plan for Rosie's."

"That sounds like a good idea." Elizabeth set a hand on the bannister. "I shouldn't really be hungry after all that pie last night, but somehow, I am."

Mary laughed. "Me too. Sometimes I wonder if I sleepwalk and burn off calories at night. I'm always starving when I wake up."

The sisters settled down in the kitchen. Mary scrambled eggs, while Elizabeth prepared toast. An easy job, but everyone liked their bread a different way, with very specific shades of brown. She started with Martha's first, since she liked it the lightest. It was a good thing too, because Martha soon made her way slowly down the stairs.

Elizabeth was pleased to see her sister was getting around a little better than she had a few days prior. Elizabeth rushed to help her to her seat and then handed her a plate with her barely toasted toast.

"Ah, just the way I like it. Thanks, Lizzie," Martha said as she sank into a chair and leaned her crutch against the wall beside her. She slathered on a copious amount of apple butter. Elizabeth prepared Mary's toast next, on the toaster's middle setting, then finished up with her own. She liked hers on the next to last setting. "Nearly charred beyond recognition," Martha would often comment.

Elizabeth decided to wait to fix Lauren's toast until she got up. She suspected she needed the rest. After several shocks to her system in a short period of time, it was no wonder the girl's brain needed time to absorb and reset.

Just after the sisters said grace and started eating, the phone rang. Elizabeth was closest to the landline, so she scraped her chair back. "I'll get it."

She picked up the receiver, balancing a slice of half-eaten toast smeared with lemon curd in her other hand. "Hello?"

Loretta's friendly, crisp voice greeted her. "Hi. Elizabeth?"

"Yes, this is Elizabeth."

"Loretta here. Look, I just got off the phone with a gentleman named Harvey Lamott. I don't expect you've heard of him before?"

"Can't say that I have."

"He's the man I mentioned yesterday. The one I asked Lauren if I could call. He might not be well known outside of the circles I work in, but his name crops up a lot in the antiques business. He's an avid collector to whom money is of little consequence. Word is his home—or homes, to be more accurate—are like museums, packed to the brim with all sorts of unique artwork, historical pieces, celebrity memorabilia, you name it."

"He sounds impressive."

"Oh, he is. And I just got done negotiating with him."

Elizabeth gripped the receiver tighter. "For Lauren's piece?"

At that moment, Lauren plodded down the stairs, her blond hair pulled into a messy ponytail and her pajamas wrinkled. "What? What's going on?" she mouthed across the room to the sisters. She'd obviously overheard Elizabeth's question.

Martha just waved a hand at her and shook her head.

Lauren sank into a chair while Mary slid a plate of eggs in front of her. "The Enigma machine, I think," Mary whispered. "Loretta may have negotiated a deal with someone."

Elizabeth, who was trying to ignore her sisters, turned her back as Loretta continued. "I talked to some people about taking the machine to auction. In all my calling around, word must have gotten out about it somehow. When I opened the store this morning, I had three voice mail messages waiting from Lamott, and five emails. I was going to contact him today, but it seems he couldn't wait."

"I stand corrected," said Elizabeth. "He sounds impressive and determined."

"Determined enough to outdo any bid that would've come up in an auction, at any rate. He apparently didn't want to leave any wiggle room for someone else to snap it up. He offered me a high-dollar amount for the item."

"How high are we talking?" Elizabeth took a small bite of toast and chewed.

"Are you sitting?"

"No. Should I be?"

"Possibly. He offered…" Loretta paused, and Elizabeth heard some papers rustle on the other end of the line. "He offered *three hundred thousand dollars*." The words hung in the air, until the monumental weight of them came crashing down on Elizabeth's consciousness. The bite of toast she'd taken a few seconds earlier felt lodged in her esophagus.

"I'm sorry?" Her voice was hoarse, and she coughed to clear her throat. "Did you say three hundred thousand dollars?" She turned back around to stare at her sisters and Lauren in disbelief. Was this real?

At her words, Lauren leapt out of her chair and broke into a wide smile. Then she grabbed onto Mary's and Martha's hands and did a little impromptu celebration dance on the kitchen floor. Mary laughingly joined in, and even Martha cracked a small smile.

"Thank you so much, Loretta. We really appreciate all you've done. Lauren is right here with us, and she's thrilled at the good news."

"Does that mean she'll accept the offer?"

Elizabeth laughed. "So do you accept this offer, Lauren?"

Lauren nodded, her laughter keeping her from speaking.

"She says yes."

"Good," Loretta said. "I'm glad. It does me good to share such good news."

Elizabeth told Loretta goodbye and hung up the phone.

Lauren's eyes shone. "Can you believe it? Now I can pay off Grandfather's house and stay there. I can settle his debts. I don't have to sell anything else in the house if I don't want to. Everything's taken care of now." She beamed at Martha and Mary, who returned her smiles. Elizabeth set her empty plate on the counter.

"Well," she said. "Not quite everything. We still have a mystery to solve."

CHAPTER THIRTY-FOUR

Elizabeth and Lauren prepared to go to Rosie's house. Mary and Martha stayed behind to run the store.

"Call me right away after you talk to Rosie," Mary said before heading to the shop. "I can't wait to find out what she has to say."

"I'll tell you when I get back," Elizabeth said. "You need to concentrate on the shop."

Mary frowned. "If I hadn't told you about her special room..."

Elizabeth smiled at her younger sister. "I'm sorry. You're right, you know. I wish I could take you with me, but I need you to take care of things here. And keep an eye on Martha. Don't let her overdo it. I wish she'd stay inside one more day, but you know how stubborn she is."

Mary offered her a small smile. "I'll watch her. Here's hoping you find the truth about Joshua... Uh, Evan Masters."

"Me too. It must be quite a story."

Elizabeth was grateful the weather was much better today. Much of the snow from the night before had been blown around. The roads were in pretty good shape.

"Shouldn't we have phoned Rosie first?" Lauren asked.

Elizabeth shook her head. "I don't want her to get rid of the evidence. She knows that Joshua became Evan Masters. I want her to tell us the truth."

"So you think she took my pictures?"

"Yes, I do."

"You know, she really hasn't done anything wrong," Lauren said slowly. "We can't force her to tell us what she knows about Joshua."

"Well, she took your pictures," Elizabeth said.

"I'd never file a police report about those pictures."

"I know that. And you're right. She doesn't have to be honest with us, but I think she will. This must have been a great burden, keeping Joshua's identity from his family all these years. She needs to look you in the face. I'm hoping she will decide you should know about your great-uncle."

Lauren sighed. "Yeah, I hope so too. I really appreciate your coming with me, Elizabeth. I'm not sure I could confront her on my own."

"Well, I care about you. And besides that, I'm the kind of person who needs resolution. I don't like unsolved mysteries. Drives me nuts."

Lauren laughed. "You're the best mystery solver I've ever seen. Boy, this has certainly been intriguing. Arthur Graves added a real twist to things." She shook her head. "Oh, Elizabeth. If he'd found the Enigma machine…" She took a deep breath. "I can't even think about it." She blinked away tears as she looked at Elizabeth. "I have you and your sisters to thank. If I hadn't known you… And if I hadn't brought those boxes to you…"

"Well, you did, and Arthur Graves is behind bars. It's all turned out for the best."

"I still can't believe it. I keep thinking I'm dreaming. A little machine like that. I'm certain Grandfather had no idea of its real worth. He probably wouldn't have kept it out where people could see it."

"Well, the important thing is that you have it, and you're going to be able to pay off your grandfather's house and live there. And you can even fix it up. It's a beautiful old house. With a little work, it could be really lovely."

Lauren nodded as she wiped away a tear. "I intend to restore it. That means more than I can say."

Elizabeth was blessed by Lauren's good fortune and grateful to be a part of it. Now she just wanted find out why Rosie Gittrich had never told Joshua's family that he was alive. Although they'd discovered that Evan Masters had died several years ago, he had a wife and three children. Did he tell them his Amish family would never welcome them? But what about Lauren? Surely they would want to know her. Elizabeth hoped God would repair the breach in this family. What worried her was finding out that Joshua had become a famous actor. How would his Amish family receive that news? She really wasn't sure it would be a blessing to them. Yet they deserved to know the truth.

She pushed away all the concerns that filled her thoughts as she pulled into Rosie's driveway. She and Lauren got out and went to the front door. Right before Elizabeth rang the bell, Lauren grabbed her arm.

"Wait a minute," she said. "I don't know—"

"Don't be afraid," Elizabeth said gently. "The truth is always better than anything your imagination might cook up."

"I know. It's just..." She took a deep breath. "Okay. Go ahead."

Elizabeth rang the doorbell, and a few seconds later Rosie opened it. She frowned at the two women and pushed the storm door open.

"You Classen sisters don't know how to call before you show up on my doorstep, do you?" she said sharply to Elizabeth. "What do you want?"

"We need to talk about Evan Masters, Rosie," Elizabeth said. "Or should I say Joshua Derksen?"

The blood drained from Rosie's face, and she grabbed the doorjamb. Elizabeth reached out to steady her, then stepped inside Rosie's living room, motioning to Lauren to follow her. They helped her over to a nearby chair.

"We're not here to accuse you of anything, Rosie," Elizabeth said. "But Joshua is Lauren's great-uncle. She deserves to know the truth, don't you think?"

Rosie let out a sigh that seemed to come from somewhere deep inside. "Yes, she does. It's been so hard. Keeping his secret. Keeping mine."

"Let's get you something to drink," Elizabeth said. She caught Lauren's eye and nodded at the front door. Lauren went over and closed it. "What would you like?"

"I have some tea on," Rosie said. "If you could bring it in here?"

"I will. Are you okay now?"

Rosie nodded and looked at Lauren, who sat down on the couch near Rosie's chair. "I'm sorry, young lady. I really am. I started out keeping secrets, and through the years it got harder to tell the truth. I was afraid…"

"Let's wait until we get you your tea, then you can explain everything," Elizabeth said.

Rosie nodded and leaned back in her chair.

Elizabeth went into the kitchen, found the tea and three cups. She put everything on a tray sitting on the counter, then took some sugar from the counter and milk from the refrigerator. She carried the tray out to the living room where she put it on the coffee table. She poured the tea into the cups and waited while everyone added whatever they liked to it. She sat down next to Lauren on the couch and waited for Rosie to talk to them. She didn't want to push her. She might shut down if she felt pressured.

Finally, Rosie put her cup down and fastened her gaze on Lauren. "Yes, Evan Masters was Joshua." She sighed. "He was just like his brother. You see, your grandfather had his own mind. He didn't hate the way he was raised, but he… Well, he felt he owed service to the country that he loved. When he told his family that he wanted to help with the war effort, they were…" She shook her head. "As you can imagine, it didn't go over well. He explained that he wouldn't fire a weapon, but that he wanted to help the soldiers who were putting their lives on the line." She smiled, and some of the weariness left her expression. "He was a wonderful man, Lauren. Really."

"I know that," Lauren said. "So his family shunned him?"

"Unfortunately, yes. I think some of them weren't in agreement with the shunning. It happened a lot more back then. Many Amish communities avoid shunning now. But back then it was simply what they did if someone had ideas that didn't agree with their *Ordnung*. Those are the rules set up for each community."

"So some of his family didn't want to shun him?" Lauren asked.

Rosie nodded. "But then Joshua decided to leave. They blamed your grandfather for influencing his younger brother. He didn't, you know. Joshua had his own reasons." She took another sip of her tea.

"Why did Joshua leave?" Elizabeth asked.

Rosie put her cup down and clasped her hands together. "He...he was in love. He left with a girl from our town."

"But why didn't anyone know about that?" Lauren asked. "It should have been pretty obvious if he left at the same time a girl he was interested in moved away."

"At her request, her family kept it quiet. Said she had a job in another city. Which was true. It wasn't their job to tell Joshua's family why he left. It was his."

"Then why didn't he?" Elizabeth asked. "Even if they didn't agree with his actions, he should have at least told them of his plans. His parents and his other siblings spent many years wondering if he was alive or dead."

"Oh my dear," Rosie said as tears ran down her face. "He did explain. And thus my sin is revealed. I've sinned against Joshua. And his family. Against you, my dear," she said to Lauren. "And there's no way to fix it. Nothing I can ever do to make things right."

CHAPTER THIRTY-FIVE

Rosie shakily stood to her feet and crossed the room to push open the door to the small room attached to the living room, the one that Mary said was plastered with pictures of Evan Masters. Elizabeth heard her rummage through a drawer, then the elderly woman returned with a yellowed note clasped in her hand. She held the paper out to Lauren. Tears glistened in her eyes.

"This was given to me by Joshua before he left," she said. "He gave it to me in full confidence—" Her voice cracked. "In full confidence that I would deliver it to his family. He wanted them to know—" She paused and hung her head low. "I'm sorry."

Lauren reached out to touch Rosie's shoulder. "You're fine. Take your time. There's no rush."

Rosie looked up, and to Elizabeth's surprise, laughed. "I suppose there isn't a huge rush, is there? This secret has been kept very well for many years, and no one's been the wiser. Oh, what fools young people are. What a fool I was."

"Why would you say such things, Rosie?" asked Elizabeth gently. "People make mistakes. Surely this one couldn't have been that grave."

Rosie tilted her head to the side. "I'm afraid it was." She motioned at the letter Lauren held in her hands. "Read that, my dear. Out loud. It will explain everything."

Lauren cleared her throat and began reading:

My dearest family,

It is with a heavy heart that I convey this news to you. I have been harboring a secret for some time, and now is the time it must come to light. I have fallen in love with a woman not of our community, and I have committed to marry her. I know that this will cause all of you grief, as the Ordnung states I must be cut off, but please know I wish it did not. I am not leaving the Plain community because I disagree with it. I cherish our heritage and the faith that accompanies it, but I cannot live against my heart any longer. I know that Amelia and I are meant to be together, and I see nothing in the Holy Scripture that forbids it. She follows Christ, as do I. She is a kind creature and is as full of love and light as any woman I have met. I count myself happy to be wed to her soon.

I know you'll believe my brother is to blame for me leaving, my wild older brother putting ill ideas in my head, but it isn't true. Not a word of it. The only similarity is that we both pursue what we feel God has for us. I pray you will forgive me for any pain I cause you by my actions, and remember that I care for you as much as ever I did. If you should ever want to reconnect with me, I plan on residing at the address below. Not sure how long we will be there.

As always, I remain,

Your Joshua

Lauren quickly scanned the rest of the letter. "Then there's an address written at the bottom. This was where Joshua lived, at least for a short period of time." She handed the note to Elizabeth, who took it. The handwriting was smeared with splotches like teardrops. Were they Joshua's…or Rosie's?

"Why did he give the letter to you? And why didn't you give it to his family?" asked Lauren. "They thought he was missing, or even dead, all these years. All this time, you knew the truth."

Rosie held up a hand. "One question at a time. You want to know why I had the letter? The answer is that we knew each other, as did our families. I was Mennonite, and he was Old Order, but when he was a young man, our church groups were allowed to mix, and we became friends. Close friends. I fell in love with him in the way that only a silly child can, and I thought he felt the same about me." She nodded to the letter Elizabeth still held. "But as you heard, that was not the case. When he gave me the letter, I thought it was a declaration of his affection for me. As soon as I found out otherwise… Well, I was devastated, as you might imagine."

"So you kept the letter, instead of giving it Joshua's family? Did he know?" asked Lauren.

Rosie shook her head, and a frown pulled at the corners of her wrinkled mouth. "Yes, I kept the letter, and no, Joshua never knew. He thought his family disowned him. All those years, he thought they hadn't forgiven him." She looked up at the women, and Elizabeth could see the regret in her eyes. "I kept the letter because I felt jilted, and I guess…" She paused. "I wanted to hurt him the way he hurt me."

"But he didn't even know you cared for him," said Lauren. "He was innocent in the whole thing."

"Oh, child. The things we do when we're young don't always make sense, do they?" Rosie leaned back in her chair. "It was a foolish mistake I made, and one I've paid for every day since. After I cooled off, I realized the magnitude of what I'd done and wanted to fix it, but then I discovered that Joshua had become an actor, which I knew wouldn't go over well with the Plain community. And then when he grew more and more popular, it became impossible to tell the truth. The lie had grown too large."

Elizabeth handed the letter back to Rosie, who carefully laid it on a table beside her. "So you just followed his career, all those years? Kept tabs on him from afar?"

"Oh, yes. I still cared about him, even if he was meant for another. I wished the best for him."

"It sounds like he had a meaningful career and a family who cared for him very much," Elizabeth said.

"Yes," Rosie said. "I'd just like to fix the mess I made as a young woman so I can live free from the weight of secrets and lies. It's been a lonely life."

It all became clear to Elizabeth. Rosie's snappish demeanor was a defense mechanism to keep anyone from getting too close and discovering her secrets. Her reclusive tendencies, the same. The obsessive shrine to Evan Masters wasn't a schoolgirl crush; it was a memorial to regret—and sacrifice. However misguided it was, Rosie had forfeited the normality of her own life in order to protect Joshua's legacy. To protect his family.

"You took the photos, didn't you?"

"I'm sorry?" asked Rosie. Her brow wrinkled in confusion.

"The photos. The ones that belonged to Lauren, from the vintage camera of her grandfather's. Arthur Graves didn't take them. It was you. You were trying to make sure no one saw the pictures or made any of the connections we made."

"Oh, that." Rosie shuffled back to the small room again. Once again they heard a drawer open and close. Rosie emerged with a folder, which she handed to Elizabeth. Inside was the original batch of photos Mary had had printed from the film, along with the negatives.

"But if it wasn't Arthur Graves who stole the pictures," began Lauren, "who left that menacing note?"

"The note that said 'forget the pictures'?" Rosie looked shamed.

"Yes," said Elizabeth slowly. "That was you?"

"I didn't actually write the note. I knew you'd recognize my handwriting right away. So I asked that fellow, the one who was ogling the photos and chomping at the bit about war memorabilia, to write it for me."

"And he agreed?"

"Oh, of course. We're both a pair of curmudgeons, and so we got along famously with each other. I just told him that I'd told you girls to hold some oil paintings for me and that the note referred to them. *Forget the pictures* meant I didn't want you to hold the items for me anymore. Of course, I knew, with the pictures being stolen, you would assume the note was a warning, not a request. I hoped you'd drop the whole thing, and I could go back to living the way I always had."

Elizabeth couldn't believe it. All this time, Rosie had been right under their nose. Not a villain in the traditional sense. Just a fragile, human woman with flaws like any of them had. A woman who had made mistakes but now was ready to own up to them.

"I have to say, though," Rosie continued, "as difficult as it is to come clean, I'm relieved you know everything now." She leaned forward in her seat and reached out to grasp the women's hands. She held on tightly and looked them each straight in the eyes. "I'm so tired of keeping secrets."

CHAPTER THIRTY-SIX

The week had flown quickly. Although the temperatures were still bitter, the snow stayed away. Business at the shop was brisk. Lauren was home, finally feeling safe because Arthur Graves was in jail. Elizabeth had asked Rachel to visit with Joshua's family and ask them to talk to her and Lauren. She instructed Rachel to tell them it had to do with Joshua but hadn't given any details. Elizabeth and Lauren felt Hilda and her family should be told the truth. All of it. If they decided to share it with anyone else, that would be their decision. Surprisingly, the family had extended an invitation to lunch. The women were surprised to be invited to eat with them and wondered if Amity and Ezra had anything to do with it.

"The Amish are usually very accommodating," Martha reminded Elizabeth over breakfast. "Visiting over food isn't unusual. Maybe Hilda felt badly about her reaction to you at the fund-raiser and wants to make things right."

"I hope so," Elizabeth said. "For whatever reason, I'm grateful Lauren has the chance to speak with them. After that, they'll have to decide if they want Lauren in their lives."

Martha was doing much better. She was cooking again, something Mary and Elizabeth were grateful for. Elizabeth had to remind herself to eat lightly this morning. She couldn't take a chance at offending Hilda this afternoon. She had just poured herself a second cup of coffee when the doorbell rang accompanied by Pal's loud barking.

"Hush, Pal," she said.

Mary got up and looked out the window next. "It's John," she said.

Elizabeth looked down at her robe and slippers. She ran a hand through her hair. "Oh my goodness. Keep him entertained for a few minutes. I've got to change clothes."

She grabbed her coffee cup and ran upstairs. It only took her a few minutes to pull on some slacks and a blouse. Then she changed her shoes and ran a brush through her hair. A little mascara and she felt pulled together enough to see John. Even though he'd stayed with them and had seen her in her robe, she would much rather it not happen again if she could help it. She gulped the rest of her coffee and went downstairs. Elizabeth assumed he'd be sitting at the table enjoying a stack of Martha's pancakes, but instead he stood near the door, talking to Martha and Mary. She noticed he was in uniform.

"Good morning," Elizabeth said as she entered the kitchen. "Do you have time for breakfast?"

John smiled. "Your sisters already asked me. Unfortunately, I had to say no. We have breakfast with the chief this morning. He puts this together every so often. The food isn't as good as Martha's, but I still look forward to it." His smile slipped a bit. "I...I wanted to drop this off." He gestured toward a large box sitting on the kitchen stool near the door. "It's that quilt. I hope you've decided to accept it. Like I said, I only purchased it as a donation to Helping Hands and because you liked it so much. I'd take it, but my mother made quilts. I have several of them. Call me nuts, but I feel like if I put a strange quilt in my house, she would be upset. I don't want to be scolded from the great beyond."

Elizabeth laughed. "All right. Just to keep you out of the doghouse. I love it. Thank you so much."

John took a deep breath and let it out. "I'm so relieved. I really hope you enjoy it."

"I know I will."

John turned toward the door but then stopped and turned back. "If you're free tonight, I wondered if you'd like to have dinner? I could pick you up around seven?"

Elizabeth nodded. "I'd enjoy that. See you at seven. Have a good time at your breakfast."

John chuckled. "It really is nice to see everyone from the station when we're not working. However, the chief seems to believe it's his job to entertain us when we get together. His jokes are the worst."

"In that case we'll pray for you," Mary said laughing.

"Thanks. I appreciate it." John smiled at them and left.

"Another date?" Martha asked with a smile.

"I guess so," Elizabeth said. She got the box off the stool and carried it upstairs, put it on her bed, and opened it. Then she took out the gorgeous quilt. In her heart she knew that today she'd taken a big step. At first she'd thought about turning down John's offer because the quilt was such an extravagant gift. How could she take something like that from a man? But accepting the quilt meant something much deeper. She'd spent too many years turning away possibilities out of fear. Fear of making a mistake. "I surrender the future to You, God," she said. "Whatever You want. If You have love waiting for me, I will receive it. Thank You."

Once she prayed, she felt as if a weight left her. Elizabeth wasn't sure John was the man God had for her. Right now, John didn't believe in God the way Elizabeth did, and she would never pursue a romantic relationship with anyone who didn't love God. But now that she'd let go of worrying about what might come, she knew that John was also in His hands. Perhaps John would see something in her—and in her sisters—that would lead him to a relationship with Christ. That still didn't mean that she and John would end up together. She would just trust that if God wanted her to be with someone, He would bring the right person. At least today, she'd opened the door for that possibility. The beautiful quilt would always remind her of her vow.

Elizabeth ran her hand over the quilt and smiled. Then she finished getting ready for her visit with the Derksens. Before she left, she prayed once again, asking God to help them today. Only God could heal a family that had been broken for so many years.

Elizabeth and Lauren stood on the front porch of the Derksens' simple white farmhouse. Lauren was nervous about the visit, and Elizabeth wasn't sure how to help her. She had put everything in God's hands and had to believe He had heard her. Of course, Joshua's family had free will. They could choose to reject Lauren. Elizabeth hoped fervently that they wouldn't do that.

Elizabeth knocked on the door, and a few seconds later it opened. Ezra stood on the other side and smiled when he saw them. He held the door open. "Welcome," he said.

Elizabeth and Lauren stepped inside. The living room was simple but inviting. A large, colorful rag rug lay in the middle of the floor in front of a huge stone fireplace. A fire crackled and popped, sending warmth into the room. Two wooden rocking chairs sat near the fireplace, and a dark blue couch hugged the far wall. Homemade lace pillows were on each side of the couch, and a lovely quilt with different shades of blue lay on one of the arms.

"Please, come with me," Ezra said, gesturing toward a room where the rest of the family had gathered. They followed him into an oversized kitchen which appeared to be the heart of the house. The table in the middle of the room was massive, obviously made by hands that took great care in its construction. Hilda sat at the head of the table. Amity busied herself at the cast-iron stove, but she turned to smile as they entered.

"We are so glad you are here," she said. "Lunch will be ready soon. I hope you like beef stew. It must simmer for a few more minutes. Perhaps we can visit for a while before we eat?"

"That would be fine," Elizabeth said.

"Please sit here," Ezra said, pulling out two chairs. He waited until the women were seated and then he sat across the table from them. Amity took a seat next to him.

"You wanted to talk to me about my brother, Joshua, ja?" Hilda asked.

Elizabeth glanced at Lauren, who looked too nervous to speak. She smiled at her, hoping to give her courage to face what was most likely going to be a tough conversation.

Lauren reached into her pocket and took out the letter Rosie had given them. She handed it to Hilda with trembling fingers.

Hilda opened it and began to read. As she did, tears filled her eyes. When she finished, she frowned at Lauren.

"I do not understand. Why are we only seeing this now? If my mother had read this, she would have known that her child was alive."

Lauren, who was also visibly moved, once again didn't seem capable of saying anything. Elizabeth stepped in.

"The letter was given to a young woman who loved your brother. Joshua trusted her to bring it to his family, but she didn't do it. She was jealous of the girl that Joshua left town with. She just gave it to Lauren a few days ago. This woman is ashamed of what she did and wanted to make it right years ago. But as time went on…"

"It became hard to face what she had done," Hilda finished for her. She sighed deeply and nodded, her eyes meeting Lauren's. "It seems this woman and I have been tempted in the same way. I should have spoken to you long ago. Told you about your uncle. I knew about you, of course. But pride kept me from doing what was right. I hope you will forgive me."

Lauren nodded as tears streamed down her face. "Of course I do. I…I always thought it was just Grandfather and me. But I have a family after all." She took a deep breath before saying, "You're his sister. You're entitled to inherit some of his property. Although he left the house to me, I recently found out that something he owned is worth a great deal of money."

Before she could say another word, Hilda waved her words away with her hand. "As you see, we live very simply. We have no need of anything. Money is not important to us. We are self-sufficient, and our needs are all met. Besides, I do not believe your grandfather would want what he left to you given to anyone else. Please, do not trouble yourself about this."

"The item he left Lauren is very, very valuable," Elizabeth said. "Lauren has sold it and intends to pay off her grandfather's house. There is enough money left for restoration and other things...."

"No," Hilda said, interrupting Elizabeth. "Please do not mention it again. I feel at peace with my decision, and I will not change my mind." She looked at her grandchildren. "Ezra and Amity believe me to be very stubborn. And they are right."

Amity laughed. "She is telling the truth. Once Grossmammi makes her mind up, it is settled. Believe me, Ezra and I have learned this lesson over the years."

Lauren smiled at her. "All right. I give up."

"Goot," Hilda said. She looked back and forth between Lauren and Elizabeth. "I see something in your expressions. Is there something else you need to tell me?"

"Joshua has passed away," Lauren said softly.

"I expected this," she responded. "He would have been very old. Older than I am. I hope he lived a happy life."

"Yes, he did," Lauren said. "He stayed married to the girl he left here with, and they had three children. I expect there are grandchildren, although I'm not sure about that. I intend to write to his family so I can find out more about them."

"That is goot," Hilda said. "I pray they are not as obstinate as I was."

Lauren chuckled. "I guess I'll find out. If it runs in the family, I could be in trouble."

Ezra and Amity broke out laughing. "Oh, Grossmammi, it seems Lauren will fit quite nicely into our lives. She teases you like we do."

"Ja, I think you are right, but I am not sure this is a goot thing," Hilda said with a grin. She looked closely at Lauren. "I feel there is more you want to tell me. Please do not reveal the identity of the woman who gave you the letter. I do not want to know. If the day comes she wants to come to me, I will listen with compassion."

"No, that's not it," Lauren said, "but I appreciate that. I would rather leave it with her as well." She turned to Elizabeth, who nodded her encouragement. Then she stared at Hilda a few moments before saying, "After he left here, Joshua changed his name to Evan Masters. He was a very famous stage and film star. I...I know this is probably something that is shameful for you to know."

Hilda shook her head. "*Ach*, Lauren. Do not concern yourself about it. Joshua made his choice to leave, and I am at peace. Again, I am just happy to know he lived a fulfilled life."

Elizabeth watched as the tension left Lauren's body, and she finally relaxed. As Amity got up to check the stew, Elizabeth offered a silent prayer of thanks to God for everything He had done for them. Mary had gained self-confidence. Martha had learned she didn't have to control everything, and Lauren had gained a family. And for herself? She'd decided to let go of her future, putting it into God's hand. She had to trust God and stop being afraid of commitment. Would something deeper come from her friendship with John? Only God knew. But like Hilda, she was at peace.

She realized Amity was saying something to her, and she smiled and joined in the fun of making new friends and laying another mystery to rest.

A NOTE FROM THE AUTHORS

Dear Readers,

What a joy to write another Guideposts cozy mystery for you! This time, the mystery, set in picturesque Lancaster County, revolved around a World War II-era camera brought into Secondhand Blessings…and an undeveloped roll of film still tucked inside it.

I (Shaen) have been fascinated with vintage cameras for many years. Studying the history of the Kodak company in college got me hooked. Having several relatives who are talented photographers and antique camera collectors cemented the interest. One day, while antiquing, I stumbled across an old camera that immediately got the gears in my mind whirring. What memories had that lens captured? How much family history had it witnessed? If a picture is, indeed, worth a thousand words, what story would those words tell? Nancy and I were both intrigued by the idea and ran with it. We hope you enjoyed reading this book as much as we enjoyed writing it!

Everyone has a story to tell and a unique purpose to fulfill. I pray that you move forward in your sense of purpose today and do the wonderful things God has uniquely equipped you to do.

Blessings!
Shaen Layle and Nancy Mehl

ABOUT THE AUTHORS

Shaen Layle

Trained as a literary novelist and with a decade of librarianship under her belt, Shaen Layle writes inspirational fiction from her home in the Midwest, where she lives with her artist husband, Danny, and their two rambunctious, but adorable, little boys. She loves drinking Lady Grey tea and discussing all things bookish with her readers on social media or on her website at shaenlayle.com. You can sign up for her newsletter at shaenlayle.com/newsletter.

Nancy Mehl

Nancy Mehl is a best-selling, award-winning author who lives in Missouri with her husband, Norman, and her puggle, Watson. She's authored over thirty books and is currently writing a new series for Bethany House Publishing. The Kaely Quinn Profiler series released book one, *Mind Games*, in December 2018, and book two, *Firestorm*, in August 2019.

Readers can learn more about Nancy through her website: nancymehl.com. She is part of the Suspense Sisters: suspensesisters.blogspot.com, along with several other popular suspense authors. She is also very active on Facebook.

BARN FINDS

If you're enthralled with World War II history, the term "Enigma machine" might not be a mystery to you. Though the rotor-based cipher machine has been around since at least 1915, the machine our story talks about is a military version, which was taken under proprietary control by the Germans at the start of the war.

Several countries, including Poland, France, and England (which included the now well-known codebreakers of Bletchley Park), banded together and worked tirelessly to crack the enigma code. They made steady progress but got their real break when they captured codebooks from a sunken German U-boat in 1942. As a result, for several weeks, the Allies were secretly able to decode Axis messages. Historians estimate that the codebreakers helped shorten the war, by possibly a few years, making the Enigma machine a vital piece of history and an extremely valuable find.

FRESH FROM ROSIE'S KITCHEN

Rosie's Italian Cream Cake

Ingredients for the cake

½ cup butter-flavored shortening

½ cup butter, softened

2 cups granulated sugar

5 eggs, separated (room temperature)

2 cups cake flour

1½ teaspoons baking soda

1 cup buttermilk (not low-fat), (room temperature)

3 teaspoons real vanilla extract

1½ cups finely shredded sweetened coconut flakes

Ingredients for the frosting

16 oz cream cheese (room temperature)

½ cup butter, softened

4 cups confectioner's sugar

2 teaspoons vanilla

1½ cups finely shredded sweetened coconut flakes

1½ cups pecan pieces

Instructions

Preheat oven to 325 degrees.

Grease and flour three 9-inch round cake pans. Set aside.

In a large bowl cream together shortening, butter, and sugar.

Add egg yolks one at a time, beating well after each addition.

In a separate bowl combine flour and baking soda.

Alternate adding buttermilk and flour mixture into sugar mixture, starting and ending with buttermilk. Be sure to mix well after each addition.

Stir in vanilla.

In a separate bowl, beat egg whites until stiff peaks form.

Fold egg whites into batter.

Stir in coconut flakes.

Pour batter into prepared pans and bake for 25–27 minutes.

Remove from oven and let cakes sit for 5 minutes before removing from pans and placing on a cooling rack to finish cooling.

Make the frosting by creaming together cream cheese and butter. Add confectioner's sugar and vanilla.

Stir in coconut flakes and pecans.

Frost and decorate cooled cake layers.

Use toasted pecans and toasted coconut flakes to garnish the cake if desired.

Store in refrigerator. Remove and let come to room temperature before serving.

Read on for a sneak peek of another exciting book
in the Mysteries of Lancaster County series!

Pride and Pettiness
by Elizabeth Ludwig

Mary Classen Baxter's stomach rumbled as the door to the Bird-in-Hand Family Restaurant & Smorgasbord swung open, and the delicious smell of warm, yeasty rolls wafted out. Despite the harsh February wind whipping across the parking lot, she came to a standstill and took a long whiff.

"Mmm. Do you smell that?" She glanced over her shoulder at her sisters, Elizabeth and Martha.

"I'd smell it better inside." Martha huffed and rubbed her gloved hands over her arms. "Come on, Mary. It's freezing out here."

Mary sighed and pulled the door open wider for her sisters to step through. Martha was sensible and organized, but sometimes it'd be nice if she put all that aside and stopped to enjoy the little things in life…like the smell of buttery steamed carrots and roasting chicken.

Her mouth watered as a waitress in a crisp green shirt and black vest strode by carrying two plates piled high with food.

Elizabeth's eyes grew round, and she rubbed her tummy. "Goodness, I didn't realize I was so hungry." She motioned toward the hostess desk. "I'll go get us a table."

"Okay." Martha pulled off her gloves and shoved them into the pocket of her coat. Dodging another hustling waitress, she unwound the muffler from around her neck. It quickly went the same way as the gloves. "Wow, this place is busy."

Mary looked around as she shrugged out of her coat. "It does seem busier than normal, but it's Thursday night. Maybe people are just getting an early start on the weekend since the weather is supposed to turn bad later."

Martha's nose wrinkled. "Hmm. Maybe."

Elizabeth returned, her red woolen scarf draped over one arm. "They'll page us when our table is ready." She eased closer to Mary as a group of teenagers angled past. "Where did all these people come from?"

Instead of stopping at the hostess booth, the teenagers made a beeline for the back dining room. Noise like the buzz of a full stadium filtered out as they entered.

"What's going on back there?" Martha asked, craning her neck to see.

Mary snapped her fingers. "The job fair."

Elizabeth glanced at her watch. "Is that tonight? I thought that didn't start until next week."

Martha shook her head and scooted out of the way of another group of teens. "No, Mary's right. I forgot all about it. No wonder this place is so packed." She glanced at the line forming behind the hostess table. "Looks like we got here just in time. They're going to be really busy once the job fair lets out. Did they say how long the wait would be?"

"Twenty to thirty minutes." Elizabeth gazed longingly at a plate of steaming roast beef drifting by atop a tray on a waitress's shoulder. "Not sure I can wait that long."

Mary slanted a glance toward the back room. "Well then, why don't we check out the job fair? We have plenty of time, and it'll keep our minds off the food."

"Why not?" Martha took hold of Elizabeth's arm and led her away from the smell of the savory beef. "Let's go."

Elizabeth sighed, her feet shuffling along the floor as she trudged behind Martha.

Mary was hungry too, but she quickly forgot the rumbling in her stomach when they ducked into the back dining room. Tables had been pushed along the walls, and lines long and short extended from each one. Most of those in line were kids, Mary noted, probably students looking for part-time work after school or during the summer, but there were plenty of adults present as well.

She leaned in toward Elizabeth. "I didn't realize there were so many jobs available."

Elizabeth grabbed a sheet of paper off the table nearest the door. "Here's the list." She squinted a little as she read over it. "Cooks, cashiers, stage usher, maintenance worker…it's a pretty wide variety."

"I'll say. Stage usher?" Martha pointed to a table with a sign that said COUNTRY ACRES CAMPGROUND. "I'm going to check that one out."

"Just don't apply for anything," Elizabeth teased, bumping her arm playfully. "As busy as we've been lately, we can't afford to lose you."

Martha smiled and melted into the crowd.

Mary motioned toward the far end of the room where the tables were smaller and the lines a little shorter. "Looks like a few of the newer businesses showed up this year." She elbowed Elizabeth and shot her a teasing grin. "How come we've never thought about signing up for a booth? We could use a little more help around the store."

"Business *has* been pretty good," Elizabeth said with a laugh. "Do you want to look around?"

Mary nodded. "Sure. Let's go."

They wandered slowly down the rows of tables, neither one speaking. The lively chatter would likely have drowned them out anyway. When they neared the end, Mary stopped to pick up a brochure touting a list of benefits and competitive pay rates.

"Mary?"

Hearing her name called by a voice she didn't recognize, she lifted her head. A couple of tables down, a woman with shoulder-length dark hair and a wide smile beckoned.

"Over here."

Elizabeth pressed into her shoulder. "Who's that?"

"I have no idea." Mary frowned and then did a double take as the woman's cheery smile stirred a distant memory. "Wait, is that—?"

The woman rounded the table and stuck out her arms. "Mary, it's me. Paige Schiller." She put her hand to her chest. "I used to be Paige—"

"Hathaway." Mary set the flyer down and moved in for her hug. "Goodness, Paige, I haven't seen you in, well, since we graduated, right? Are you back in town?"

She stepped away as Paige nodded.

"Unfortunately, yes." She chuckled and held up her left hand. "I mean, I'm glad to be back in Bird-in-Hand. I just hate that it's because of my divorce."

"Oh, I'm so sorry."

Her smile faded. "Thank you, but it was sort of inevitable, really."

Though her tone remained light, the lines around her lips and eyes spoke of a wealth of heartache—something Mary remembered from her own divorce. Other than that, the years had been kind to Paige. She still had the slender, athletic figure Mary remembered from high school, and a sort of fresh, youthful energy about her Mary could easily envy. She turned and introduced her childhood friend to Elizabeth. Paige stuck out her hand and gave Elizabeth's a shake. "Pleased to meet you," she said.

Elizabeth smiled at her. "It's good to meet you too," she said.

Paige motioned around the room. "Crazy, huh? The number of people that turned out for this is way better than I expected."

Mary followed her gaze. "I'll say." She pointed to Paige's table. "So, what are you here for?"

"I just opened a beauty salon and could really use some help." Her gaze flicked from Mary to Elizabeth. "Any chance either of you do nails?"

Elizabeth shot Mary a sly smile. "Say, that's something you haven't done before."

Mary laughed and followed Paige back to her table. She'd held a variety of jobs over the years, from coffee barista to teaching art lessons, but she'd never worked in a salon. "Sorry, Paige, my sisters and I aren't looking for a job. We're just here for dinner."

"Aw, that's too bad." Paige smiled and handed her a sheet with the details of the position and the pay. "In case you change your mind."

Mary laughed and tucked the paper into her purse. "So? What have you been up to? Any kids? Or grandkids?"

Paige shook her head. "No grandkids yet. Kailey, my daughter, just turned fifteen." She glanced at Elizabeth. "I was thirty-six when she was born. Jack and I didn't think we could have kids. She sort of surprised us both when she was born."

"That's one of life's *good* surprises," Mary said.

Paige smoothed the edges of the tablecloth next to her display and nodded. "Absolutely. Wouldn't trade her for the world. Of course, Jack wasn't too happy when I decided to move away from Pittsburgh to come back to Bird-in-Hand, but..." She dropped her gaze and shuffled the papers on her table into a neat stack. "Anyway, I did what I thought was best for Kailey and me. She wasn't very happy at her old school. It was too big, and Kailey's so shy, she felt lost. I thought moving to a small town would be good for her."

Strain marked Paige's features, and Mary knew how tough the decision to uproot her family must have been for her. She reached out and squeezed her hand. "You'll have to come by our shop. We opened a thrift store and gift shop called Secondhand Blessings in the barn on my parents' old farm. Do you remember where it is?"

"I do. Oh, I used to love that old Victorian farmhouse. I remember your mother always used to hang that beautiful red, white, and blue bunting on the porch railing every Fourth of July. And those gorgeous stairs that led up to the porch." She feigned a dreamy roll of her eyes. "Does it still look the same?"

Mary smiled proudly. "Pretty much. We've made a few renovations inside, but for the most part, we wanted to keep it looking the way it did when we were growing up."

"Well, I'm glad to hear it's still in the family." Paige's eyes sparkled with excitement, and she returned the squeeze on Mary's fingers. "I can't tell you how good it is to see a familiar face. It makes me feel so much better about everything."

Warmed by Paige's words, Mary smiled. "I'm so glad."

"Mary." Elizabeth held up the pager, which was flashing bright red. "Our table is ready."

"Oh, we've got to go." Mary dropped Paige's hand and jerked her thumb toward the main dining room. "Do you want to join us? I'm sure we could add one more person."

"I'd love to, but I can't." She frowned and tapped the stack of papers. "I'll be here for another hour at least. But I'll definitely stop by your store."

"Great. It's open Monday through Saturday, though we close a little earlier on Tuesdays." Mary circled around the table and gave her friend one last hug. "Bye, Paige. I can't wait to meet your daughter."

"Bye, Mary." She waved to Elizabeth. "Nice to meet you."

"You too." Elizabeth smiled and then waited for Mary before heading toward the dining room. "She seems nice. Why don't I remember her?"

"She was into a lot of sports in high school. Plus, she was pretty shy." Mary waved to Martha, who extricated herself from the cluster of people gathered around the campground booth and joined them.

"Is our table ready?"

Elizabeth held up the pager and then wove toward the hostess stand. In minutes, they were seated and digging with gusto into the variety of home-style items the smorgasbord offered. And almost as quickly, the noise of the job fair melted into a cloud of fluffy mashed potatoes.

Mary yawned and stepped away from the cash register in Secondhand Blessings. It was only two thirty, but the busy morning, combined with a late night tossing and turning, had put a kink in her back and left her wishing for a nap. A lock of her hair fell into her eyes, and she immediately thought of Paige as she pushed it away. How good it would be to have a friend from high school back in town!

The doors whooshed open, and as though she'd been conjured by Mary's musing, Paige ducked into the store. Next to her was a girl with hazel eyes and long hair the same dark shade as her mother's.

Mary smiled and circled the counter to greet them. "Hey, you found us." She stopped in front of the girl and held out her hand. "You must be Kailey. It's such a pleasure to meet you."

The girl neither responded nor looked Mary in the eyes. Instead, she slipped one hand around her waist and laid the other limply in Mary's palm.

Paige draped her arm around Kailey's shoulders. "Kailey, this is Mary Baxter, an old friend of mine from high school."

A blush colored Kailey's cheeks, making her look even more like the friend that Mary remembered from high school. She pulled her hand away then ducked her head and shuffled her feet, her discomfort obvious.

Mary offered a kind smile. "Welcome to Bird-in-Hand, Kailey. How do you like it so far?"

"It's okay." She glanced at her mother. "Can I look around?"

"Sure, baby." Paige dropped her arm and nodded encouragingly. Kailey disappeared down one of the aisles.

"She's beautiful," Mary said. "She looks just like you at that age."

"Thank you." Paige shook her head sadly. "She's really having a tough time with the divorce though. She used to be a lot more outgoing before Jack and I split up."

"Hopefully that will come back in time," Mary said gently. A customer approached the cash register, and she frowned apologetically. "Sorry, I need to help this person."

Paige fluttered her hand. "No, no, you go right ahead. I'm going to go find Kailey and then have a look around."

Mary nodded and was soon wrapped up in helping customers. A short while later, Paige reappeared at the cash register, an antique pair of barber's shears in her hand. Kailey hovered at her elbow, a slim and silent shadow.

"Ooh, those are nice." Mary ran her finger along the finely scrolled blades. "I forgot we had them."

Paige set the shears on the counter. "Something for the salon. I thought they would look neat mounted in a shadow box on the wall in my office."

"Absolutely." She looked past Paige at Kailey. "How about you, Kailey? Find anything you like?"

Kailey jammed her hands into her pockets and her gaze jerked toward the door. "We don't have a lot of room in our apartment."

Mary glanced at Paige. Kailey's sharp words sure sounded like an indictment. Paige ignored it and handed Mary a twenty-dollar bill. Mary started to push the money back to her, but something in the steady way Paige met her eyes told her she didn't want that. She rang up the sale and handed Paige her change.

"So, Paige, I've been looking for a good hairdresser." Mary reached under the counter for a bag to package up the shears. "Tell me about your salon. Have you been open long?"

Paige pulled her purse strap over her shoulder. From a pocket on the side, she pulled out a business card and handed it to Mary. "It's been a couple of weeks. We moved here after the holidays, but it took me a while to find a place and get set up. Plus, it took us a few days to get settled in our new apartment."

"Of course."

"I'd be happy to do your hair," Paige continued. "I mean, if you're serious about looking for a new hairdresser."

Mary tucked the card into her apron pocket and then pushed the bag with the shears across the counter. "Oh, I'm serious. Do I need to make an appointment?"

"Nope," Paige said, her expression brightening. "Just come on by. I'm taking walk-ins until I can build up my client list. And if you like your hairdo, maybe you can tell your friends?" She widened her eyes hopefully then pretended to bite her nails.

Mary laughed. "Of course I will."

Mary waved as Paige and Kailey made their way to the door. "Thanks for coming!"

More customers lined up at the cash register, so Mary concentrated on the task at hand. Eventually, though, she was ready for a break and was only too glad to hand the job over to Elizabeth.

"Maybe we'll need to take on that additional help sooner than I thought," Elizabeth joked, tipping her head toward the customers coming in through the door.

Mary sucked in a breath. Wade Jameson paused just inside the entrance, his customary baseball cap in his hand and sunglasses tucked into the collar of his shirt.

Elizabeth tilted her head. "Hey, isn't that—?"

"The high school baseball coach," Mary said.

"And Bird-in-Hand's most eligible bachelor," Elizabeth said, echoing Mary's thoughts. She slanted a sly smile at her sister. "Wonder what he's doing here."

Catching sight of them, Wade lifted his hand and stepped toward them, a wide smile on his lips "Hey, Mary. I was hoping you'd be here today."

266 | MYSTERIES *of* LANCASTER COUNTY

At his words, Elizabeth snorted playfully and disappeared down one of the aisles.

Mary dropped her hand to her shirt, smoothing the wrinkles from the deep blue fabric, and circled the counter to meet him. "Good afternoon, Wade. Something I can help you find?"

A dimple appeared on his right cheek. "Last time I bumped into you, I mentioned I might stop by, remember?" His smile widened, and he leaned in closer. "Were you leaving?"

Mary took a steadying breath. "Actually, I was just about to take a short break."

"Then my timing is perfect." A twinkle lit his hazel eyes, and he motioned toward a patch of sun glinting through one of the shop windows. "Mind if we talk a minute?"

Not at all sounded too proper. *No* was too abrupt. Mary pressed her lips tight and led the way to the back of the store.

Wade was tall and lean. No wonder women swooned when he passed. Okay, so maybe that was an exaggeration, but he still made Mary's heart beat fast. She crossed her arms over her chest and turned to him.

"What can I do for you, Wade?"

The smile slipped a bit, and a glimmer of uncertainty shone in his eyes. Mary groaned. She was coming across all wrong. She dropped her arms and smiled. "I'm surprised you were able to get out of class."

He grinned and slid one hand into his pocket. "This is my conference period. I thought I would try to catch you before I head to practice."

"Baseball practice already?" She glanced out the window at the light dusting of snow on the ground.

"Spring training is just around the corner. I'm working on lining up some scrimmages."

"I see." She waited.

He shrugged his shoulder. "So, Mary, I was wondering, if you're not busy tomorrow, would you like to catch a movie or something?"

"Saturday?" Her pulse ratcheted. Were her palms sweating? She clasped her hands. They were definitely sweating. "Uh, yeah, that sounds fun."

"Yeah?" He lifted one sandy-brown brow and thwacked the baseball cap lightly against his leg. "Cool. How about five thirty? That would give us time to head over to Lancaster for something to eat before the show."

She hesitated. "Could we make it a little later, say around six? The store closes at five, so that will give me plenty of time to get ready. N-not that I need an hour to get ready." She stumbled to a stop, heat flooding her cheeks.

Wade laughed. "Okay. So I'll see you then?"

She nodded. "Looking forward to it."

"Good." He pulled a business card out of his pocket and handed it to her. "Here's my number in case anything comes up. See you tomorrow, Mary." He paused, a funny sort of half-smile on his face as he looked at her. Finally, he clapped the cap back on his head and turned, freeing her to breathe normally.

Martha poked her head around a bookshelf, her gaze darting from Wade's retreating back to Mary. "Was that Wade Jameson, the baseball coach?"

"It was." Mary scrambled to pull Paige's card from her pocket. Across the front, the words PAIGE'S PLACE scrolled in flowing brown script. "Hey, Martha?" she asked distractedly.

Her sister stepped out from behind the bookshelf, eyebrows raised questioningly.

"Would it be all right if I take off a couple of hours tomorrow?" Mary smiled and lifted her gaze from the card in her hand to the man outside the window climbing into a shiny new Dodge Challenger. "I'm going to need to get my hair done."